Rocky Mountain Promise

VIVIAN BELLE

STERLING RIDGE PRESS LLC

Cover designed by Sterling Ridge Press LLC

Published by: Sterling Ridge Press, LLC www.sterlingridgepress.com

ISBN: 978-1-966093-22-0
Printed in the United States of America

First Edition: April 2025

For permissions, contact: support@vivianbelle.com or visit www.vivianbelle.com

Dedication

For all who find healing in the wilderness of their hearts,
Who brave the storms of doubt to discover faith,
And who learn that love arrives not when we seek it,
But when we open ourselves to serve others.
To those who stand at the intersection of science and faith,
Finding harmony where others see only discord.
And especially for the quiet healers in forgotten places.
The nurses, doctors, midwives, and caregivers
Who tend wounds both seen and unseen,
Who hold vigil in the darkest hours,
And who believe in healing
Even when a cure seems impossible.
May you, like Laura and Moses,
Discover that in tending others,
You find yourself most truly healed.
Vivian Belle

About The Author

Vivian Belle is a talented author known for her sweeping **Historical Christian Romance** novels set against the untamed beauty of the American frontier. With a deep love for history and storytelling, she brings to life **resilient heroines, steadfast heroes, and faith-filled journeys** in the vast, rugged landscapes of the past.

Nestled in the **majestic mountains of northern West Virginia,** Vivian finds endless inspiration in the rolling hills, winding rivers, and boundless sky that mirror the spirit of her stories. When she's not writing, she enjoys **kayaking on tranquil waters, hiking through breathtaking mountain trails, and, of course, getting lost in a good book.**

Vivian's novels capture the heart of **faith, love, and perseverance**—where strong women and honorable men overcome life's trials to find hope, home, and happily-ever-after. Whether she's exploring the great outdoors or crafting her next frontier romance, Vivian's passion for adventure and storytelling shines through in every word she writes.

You can find out more about Vivian and her latest releases at www.vivianbelle.com or follow her on social media for updates and behind-the-scenes glimpses of her writing process. Stay connected—you won't want to miss the heartfelt stories of love and family she has in store!

Also by Vivian Belle

Where the Heart Finds Home
Faith on the Frontier
Love in Hopewell Creek
Abigail's Promise
Beneath Montana Skies
Rocky Mountain Promise

Contents

Chapter 1

The stagecoach lurched to a halt, sending Laura Smythe sliding forward on the worn leather seat. She steadied herself against the jostling, one hand clutching the seat while the other gripped the edge of the window frame. For six days, she had endured the bone-jarring journey from Denver, climbing ever higher into the rugged Colorado mountains, and now, finally, they had arrived.

"Aspen Hollow!" the driver called out, his voice carrying over the snorting of exhausted horses.

Laura peered through the window, taking in her first glimpse of her new home. The valley cradled a collection of weathered wooden buildings, their facades plainly practical rather than ornamental. Aspen Hollow wasn't grand or imposing, but nestled against the majestic backdrop of towering mountains. It possessed a certain rugged charm. The late autumn air had painted the namesake aspen groves in brilliant gold, their trembling leaves standing out against the dark evergreens climbing the mountainsides.

As the driver opened the door, Laura straightened her skirts and adjusted her hat, determined to make a proper impression despite the dust of travel that clung to her navy blue traveling suit. Six days in a cramped stagecoach had left her tired and sore, but anticipation gave her strength. This was where God had called her to serve, to fulfill the promise she'd made after her family's tragic deaths.

"I'm ready, Lord," she whispered, her prayer barely audible above the bustle of arrival. "Use me as Your hands of healing here."

Laura stepped down from the coach and breathed deeply, savoring the clean mountain air after the stuffiness of the coach.

A small crowd had gathered at the stage depot, mostly men collecting mail or parcels. A few curious glances came her way, but most seemed preoccupied with their own business. Laura scanned the faces, wondering if anyone had come specifically to greet her.

"Miss Smythe?" A warm voice drew her attention to a tall, slender man approaching with a broad smile. His dark coat and white collar identified him immediately as a clergyman. "I'm Pastor Simon Lewis. Welcome to Aspen Hollow."

Relief washed over her at this friendly greeting. "Pastor Lewis, how wonderful to meet you." She extended her hand. "Thank you for arranging everything. I can't tell you how grateful I am for this opportunity to serve."

The pastor clasped her hand firmly. Gray streaked his dark hair at the temples, and the fine lines around his eyes spoke of both joy and hardship. "The pleasure is ours, Miss Smythe. We've been praying for someone with your nursing training for quite some time."

"I've been praying, as well, for guidance to wherever I might be most needed." Laura smiled, grateful for this immediate connection.

While the driver unloaded all the passenger luggage and various mail parcels, Laura took in more of her surroundings. The main street stretched before her, lined with various establishments.

"I've brought my wagon to transport your belongings," Pastor Lewis said, gesturing to a simple buckboard nearby. "Mrs. Williams has prepared a room for you at the Aspen Rest boarding house. It's quite comfortable, and right here on Main Street."

"That sounds perfect."

"I'd hoped Dr. Grant would be here to greet you as well," Pastor Lewis added, a slight frown creasing his brow as he glanced around the depot.

"I'm eager to meet him," Laura replied, though in truth, her stomach fluttered with nerves at the prospect. Her missionary assignment had mentioned she would assist the local doctor, but provided few details about him or what their working relationship would entail.

"Well, I believe that's him now," Pastor Lewis said, nodding toward the general store across the street.

Laura followed his gaze to see a tall man emerging from the establishment, carrying a small crate of supplies. Even from a distance, she could see his face was set in stern lines, his movements purposeful and efficient. His dark hair was slightly too long, and a shadow of stubble defined his jaw.

"Dr. Grant!" Pastor Lewis called, raising his hand in greeting.

The man glanced up, his expression unchanging as he spotted them. After a moment's hesitation, he set his crate in the back of a nearby wagon and crossed the street toward them. His stride was long and measured, his posture straight despite the obvious weariness in his bearing.

"Doctor, allow me to introduce Miss Laura Smythe," Pastor Lewis said as the man reached them. "She's the nurse I mentioned, sent by the missionary board in Philadelphia."

Up close, Dr. Grant was even more imposing. Tall and lean, with broad shoulders and hands that spoke of hard work. His deep-set blue eyes studied her with unsettling intensity beneath dark brows. Laura extended her hand, summoning a warm smile despite his forbidding expression.

"Dr. Grant, I'm so pleased to meet you. I've been looking forward to assisting you in caring for the people of Aspen Hollow."

The doctor made no move to take her hand. "Miss Smythe," he acknowledged with a curt nod, his voice deep and gravelly. "I wasn't aware they were sending someone so..."

"So...?" she prompted when he didn't continue.

"Young," he finished, though something in his tone suggested he might have been thinking something else entirely. His gaze traveled over her, taking in her city clothes and the medical bag clutched in her hands. "And clearly city-bred. This isn't Philadelphia, Miss Smythe. People here live and die by different rules than what they teach in those fancy eastern schools."

Laura slowly lowered her hand, her cheeks warming. "I'm well aware that frontier medicine presents unique challenges, Dr. Grant. That's precisely why I requested a position in a community like Aspen Hollow."

"Did you?" His expression remained skeptical. "And what exactly do you know about 'communities like Aspen Hollow'?"

Pastor Lewis cleared his throat. "Dr. Grant Miss Smythe has traveled a long way. Perhaps we should allow her to settle in before discussing medical matters."

The doctor's gaze lingered on Laura for another moment before he shrugged. "As you wish, Pastor. I have patients to attend to, anyway." He turned to Laura. "You can find me at my clinic when you're ready to discuss your... duties." He emphasized the last word as if doubtful she could fulfill them.

With that, he turned and strode back toward his wagon.

Laura stood rooted to the spot, her earlier excitement dampened by the cold encounter. She had expected challenges in Aspen Hollow, but she hadn't expected such immediate dismissal from the very person she was sent to assist.

"Please don't mind the doctor," Pastor Lewis said gently. "He's a good man at heart, just... wearied by the demands of being the only physician for twenty miles."

Laura nodded, though she couldn't quite hide her disappointment. "Of course. I'm sure we'll establish a professional relationship in time."

As they loaded her belongings onto the pastor's wagon, Laura found her gaze drawn back to Dr. Grant. Despite his rudeness, she couldn't help noticing the respectful nods he gave to townsfolk who greeted him, and the natural authority in his bearing. There was something compelling about him, even in his gruffness with her. A depth and intensity that suggested more beneath the harsh exterior.

She quickly dismissed her thoughts. Her purpose here was to serve, not to concern herself with the temperament of a cynical doctor. Yet, she couldn't deny the unexpected flutter of awareness she'd felt in his presence, irritating as it was.

"Everything alright, Miss Smythe?" Pastor Lewis asked as he helped her onto the wagon seat.

"Yes, thank you. Just taking in my new home." She said with a determined smile. "Tell me about Aspen Hollow. How many residents are there?"

As the wagon pulled away from the depot, Pastor Lewis provided a detailed overview of the town and its inhabitants. Founded just fifteen years prior after silver was discovered in the mountains, Aspen Hollow had grown from a handful of tents to a proper town of nearly five hundred souls, with more in the surrounding homesteads and mining camps.

They passed the general store, Abernathy & Sons, according to the sign, where several women in practical frontier dresses could be seen through the large windows examining bolts of fabric. A smithy rang with the sound of hammering metal, and children darted between buildings in a game of chase. Despite Dr. Grant's chilly reception, the town itself felt alive with possibility.

"That's the schoolhouse," Pastor Lewis pointed out a simple wooden building. "And just beyond is our church. You're welcome to attend services this Sunday, of course."

"I wouldn't miss it," Laura assured him. Her faith had sustained her through her darkest hours, and she knew it would be her anchor in this new chapter of her life.

"And here we are," the pastor announced as they pulled up before a two-story building with a wide, welcoming porch. A sign above the door read "Aspen Rest—Rooms & Meals" in careful lettering. "Mrs. Williams runs the finest boarding house in town—though I should mention it's also the only one."

A plump, motherly woman in her forties emerged from the front door, wiping her hands on her apron. Her face brightened as she spotted them.

"You must be our new nurse!" she called, hurrying down the steps. "I'm Sera Williams. We're so pleased to have you staying with us."

Laura immediately warmed to the woman's genuine welcome. "Thank you, Mrs. Williams. I'm Laura Smythe. I hope my arrival hasn't troubled you."

"No trouble at all! We've been preparing your room all day. It's not fancy, mind you, but it's clean and comfortable." Mrs. Williams gestured to a weathered man emerging from around the side of the house. "Lester, come help with Miss Smythe's things."

Mr. Williams, a quiet man with kind eyes, helped unload Laura's trunk and valises. The pastor excused himself, promising to check on her tomorrow and extending another invitation to Sunday services.

As Mrs. Williams showed Laura to her room on the upper floor, the older woman kept up a steady stream of information about meal times, laundry arrangements, and the other boarders—currently a young schoolteacher named Millie Abernathy and an elderly gentleman who worked as the telegraph operator.

The room was indeed small but charming in its simplicity: a narrow iron bed with a colorful patchwork quilt, a washstand with a porcelain basin and pitcher, a small wardrobe, and a bedside table with an oil lamp. A window overlooked Main Street, offering a view of the bustling town below.

"It's perfect," Laura said sincerely. After the stagecoach journey, even the modest accommodations felt luxurious.

"Dinner's at six sharp," Mrs. Williams informed her. "That gives you time to rest and freshen up. You must be exhausted from your journey."

When Mrs. Williams departed, Laura sat on the edge of the bed, the reality of her situation settling around her. She was really here, hundreds of miles from everything familiar, in a rugged mountain town where at least one person already seemed convinced she didn't belong.

She reached into her medical bag and withdrew her most treasured possession: a small, worn Bible that had been her mother's. Opening it, she ran her fingers over the familiar passage from Isaiah that had guided her through her darkest hours: "Fear not, for I am with you; be not dismayed, for I am your God; I will strengthen you, I will help you, I will uphold you with my righteous right hand."

"I'm here, Lord," she whispered. "Guide my hands and heart. Help me serve these people, even if they don't want me yet."

Rising from the bed, she moved to the window. From this vantage point, she could see further down Main Street to a small building with a sign that read: "Dr. M. Grant—Physician & Surgeon." As she watched, the doctor himself emerged, medical bag in hand, and strode purposefully down the boardwalk. Despite his earlier coldness, there was no denying the dedication evident in his hurried pace.

A knock at the door interrupted her thoughts.

"Yes?" she called.

Mrs. Williams poked her head in. "I thought you might like to wash up before dinner. I've brought some hot water for your basin."

"That's very thoughtful, thank you." Laura accepted the steaming pitcher gratefully.

"I should mention," Mrs. Williams added hesitantly, "folks around here can be a bit... cautious with newcomers. Especially those with city ways."

Laura nodded, thinking of Dr. Grant's dismissive attitude. "I understand."

"Don't you worry, though. They'll come around once they see what you can do for our town. It's quite wonderful knowing we have a nurse now to assist Dr. Grant." Mrs. Williams patted her arm. "I must say,

Dr. Grant's bark is worse than his bite, by the way. He's saved more lives in this valley than anyone can count."

"I'm sure he's very skilled," Laura acknowledged. "I just hope he'll allow me to contribute my skills as well."

"He will, in time." Mrs. Williams moved toward the door. "He's had a hard go of it, that one. Been the only doctor here for five years, ever since old Doc Murphy passed. Works himself to the bone, he does."

After Mrs. Williams left, Laura washed away the dust of travel, changed into a fresh blouse and skirt, and braided her chestnut hair. Refreshed, she took a brief walk before dinner to orient herself to the town that would be her home for the foreseeable future.

The main street bustled with evening activity, miners returning from shifts, shopkeepers closing up for the day, and children being called home for supper. Laura nodded politely to those who met her gaze, receiving curious looks in return. She was clearly a novelty in Aspen Hollow.

She walked toward Dr. Grant's clinic. The building was weathered but sturdy, with a small sign above the door. The lower windows were dark, suggesting he was still out on house calls.

What kind of man was he? Laura wondered. Pastor Lewis and Mrs. Williams both seemed to think well of him, despite his gruff manner. And there had been something in his eyes, a weariness, yes, but also a depth of something carefully guarded.

"He's just a colleague," she reminded herself firmly. "And right now, not even a friendly one."

As she turned to head back to the boarding house, she nearly collided with a young woman hurrying down the street.

"Oh! I'm so sorry," Laura apologized, steadying the woman by her shoulders.

"No harm done," the woman replied with a smile. She was young, with blonde hair tucked beneath a practical bonnet and bright, curious eyes. "You must be the new nurse everyone's talking about."

"Word travels fast," Laura said, returning the smile. "I'm Laura Smythe."

"Millie Abernathy. I teach at the school, and I'm staying at Aspen Rest, as well." She glanced at Dr. Grant's clinic behind Laura. "Were you looking for the doctor?"

"No, just familiarizing myself with the town," Laura explained.

"I'm so pleased to have another young woman around. Aspen Hollow is wonderful, but it can be a bit lacking in female companionship at times." Millie linked her arm through Laura's. "Come, we should head back if we don't want to miss Sera's pot roast. It's the best in the territory."

As they walked, Millie chatted easily about the town and its inhabitants. Laura warmed to the young teacher's friendly nature, grateful for this immediate connection.

"Have you met Dr. Grant yet?" Millie asked as they approached the boarding house.

"Briefly," Laura replied. "He seemed... rather skeptical of me."

Millie squeezed her arm sympathetically. "He's like that with everyone at first. My younger brother Tommy came down with a terrible fever yesterday, and Dr. Grant barely spoke ten words while treating him. But he sat by Tommy's bedside all night, and when I thanked him, he just shrugged and said it was his job." She paused. "The thing is, Tommy wasn't just his only ill patient last evening. The mine had an accident that too, and he'd been treating injured miners for hours before he came to us. He was dead on his feet, but he still stayed."

Laura absorbed this new information. "He must be dedicated to his patients."

"He is. But between you and me, I think he could use some help." Millie lowered her voice. "He looks after everyone but himself."

They reached the boarding house, where delicious aromas wafted from the kitchen. As they entered, Laura couldn't help glancing back down the street toward Dr. Grant's clinic. Perhaps there was more to the town's physician than his cold greeting suggested.

Chapter 2

Moses Grant pressed the back of his knuckles against Tommy Abernathy's forehead, noting with satisfaction that the boy's fever had broken overnight. The young man's eyes, bright with relief rather than illness, watched him carefully.

"Better?" Moses asked, his voice gruff but not unkind.

Tommy nodded. "Yes, sir. My throat doesn't hurt so bad now."

"Good. Keep drinking that willow bark tea your mother's been making. Rest for another day." Moses packed his stethoscope into his medical bag. "And no sneaking outside to play with the Holcomb boys. I'll know if you do."

Twila Abernathy hovered at her son's bedside, her hands clasped tightly at her waist. "Thank you, Doctor. We were so worried when the fever wouldn't break."

Moses nodded curtly. He'd seen this pattern before, parents terrified over common childhood ailments. Not that he blamed them. In these mountains, even a simple fever could turn deadly if not watched carefully.

"Just a seasonal throat inflammation. Nothing serious." He snapped his bag closed. "I'll check back tomorrow."

As he descended the stairs into the mercantile, Silas Abernathy approached from behind the counter. "How is he?"

"He'll be fine. Keep him indoors today."

Relief flooded the shopkeeper's face. "What do I owe you for this visit?"

Moses considered the ledger he kept in his mind. The Abernathy's had provided him with supplies last month, when his funds were tight. "We're square for now. That coffee you gave me last month more than covers it."

Silas nodded, understanding the unspoken system of barter and exchange that kept Aspen Hollow functioning. "Heard the new nurse arrived yesterday. Quite the commotion at the stage depot, I'm told."

Moses grunted noncommittally, hoping to avoid the subject.

"Clara Bellweather was in here first thing this morning, going on about how the young lady seems 'mighty refined' for our little town." Silas raised an eyebrow. "Reckon you'll be glad for the help, though?"

"We'll see," Moses replied, adjusting his hat. "Frontier medicine isn't something they teach in those fancy eastern schools."

The bell above the mercantile door jangled as he stepped out into the crisp morning air. Aspen Hollow was already alive with activity, miners heading up to the Flint operation, the blacksmith's hammer ringing out, and women sweeping the boardwalk and exchanging news across the street.

His clinic was only a short walk away, but Moses took his time, nodding to those who greeted him. Five years in Aspen Hollow had made him a fixture here. Not necessarily well-liked. He wasn't the sort to join the sociables at the church or drink with the miners at Jasper McCoy's saloon, but he was respected. Needed.

And now they'd brought in some city-trained nurse, probably full of modern theories with no practical application in a place where the nearest hospital was a four-day journey away.

Moses climbed the steps to his clinic, unlocking the door with a key worn smooth from years of use. The familiar smell greeted him—carbolic acid, herbs, and the mustiness of old books. He moved through the small waiting area with its hard benches into his consulting room, where morning light fell across his desk, illuminating the disorganized stacks of patient notes and medical journals.

He hung his coat and hat on the rack, rolled up his shirtsleeves, and began preparing for the day. Mrs. Sterling would be coming in for her arthritis treatment, and Jonah Crawford needed another look at the mining cut on his arm.

Moses examined his supplies, mentally cataloging what needed replenishing. Quinine was running low again. He'd have to send for more, though who knew when it would arrive. The higher passes would be snowed in soon, making deliveries uncertain until spring.

He sank into the chair behind his desk, suddenly weary, though the day had barely begun. The familiar ache settled between his shoulder blades, a permanent companion these days. At thirty-two, he sometimes felt decades older, worn down by the weight of responsibility, by the lives he'd saved and the ones he'd lost.

His gaze fell on the small Bible sitting on the corner of his desk, gathering dust. It had been his father's, a reminder of a faith that once burned bright but now barely flickered. What kind of God allowed good people to suffer while the wicked prospered? What kind of divine plan included children dying of fevers while their parents prayed desperately for intervention?

Moses pushed the thought away. There was no use in such ruminations. He had work to do, patients who needed him. That was reality—not some comforting platitude about God's mysterious ways.

A knock at the clinic door interrupted his dark thoughts.

"Come in," he called, expecting Mrs. Sterling and her arthritic complaints.

The door opened, and instead of the elderly widow, Laura Smythe, stepped into his consulting room.

Moses stiffened. She looked different this morning, less travel-worn, more determined. Her chestnut hair was neatly arranged, her simple blue dress practical but undeniably fine compared to the homespun most Aspen Hollow women wore. She carried a medical bag similar to his, though newer and less scarred by use.

"Good morning, Dr. Grant," she said, her voice clear and confident.

"Miss Smythe." He didn't stand or invite her to sit. "I wasn't expecting you so early."

"I thought it best to establish our working arrangement promptly." She moved further into the room, seemingly undeterred by his lack of welcome. "I wanted to discuss how I might best assist you in caring for Aspen Hollow's residents."

Moses leaned back in his chair, studying her with narrowed eyes. Up close, in the clarity of morning light, he noticed details he'd missed during their brief encounter at the stage depot. Her eyes weren't hazel as he'd initially thought, but a clear blue that reminded him of the alpine lakes high in the mountains. Her posture was straight, almost defiant, but her hands, clasped before her, betrayed a slight nervousness.

"I'm not sure what Pastor Lewis told you," he said finally, "but I don't need an assistant. Especially not one whose experience is limited to city hospitals with their fancy equipment and endless supplies."

A flash of irritation crossed her features, quickly controlled. "My training at Philadelphia Medical College for Women was thorough, Dr. Grant. I assure you, I'm quite capable of adapting to frontier conditions."

Moses scoffed. "Are you? Have you ever delivered a baby by lamplight during a blizzard? Set a bone without chloroform? Treated gangrene with nothing but a knife and whatever whiskey was handy?"

"No," she admitted. "But I've—"

"Treated well-to-do patients in clean hospital beds? Worked with the latest instruments and medicines?" He shook his head. "This isn't Philadelphia, Miss Smythe. People here live hard and die hard. They don't need fancy theories or gentle bedside manner. They need results."

She tensed visibly, but didn't back down. "If you'd allow me to finish, Dr. Grant, I was going to say that while my hospital experience is certainly different from your frontier practice, I've also worked in Philadelphia's poorest neighborhoods. I've treated diphtheria outbreaks in tenements, delivered babies in conditions that would horrify you, and managed gunshot wounds with limited supplies."

Her voice grew more passionate as she spoke, and Moses found himself reluctantly impressed by her conviction, if not her claims.

"Moreover," she continued, "modern medical science has made significant advances that could benefit your patients. Proper hygiene alone could prevent countless infections."

At this, Moses rose from his chair, anger flaring. "Are you suggesting I don't know how to keep my instruments clean?"

"I'm suggesting that new understanding of germ theory has revolutionized surgical outcomes. Simply washing hands thoroughly between patients can—"

"I know about Lister's theories," he interrupted, irritated that she thought him some backwoods hack. "But when you are elbow-deep in a mining accident victim with five more waiting, there's precious little time for such niceties."

Laura's eyes widened slightly, perhaps surprised he was familiar with modern developments. "Then you understand the value of antiseptic techniques. Why not implement them more consistently?"

Moses moved around his desk, closing the distance between them. He noted with grim satisfaction that she didn't step back, despite his attempt to intimidate with his height advantage.

"Let me explain something, Miss Smythe. In Aspen Hollow, we deal with reality, not ideals. When a man comes in with his arm crushed by mining equipment, I don't have time to engage in elaborate sterilization rituals. I need to stop the bleeding and save what I can of the limb before he dies on my table. When a child is choking with diphtheria, the mother doesn't care if my hands are scrubbed raw—she just wants her child to breathe again."

"But those very practices might be why some patients don't recover," Laura countered, holding her ground. "Infections following surgery—"

"Is a fact of frontier life," he cut in. "You think I don't know the risks? That I haven't seen good men die from infection after I've done everything possible to save them?" The memory of his brother-in-law surfaced unbidden, a young miner whose leg he'd amputated after an accident. He'd seemed to be recovering until infection set in. Moses had watched helplessly as the poison spread through his system.

Laura must have seen something in his expression, because her voice softened slightly. "I'm not questioning your dedication or skill, Dr. Grant. I'm simply suggesting that incorporating some newer practices might improve outcomes for your patients. Isn't that what we both want?"

Moses turned away, disturbed by her perception and the unwelcome memories she'd stirred. He moved to the cabinet where he kept his surgical instruments, opening it more forcefully than necessary.

"What I want," he said, his back to her, "is to continue treating my patients as I have been, effectively and practically. What I don't need is someone with book learning and no real experience questioning methods that have kept people alive in these mountains for years."

"I have more than book learning," Laura insisted, her voice taking on an edge of frustration. "And I didn't come all this way to be dismissed without a fair chance to prove my worth."

"No one asked you to come all this way," Moses pointed out, turning back to face her.

"Actually, Dr. Grant, they did." Her chin lifted slightly. "Pastor Lewis wrote to the missionary board specifically requesting a trained nurse to assist with the growing medical needs of Aspen Hollow. The board selected me because of my training and my expressed desire to serve in a frontier community."

Moses silently cursed Simon Lewis for his interference. The pastor meant well, but he didn't understand the practical realities of frontier medicine.

"The pastor is not a medical professional," he said flatly. "He has no business determining what this practice needs."

"Perhaps not, but he cares about this community's well-being. As do I." Laura stepped closer, her expression earnest. "Dr. Grant, I understand your skepticism. I'm a stranger, and you've been solely responsible for medical care here for years. But I'm not here to challenge your authority or criticize your methods. I'm here to help, to learn from your experience, and yes, perhaps to offer some newer approaches that might complement your own."

Something in her impassioned speech struck a chord, though Moses was loath to admit it. There was a sincerity in her voice, a conviction that seemed at odds with the delicate appearance she presented. And despite his protestations, he knew he could use help. The burden of being Aspen Hollow's only medical professional wore on him more with each passing season.

But accepting help meant relinquishing control, opening his practice to change, to potential failure. And failure, in his profession, meant death.

"You say you want to help," he said, his voice low. "But you've already made it clear you think my methods are outdated, even dangerous. How exactly do you propose we work together when our approaches are so fundamentally different?"

Before Laura could respond, the clinic door swung open. Jasper McCoy, the saloon owner, stood in the doorway, his face tense with urgency.

"Doc, you're needed at the mine. There's been an accident—Jonah Crawford's caught under a collapsed support beam."

Moses was already moving, grabbing his medical bag and coat. "How bad?"

"Bad enough. They're trying to get him free now."

Moses nodded grimly, then glanced at Laura, who was watching the exchange with alert concern. A decision formed quickly—not one he was entirely comfortable with, but necessary.

"Miss Smythe, if you're serious about proving your worth, come along. Let's see how your Philadelphia training holds up against a real frontier emergency."

Laura didn't hesitate. "I'll need my bag from the boarding house."

"No time," Moses said, already heading for the door. "You can use mine."

Outside, Jasper had brought a horse for Moses. "Got another?" Moses asked, nodding toward Laura.

"Not with me. She'll have to ride double with you."

Moses suppressed a groan. "Fine. Miss Smythe, have you ridden before?"

"Yes," she replied simply, moving toward the horse with determined steps.

Ignoring the curious stares of passersby, Moses mounted and then extended his hand to Laura. She grasped it firmly, allowing him to pull her up behind him.

"Hold on," he instructed gruffly, and then urged the horse into a rapid trot toward the mine on the mountainside above Aspen Hollow.

Laura's arms circled his waist, her grip secure but not clinging. Despite the circumstances, Moses was acutely aware of her presence, the slight weight against his back, and the subtle scent of something clean and floral that was distinctly out of place in his world of carbolic acid and mining dust.

"The mines here primarily extract silver," he explained as they rode, falling into his habit of providing practical information in tense situations. "Accidents are common. Support beams give way, dynamite misfires, air goes bad. Jonah's a good kid—barely twenty-two. Smart enough to be doing something safer, but mining pays better than most work around here."

"Has he had accidents before?" Laura asked, her voice close to his ear.

"Cut his arm a few weeks back. Should have had stitches, but he kept working, and it tore open again. Might have developed infection if Mrs. Hayes, the local herbalist, hadn't packed it with a poultice that drew out the poison."

"You work with a local herbalist?" Surprise colored her voice.

"Clementine Hayes knows more about healing plants than any book I've studied," Moses replied matter-of-factly. "I'd be a fool not to use her knowledge. Unlike some, I don't dismiss what works just because it doesn't come with a fancy medical school stamp of approval."

He felt rather than saw Laura stiffen slightly at the barb, but she didn't rise to it.

The trail steepened as they approached the mining camp. Rough shacks and tents clustered on the hillside, home to the men who spent their days underground hunting for silver veins. Ahead, a crowd had gathered at the mine entrance, where the large wooden structure of the hoist house stood.

Moses dismounted quickly and helped Laura down, then pushed through the gathered miners. Inside the mine entrance, a group of men worked frantically around a fallen timber. Beneath it lay Jonah Crawford, pale and still, but conscious.

"Move back," Moses commanded, and the men immediately gave way.

He knelt beside Jonah, quickly assessing the situation. The support beam lay across the young man's legs, not his torso, which was a small mercy. But from the awkward angle of his right leg, Moses suspected a break, possibly a compound.

"Hey, Doc," Jonah managed, his voice tight with pain. "Seems I'm making a habit of needing your services."

"I'd prefer you found a less dramatic way," Moses replied, beginning his examination. He checked Jonah's pulse, rapid but strong, and pupils, which reacted normally.

"How long has he been trapped?" he asked the mine foreman, a burly man named Blackwood.

"About thirty minutes. Beam came down sudden-like. We've been trying to lift it, but it's pinned good, and we're afraid of shifting it wrong and crushing him more."

Moses nodded, his mind working through options. "We need to get it off without doing more damage. Get me four strong men and those support posts you use for the new shafts."

As the foreman bellowed orders, Moses turned to check Jonah more thoroughly. The young miner's face was contorted with pain, his breathing shallow.

"My legs... can't feel the right one anymore," Jonah said, fear evident in his eyes.

"That might be a blessing for now," Moses told him honestly. "When we get this beam off, the pain's going to be substantial."

Jonah nodded bravely, then his gaze. "You're the new nurse, ain't you? The one from back East?"

Moses suddenly remembered Laura's presence. She had moved quietly to Jonah's other side, her expression composed despite the chaotic scene.

"Yes, I'm Laura Smythe," she said, her voice calm and reassuring. "I'm going to help Dr. Grant take care of you."

Before Moses could object to her presumption, she continued, addressing him directly. "Should I check for other injuries while you plan the beam removal?"

Her calm professionalism in the face of the emergency caught him off guard. He had half-expected her to blanch at the sight of blood or the grime of the mining tunnel.

"Yes," he agreed tersely. "Check for head injuries, broken ribs, internal bleeding."

While Moses directed the miners in positioning supports to lift the beam, Laura worked methodically, her hands gentle but efficient as she examined Jonah. She spoke softly to him, keeping him engaged and distracted from his predicament.

"You've done good work setting up a brace for his neck," Moses acknowledged, surprised by her initiative. He hadn't instructed her to do so, but it was precisely what he would have done if concerned about potential spinal injuries.

"Standard procedure for crush injuries," she replied without looking up. "He has some bruising on his abdomen that concerns me. Possible internal bleeding."

Moses frowned, moving to examine the area she indicated. The bruising was indeed worrisome, spreading across Jonah's lower-right side.

"Good catch," he admitted grudgingly. "That changes our priorities."

He turned to the foreman. "We need to move faster. He might be bleeding internally."

The men worked with renewed urgency, positioning wooden supports under the beam to create a lever system. Moses returned to Jonah's side, preparing a dose of laudanum from his bag.

"This will help with the pain," he explained, administering the medicine. "Miss Smythe, when we lift the beam, we'll need to move him immediately. Are you strong enough to help?"

"Yes," she said firmly. "I'll support his head and shoulders while you focus on his legs."

The strategy was sound, exactly what Moses would have suggested. He gave her a short nod of approval, then moved to direct the final preparations.

"On my count," he told the miners. "Lift slow and steady. Three, two, one—"

The men strained against the makeshift levers, and gradually, the heavy beam began to rise. As soon as there was clearance, Moses and Laura moved as one, sliding Jonah free of the beam's weight.

The young miner cried out as the movement jostled his injured leg, the sound echoing harshly in the tunnel. The right leg was indeed broken, bone protruding through torn trousers and flesh.

"Get him outside where the light's better," Moses ordered, and several miners stepped forward with a stretcher fashioned from canvas and wood.

Working together, they carefully transferred Jonah to the stretcher. Laura moved to his head, keeping him calm with quiet reassurances as the miners carried him from the tunnel into the daylight.

Outside, Moses directed them to lay the stretcher on a flat area near the hoist house. A crowd had gathered, but kept a respectful distance as he and Laura went to work.

"I need to set the leg before we move him down the mountain," Moses said, rolling up his sleeves. "The laudanum will help, but it's still going to be painful. Miss Smythe, I need you to hold him steady."

Laura positioned herself at Jonah's shoulders, her hands firm but gentle. "I'm right here, Jonah," she told the young miner. "You're doing wonderfully."

Moses cut away the blood-soaked trouser leg, revealing the full extent of the injury. The bone had broken cleanly, though the skin and muscle damage was severe. Setting it would be challenging, but necessary before transport.

"Ready?" he asked, looking at Laura.

She met his gaze steadily. "Yes."

"Jonah, this will hurt, but it needs to be done," Moses warned. "On three. One, two—" He moved on two, a trick he often used to catch patients unprepared.

Jonah's scream tore through the air as Moses pulled and manipulated the limb, realigning the bone with practiced movements. Laura held the young man firmly, murmuring encouragements and prayers as he writhed in agony.

"Almost there," Moses grunted, feeling the bone slip back into place. "Get me splints and bandages from my bag."

Laura reached for the medical bag with one hand, still supporting Jonah with the other. She extracted what Moses needed without fumbling or hesitation, passing them to him efficiently.

Once the leg was splinted and stabilized, Moses turned his attention to the potential internal bleeding. The bruising had spread slightly in the short time since they'd first noticed it.

"We need to get him down to the clinic," he told Laura. "I want to monitor that bruising closely."

She nodded. "Should we use the wagon I saw at the camp entrance?"

"Yes, but we'll need to pad it well. The road down is rough."

Moses gave instructions to the foreman about preparing the wagon, then turned back to find Laura already assembling makeshift padding from blankets and canvas sacks around Jonah on the stretcher.

"You've done this before," he observed, watching her arrange the materials with practiced efficiency.

"Emergency transport? Yes, though usually through city streets, not mountain trails." She glanced up at him. "Principles are the same—minimize movement, maximize comfort, maintain vigilance."

Her competence was undeniable, Moses admitted to himself reluctantly. She worked with the confidence of experience, not just book learning. And she hadn't flinched at the blood or the screams or the filth of the mining camp.

As they prepared to transfer Jonah to the wagon, Laura approached Moses, speaking quietly, so the injured miner couldn't hear.

"The internal bleeding concerns me. If it's severe, he might not survive the journey to your clinic."

Moses nodded grimly. "I know. But we have no choice. I can't operate here."

"What if..." she hesitated, then continued more firmly, "What if we try to slow the bleeding first? Cold compresses might constrict the blood vessels enough to buy us time."

It was a sound suggestion. "There's a spring nearby with cold water," Moses said. "And ice in the shadowed parts of the ravine."

He dispatched one of the miners to gather what they needed, and soon they were applying cold compresses to Jonah's abdomen. The young man's color improved slightly, and his pulse, which Laura monitored constantly, steadied.

"It's working," she said, relief evident in her voice. "Not a permanent solution, but it might get us down the mountain safely."

Moses nodded. "Good thinking."

The wagon was ready, and with careful coordination, they transferred Jonah. Laura climbed in beside him, continuing to monitor his condition and maintain the cold compresses.

"I'll ride ahead and prepare the clinic," Moses told her. "Keep him as still as possible and watch that bruising. If it spreads rapidly or his pulse weakens significantly, send one of the miners riding with you to find me."

She nodded, her focus already returned to her patient. "We'll manage, Dr. Grant."

Something about her calm confidence in the face of crisis stirred a reluctant respect in Moses. He mounted his horse and rode ahead, his mind filled with preparations for the surgery that likely awaited them, and unexpected thoughts of the capable young nurse he'd been so quick to dismiss.

At the clinic, Moses worked rapidly to prepare his surgical table and instruments. He boiled water for cleaning the wound, arranged his surgical implements, and prepared a stronger dose of laudanum for the operation.

When the wagon arrived, Jonah was still conscious, though weakened from pain and blood loss. The bruising hadn't spread significantly, suggesting the internal bleeding might be slower than they'd feared.

"His pulse has remained stable," Laura reported as they transferred Jonah to the surgical table. "Weak, but not declining. The cold compresses seem to have helped."

"Good work," Moses acknowledged. "Now we need to address both injuries—the compound fracture and the internal bleeding."

He washed his hands thoroughly in the carbolic solution he kept prepared, a concession to modern practices he'd adopted years ago, though he'd been disinclined to mention this to Laura during their earlier argument.

To his surprise, Laura was already washing her hands as well, then donning a clean apron she'd found hanging on his rack.

"I assume you'll want assistance?" she asked, rolling up her sleeves.

Moses hesitated only briefly. Under normal circumstances, he operated alone, but this case would require multiple areas of attention. And she had proven herself capable at the mine.

"Yes," he decided. "You'll assist. Follow my instructions exactly."

For the next two hours, they worked together over Jonah's broken body. Moses operated on the internal bleeding first, making a careful incision to repair a torn blood vessel in the abdomen. Laura handed him instruments before he asked for them, administered ether with practiced precision, and managed bleeding with efficient pressure and sutures.

When Moses moved to the leg, cleaning and properly setting the compound fracture, Laura anticipated his needs without prompting. She held retractors steady, provided clean gauze, and maintained a watchful eye on Jonah's vital signs throughout.

By the time they finished, Jonah was stabilized, his wounds cleaned and dressed, his broken leg properly set and splinted.

"He needs constant monitoring," Moses said, washing blood from his hands in a basin. "Infection is the greatest risk now, especially with the abdominal wound."

Laura nodded, her face showing fatigue, but no sign of the squeamishness or distress. "I can stay with him."

Moses shook his head. "No, I'll take the first watch. You should rest. It's been a long day, and you're still adjusting to the altitude."

She looked about to argue, then nodded, acknowledging the wisdom of his suggestion. "I'll return this evening to relieve you, then. Say around eight o'clock?"

The offer surprised him. He was accustomed to handling post-operative care alone, often staying awake for days monitoring critical patients.

"That would be... helpful," he admitted, the words feeling strange on his tongue.

Laura removed her bloodied apron and washed her hands once more. As she dried them on a clean towel, she looked around the surgical room with an appraising eye.

"You're well-equipped for a frontier clinic," she observed. "And your surgical technique is excellent."

The compliment, delivered without flattery or condescension, caught Moses off guard. "I trained in Chicago before coming west," he said, offering the information without really understanding why. "Worked in a hospital there for three years."

"It shows," she replied simply. "Your sutures are precise, and you're economical with your movements. Very effective."

Moses shifted uncomfortably under her professional assessment. He wasn't accustomed to discussing his methods or receiving commendation for them.

"Necessity teaches efficiency," he said finally. "When you're the only doctor for miles, you learn to work clean and fast."

Laura smiled slightly, the expression transforming her serious face. "Indeed. Though, I hope you'll consider having an assistant regularly now. Four hands are certainly better than two in cases like Jonah's."

Moses couldn't argue with the logic, especially after witnessing her competence firsthand. But accepting her assistance meant accepting change—to his practice, his routines, and his solitary existence.

"We'll discuss a working arrangement tomorrow," he said, neither accepting nor rejecting her implied offer. "After we see how Jonah fares through the night."

"Of course." She moved toward the door, then paused. "Dr. Grant, I want to apologize for my comments earlier about hygiene practices. I noticed you use carbolic solution, and your surgical technique is impeccable. I should have observed before making assumptions."

The apology surprised him almost as much as her competence had. "And I should have given your training more credit," he admitted, the words difficult but necessary. "You handled yourself well today. Better than many interns I've seen in Chicago hospitals."

A genuine smile brightened her face. "Thank you. That means a great deal, coming from you."

As she turned to leave, Moses found himself studying her—really seeing her for the first time. Beneath the travel dirt yesterday and the surgical blood today, Laura Smythe was a striking woman. Not in the conventional way of the girls who occasionally caught his eye at town socials or meetings, but in a manner entirely her own.

There was a strength in her bearing, a confidence in her movements that spoke of someone comfortable with her abilities, yet not prideful about them. Her hands, he'd noticed during surgery, were capable and steady. The hands of someone accustomed to practical work despite her refined appearance.

"Miss Smythe," he called as she reached the door.

She turned, eyebrows raised in question.

"Eight o'clock," he confirmed. "And bring a change of clothes. Frontier emergencies don't keep regular hours."

Her smile returned, a flash of warmth in his austere clinic. "I'll be prepared, Dr. Grant."

After she left, Moses checked on Jonah once more, then sank into the chair beside the surgical table, suddenly aware of the bone-deep weariness that followed intense concentration and physical exertion.

Against his will, his thoughts returned to Laura. He'd been determined to dismiss her, to prove her city training inadequate for frontier demands. Instead, she'd demonstrated skill and adaptability he hadn't expected.

More disturbing than her competence, however, was his reaction to her. He'd noticed things he had no business noticing. The graceful efficiency of her movements, the way her eyes brightened when she spoke of patient care. The subtle floral scent somehow persisted even through the smells of blood and ether.

"Don't be a fool, Grant," he muttered to himself. "She's a colleague, nothing more. And a temporary one, more than likely."

But as he settled in for his vigil at Jonah's bedside, Moses couldn't entirely banish the image of Laura's confident hands working alongside his own, or the unexpected sense of relief at the prospect of sharing his burden. If only for a time.

Chapter 3

Laura stepped into Abernathy & Sons General Store, the bell above the door announcing her arrival with a cheerful jingle. After returning to the boarding house to wash away the blood and grime from Jonah's surgery, she'd changed into a clean dress and decided to explore Aspen Hollow properly. The mercantile seemed the perfect place to start.

The interior was dim after the bright afternoon light, but her eyes quickly adjusted to reveal a space packed floor to ceiling with goods of every description. Wooden barrels of flour, sugar, and coffee beans lined one wall. Shelves crowded with canned goods, tools, and housewares stretched to the ceiling. Glass cases displayed more precious items, watches, jewelry, and small bottles of perfume that seemed oddly delicate against the rugged backdrop of the frontier store.

"Well, if it isn't our new nurse!" A round-faced woman with graying hair bustled around the counter, her eyes alight with curiosity. "I'm Twila Abernathy. My husband, Silas, and I run this establishment." She wiped her hands on her apron before extending one to

Laura. "We're mighty pleased to meet you, especially after what you did for Jonah Crawford today."

Laura shook her hand, surprised by the warm greeting. "News travels quickly in Aspen Hollow, I see."

"Quicker than a mountain storm." Twila chuckled. "Three miners came straight down to report how you helped Dr. Grant at the mine, and Felix—that's my oldest boy—was at the clinic delivering supplies when they brought poor Jonah in. Said you worked alongside the doctor like you'd been doing it for years."

"I was simply doing my job," Laura replied, though she couldn't help feeling pleased that her first emergency in Aspen Hollow had apparently made a positive impression.

"Modest too! That's refreshing." Twila turned toward the back of the store. "Marybeth! Come meet Miss Smythe!"

A young woman with blonde hair tucked neatly under a simple cap emerged from behind a display of fabrics. Her expression brightened when she saw Laura.

"The new nurse! I've been hoping to meet you." Her smile was genuine and immediate. "I'm Marybeth Flanagan. I help the Abernathy's here at the mercantile."

"A pleasure to meet you both," Laura said, returning the smile. "I'm just getting acquainted with the town."

"Then you must let me show you around the mercantile at least," Marybeth offered eagerly. "Mrs. Abernathy, might I take a few minutes?"

"Of course, dear. I need to check on the order from Denver, anyway." Twila patted Laura's arm. "You're in good hands with Marybeth. And do come by our home sometime. My Tommy's been under the weather, and Dr. Grant says he's on the mend, but a second opinion from a trained nurse would ease a mother's heart. We live upstairs."

"I'd be happy to check on him," Laura replied, touched by the invitation.

As Twila moved away, Marybeth linked her arm through Laura's with an easy familiarity that was unexpected but welcome.

"You must tell me everything about Philadelphia," Marybeth said, her voice low with excitement. "I've never been farther east than Denver, and that was only once, three years ago."

"Philadelphia is quite different from Aspen Hollow," Laura admitted, allowing Marybeth to guide her through the store. "Though perhaps not as different as one might think. People are people wherever you go. They all love, struggle, and need care."

"But you must have theaters! And restaurants, and museums!" Marybeth's eyes shone. "And I've heard the fashions are months ahead of what we get here."

Laura couldn't help smiling at the young woman's enthusiasm. "Yes, to all of that. Though I spent more time in hospitals and clinics than at the theater, I'm afraid."

"Still, it must be wonderful to have choices," Marybeth sighed, then caught herself. "Not that Aspen Hollow isn't a fine place to live. We have everything we need, truly."

Laura glanced around the well-stocked mercantile. "It seems that way. Mr. Abernathy carries an impressive variety of goods."

"Oh yes. Silas prides himself on anticipating what the town needs before they know it themselves. That corner there—" she pointed to where bolts of fabric were displayed alongside sewing notions, "—that's my domain. I help ladies select patterns and fabrics."

As they continued their tour, Laura noticed two older women whispering while examining a display of canned goods, their gazes repeatedly darting toward her.

"—from Philadelphia, imagine that—"

"—modern notions—"

"—working alongside Doc Grant at the mine—"

Marybeth followed Laura's gaze and leaned closer. "That's Mrs. Whitman and Mrs. Holcomb. The town's two most dedicated gossips, though Mrs. Holcomb at least usually gets her facts straight."

"I see," Laura murmured. "I suppose I'm quite the novelty."

"The most exciting thing to happen since the church roof caught fire during Easter service last spring," Marybeth confirmed with a suppressed laugh. "Don't mind them. They mean well, mostly."

The bell over the door jingled, and a stout, gray-haired woman entered, removing her gloves with precise motions. Her clothes, while practical, were of a finer quality than most Laura had seen in town so far.

"That's Mrs. Evelyn Sterling," Marybeth whispered. "Widow of one of the founding miners. She's quite particular about everything."

Mrs. Sterling caught sight of Laura and Marybeth and made a direct line toward them, her expression appraising.

"So you're the nurse from back East," she declared without preamble, her sharp eyes taking in every detail of Laura's appearance. "Clara Bellweather mentioned to me, you had arrived. I'm Evelyn Sterling."

"Laura Smythe," Laura replied, extending her hand. "It's a pleasure to meet you, Mrs. Sterling."

The older woman accepted the handshake briefly. "Philadelphia, I understand. Very different from our little town."

"Yes, but I'm finding Aspen Hollow has its own unique character and charm."

Mrs. Sterling nodded, seeming to approve of this diplomatic answer. "I hear you assisted Dr. Grant with young Crawford today."

"Yes, there was an accident at the mine. Jonah was injured, but Dr. Grant performed surgery successfully. We're hopeful for his recovery."

"We've managed just fine with Dr. Grant's care these past five years," Mrs. Sterling remarked, her tone suggesting a question.

Laura recognized the subtle challenge. "Dr. Grant is clearly very skilled. I hope to complement his practice with my training and experience."

"Hmm. Well, I do hope you'll adjust to our ways, Miss Smythe. We're practical folk here. No patience for fancy theories that don't hold up in the mountains." With a slight nod, Mrs. Sterling moved toward the counter, where Twila had reappeared.

"Don't worry about her," Marybeth whispered once Mrs. Sterling was out of earshot. "She tests everyone new. If she decides she likes you, she'll be your staunchest supporter."

"And if she doesn't?" Laura asked with a raised eyebrow.

Marybeth grimaced. "Let's hope it doesn't come to that."

Their conversation was interrupted by the arrival of Clara Bellweather, a thin woman with an animated face, who immediately joined Mrs. Sterling at the counter. Her voice carried clearly through the store.

"Did you hear about Barnaby Flint's latest outburst at the town council meeting?" she asked Mrs. Sterling. "Ranting again about how the founding families cheated him out of his rightful claim. Your Herbert was one of those he named specifically."

"Barnaby Flint has been telling that tired tale for fifteen years," Mrs. Sterling replied dismissively. "The man is bitter and growing more unpleasant with age."

"Yes, but this time he threatened... well, something about 'this town will regret the day they crossed Barnaby Flint.' Made quite a scene before Pastor Lewis calmed him down."

Laura glanced at Marybeth questioningly.

"Barnaby Flint owns the main silver mine," Marybeth explained quietly. "He's... not the most pleasant man in town. Convinced himself that the original settlers somehow stole part of his claim, though most say he's just greedy and resentful because others struck richer veins."

"The mine where Jonah was injured today?"

"The very same. Flint Mining Company employs half the men in town, so people tolerate his moods." Marybeth shrugged. "He pays well enough, even if he complains constantly about his supposed mistreatment."

Laura filed this information away, finding it an interesting glimpse into the town's dynamics. Every community had its conflicts and personalities. Aspen Hollow was no different in that regard.

"I should introduce you to Mr. Abernathy while you're here," Marybeth suggested, changing the subject. "He's in the back office going over the books."

Laura followed her to a small room partitioned off from the main store, where a tall, sandy-haired man sat at a desk covered with ledgers.

"Mr. Abernathy," Marybeth called softly. "I've brought Miss Smythe to meet you."

Silas Abernathy looked up, removing his spectacles as he rose. "Miss Smythe, welcome to our establishment. I understand you've already made quite an impression at the mine today."

"Your wife mentioned the same thing," Laura said, shaking his offered hand. "Word certainly travels quickly here."

"It's both the blessing and curse of a small town," he replied with a slight smile. "Nothing stays private for long, but we also know when our neighbors need help."

"I'm discovering that. Everyone has been very welcoming."

"Well, most everyone," Marybeth interjected with a knowing look.

Mr. Abernathy cleared his throat. "Yes, well... Dr. Grant can be... abrupt. But he's a good man, and this town owes him a great deal."

"So I'm learning," Laura acknowledged, thinking of the doctor's surprising skill during Jonah's surgery. "His medical abilities are impressive."

"He saved my boy's life last winter when pneumonia nearly took him," Mr. Abernathy said quietly. "Stayed by Tommy's bed for three days straight, barely sleeping. Doc Grant's been tending to Tommy again the past couple days. He's been down with the flu or some such bug going around. That's the kind of doctor he is, gruff as a bear but devoted to his patients."

This glimpse into Moses Grant's character gave Laura pause. She'd seen his surgical skill firsthand, but this level of dedication spoke to something deeper than mere professional competence.

"I didn't mean to speak ill of the doctor," Marybeth said quickly. "Only that he's not always the most welcoming to newcomers."

"No offense taken," Laura assured her. "First impressions aren't always accurate."

"Well, I for one am glad you're here," Mr. Abernathy said firmly. "Doc Grant works too hard, has for years. Town this size needs more than one medical professional."

A bell rang at the counter, and Mr. Abernathy excused himself to help a customer, leaving Laura and Marybeth alone again.

"Would you like to see more of the town?" Marybeth offered. "My shift ends in ten minutes, and I'd be happy to show you around."

"I'd appreciate that," Laura replied, genuinely pleased by the suggestion.

After Marybeth completed her duties, the two young women set out into the afternoon sunshine. Aspen Hollow revealed itself as they walked, a patchwork of practical structures nestled against the dramatic backdrop of the mountains. The town had grown organically, buildings clustered together where the terrain allowed, with no formal planning evident in its layout.

"Main Street is the heart of things," Marybeth explained as they walked. "Most businesses are here or within a block or two. The Golden Nugget Saloon is down that way—" she nodded toward the far end of the street, "—though I imagine that's not a place you'll frequent much."

"Probably not," Laura agreed with a smile. "Though I expect some of my patients might come from there."

"No doubt. Jasper McCoy runs it. He's gruff but fair. Doesn't allow too much trouble in his establishment, which is why it's lasted when other saloons came and went."

They continued walking, Marybeth pointing out various buildings and explaining their significance.

"That's the schoolhouse where Millie Abernathy teaches," Marybeth said, indicating the simple wooden building. "Twenty-seven students of all ages, and she manages them beautifully."

Beyond the schoolhouse stood a white-painted church with a modest steeple. "First Mountain Chapel," Marybeth continued. "Pastor Lewis preaches powerful sermons, though he's never harsh about it. Services are at ten on Sundays, and many attend."

"I'll be there this Sunday," Laura said, noting how the church seemed to occupy the literal and figurative high ground in the community. "My faith is very important to me."

"Mine too," Marybeth said simply. "It's what gets us through the hard winters and harder times."

As they walked, Laura became increasingly aware of the curious glances and whispers that followed them. People nodded politely when Marybeth introduced her, but there was a reserved quality to most interactions, and a sense of judgment.

"Don't mind them," Marybeth said after they passed a group of miners who had fallen silent at their approach. "New faces are rare here, especially pretty educated women from the East. They're curious, that's all."

"I understand. I just hope I can prove myself useful to the community."

"After today's work with Jonah, you're already on your way," Marybeth assured her. "Look, there's Clementine Hayes's place. She's our local herbalist?"

Laura followed Marybeth's gaze to a small cabin set slightly apart from the main thoroughfare. A garden stretched behind it, still showing signs of life despite the advancing autumn season. Herbs hung drying from the porch rafters, and the scent of something pungent but not unpleasant drifted toward them.

"Dr. Grant spoke highly of her knowledge," Laura recalled. "Perhaps I should introduce myself?"

"Another time might be better," Marybeth suggested. "She's particular about interruptions while she's working, and that smoke suggests she's preparing remedies."

They continued their tour, passing Dr. Grant's clinic. Laura studied the building with newfound interest. The weathered exterior gave little indication of the surprisingly well-equipped surgery room within. She thought of Moses's hands, steady and precise as they worked to save Jonah's life, and felt a surprising flicker of admiration.

"Penny for your thoughts?" Marybeth asked.

Laura shook herself from her reverie. "I was just thinking about the surgery today. Dr. Grant is a skilled physician, despite his... challenging demeanor."

"That's one way of putting it," Marybeth laughed. "Most just call him ornery."

"There's more to him than that," Laura said. "The way he handled Jonah's case—there was genuine care beneath the gruffness."

"Interesting," Marybeth commented with a sidelong glance that made Laura blush slightly.

"From a professional perspective, of course," she clarified quickly.

"Of course," Marybeth agreed, though her expression remained amused. "Oh, there's Mrs. Bellweather again, and she's spotted us. Brace yourself."

Clara Bellweather approached with determined steps, her face alight with the pleasure of having new information to share.

"Miss Smythe! I was just telling Evelyn Sterling how exciting it is to have a nurse from Philadelphia among us. Such a grand city. My cousin visited once and could hardly stop talking about the buildings and carriages and fashionable people."

"It's a beautiful city," Laura agreed, "though Aspen Hollow has its own unique beauty."

"How diplomatic of you! But surely, you must find us terribly provincial after Philadelphia society. I hear the medical college there is most impressive, all those modern theories and scientific advances." Mrs. Bellweather leaned closer. "Tell me, is it true what they say about city doctors washing their hands dozens of times a day? Seems a terrible waste of good soap!"

Laura bit back a smile. "Handwashing is indeed emphasized in modern medical practice, Mrs. Bellweather. It's been shown to reduce infections significantly."

"Imagine that! Though our Dr. Grant does well enough without such fussiness, I'd say. He saved my Arthur's foot after that logging accident, just took a swig of whiskey, poured some on the wound, and set to work right there on our kitchen table!" She seemed almost proud of this crude approach. "No handwashing to speak of."

"Actually," Laura corrected gently, "I observed Dr. Grant using a carbolic solution today before surgery. He's clearly familiar with antiseptic practices."

"Is that so?" Mrs. Bellweather looked almost disappointed at being deprived of this contrast. "Well, I suppose even our cantankerous doctor can learn new tricks. Speaking of which, how did you find working with him today? I hear he's not made you particularly welcome."

Before Laura could respond, another voice interrupted.

"Clara Bellweather, are you interrogating the poor girl in the middle of the street?" Sera Williams approached, a market basket on her arm. "Miss Smythe barely has her bearings, and you're pestering her with questions."

Mrs. Bellweather drew herself up indignantly. "I'm merely making our new nurse feel welcome, Sera!"

Despite her apparent annoyance, there was no real heat in the exchange, suggesting to Laura that this was a familiar and almost affectionate pattern between the two women.

"I've been running my boarding house for twelve years, and that's long enough to know when someone might appreciate a respite from endless questions," Mrs. Williams replied good-naturedly. She turned to Laura. "I was just heading back to prepare supper. Would you care to join me, dear? Marybeth, you're welcome as well, of course."

"Thank you, but I promised Mother I'd help her with the mending," Marybeth declined. "But I'll see you soon, Laura. Perhaps we can continue our tour another day?"

"I'd like that," Laura said sincerely. She'd enjoyed the young woman's company and practical insights into Aspen Hollow.

As she walked back to the boarding house with Mrs. Williams, Laura reflected on her impressions of the town. Beneath the rough exterior and initial wariness, there seemed to be a genuine sense of community and care. People looked after one another here, which aligned perfectly with her calling to serve.

"You've had quite a first day in Aspen Hollow," Mrs. Williams commented as they climbed the steps to the boardinghouse porch. "Arrived yesterday and already assisted in a major surgery. I imagine Dr. Grant must have been impressed with your skills."

"I'm not sure 'impressed' is the right word," Laura admitted. "But I think he was surprised to find I wasn't completely useless."

Mrs. Williams chuckled. "High praise from our doctor, believe me. Lester says Jonah might not have survived if you both hadn't acted as fast as you did. You've already made a difference here, Laura."

"I hope so," Laura said.

Inside, delicious smells emanated from the kitchen, where Mr. Williams was stirring something on the stove.

"I put the stew on as you asked, dear," he told his wife. "Added those carrots from the Holcombs' garden too."

"Perfect," Mrs. Williams said, giving her husband an appreciative pat on the arm. "Supper will be ready in about an hour, Laura. That should give you time to rest a bit."

"Actually, I'm supposed to return to the clinic at eight to relieve Dr. Grant from watching over Jonah. Would it be possible for me to take my dinner and something for Dr. Grant to eat as well, instead of my dining alone here?" Laura asked. "I imagine he's hungry."

"Night watch already! He must trust your nursing skills," Mrs. Williams observed. "I'll pack some food for you both. I guarantee Doc Grant hasn't eaten anything decent today."

"That's very kind of you."

"Not at all. Looking after folks is what we do here." Mrs. Williams headed toward the kitchen. "Go freshen up. I'll have a basket ready when you come down."

In her room, Laura collected a clean dress, basic toiletries, her bible, and a medical journal. She changed into a more practical garment suitable for a night of patient monitoring, then knelt beside her bed.

"Lord," she prayed, "thank You for bringing me safely to this place and for the opportunity to serve You here. Guide my hands and heart as I care for Jonah and work with Dr. Grant. Help me to bring Your healing presence to Aspen Hollow, and to be patient as I earn the trust of these good people."

She remained kneeling for several minutes, drawing strength from the familiar ritual of prayer that had sustained her through the darkest days after her family's deaths. The memory of that terrible accident still lurked beneath the surface of her thoughts. The splintering of wood, the screams, the helplessness as she watched her parents and younger brother slip away despite her desperate efforts to save them.

Laura tucked her Bible into her bag alongside the medical journal. Both represented essential aspects of her calling, scientific knowledge and spiritual guidance working in harmony. Dr. Grant might scoff at what he perceived as impractical idealism, but Laura had seen first-hand how faith and modern medicine could complement each other.

The image of the doctor rose unbidden in her mind, his intense concentration during surgery, the sure movements of his hands, and the unexpected gentleness when he'd examined Jonah's injuries at the mine. There was more to Moses Grant than his gruff exterior suggested, layers that intrigued her despite her initial negative impression.

She recalled the ride to the mine, the solid strength of him as she'd held on during their hurried journey, the way he'd efficiently explained mining dangers even while rushing to Jonah's aid. There was something compelling about his focused competence, his evident dedication to his patients despite his cynical manner.

Laura shook her head, dismissing these thoughts as irrelevant. Professional respect was one thing, and she did respect his medical skills, but anything beyond that was foolish to contemplate. She was here to serve the community and practice her nursing, not to be intrigued by a cantankerous doctor who'd made it clear he barely tolerated her presence.

After quickly freshening up, she gathered her things and headed downstairs, where Mrs. Williams waited with a covered basket.

"Beef stew, fresh bread, and apple pie," she announced. "Enough for you and Dr. Grant both."

"I appreciate your thoughtfulness, Mrs. Williams."

"Call me Sera, dear. And it's no trouble." She handed Laura the basket. "Will you be all right walking to the clinic alone? Lester could escort you."

"Thank you, but I'll be fine."

The evening air had cooled considerably as Laura made her way down Main Street toward the clinic. Stars were appearing in the darkening sky, their brilliance undiminished by city lights. Lanterns glowed in windows, and voices and laughter spilled from the Golden Nugget Saloon as she passed. A few men nodded respectfully as she walked by.

The clinic windows glowed with lamplight, and Laura took a deep breath before climbing the steps and knocking on the door.

Chapter 4

Moses checked Jonah's pulse for the third time in an hour, noting with satisfaction that it remained steady despite the trauma of surgery. The young miner slept fitfully, occasional murmurs escaping his lips as the laudanum kept the worst of the pain at bay. Satisfied with his patient's condition, Moses settled back into the worn chair beside the surgical table, his body aching from the day's exertions.

The clinic was quiet except for Jonah's breathing and the occasional creak of the building settling. Moses rubbed his eyes, feeling the familiar weight of responsibility pressing down on him. Five years of being Aspen Hollow's only physician had carved permanent lines into his face and turned portions of his dark hair prematurely gray at the temples.

He glanced at the small clock on his shelf. Not quite six. Miss Smythe wouldn't arrive for another two hours. He could use that time to organize his thoughts on their working arrangement, though part of him still resisted the idea of accepting her assistance.

The image of Laura's capable hands working alongside his during surgery rose in his mind. She had moved with practiced efficiency, anticipating his needs before he voiced them. Not the fumbling uncertainty he'd expected from a young city-trained nurse confronted with frontier realities, but genuine competence.

"Stop it, Grant," he muttered to himself. One successful surgery didn't erase the fundamental differences in their approaches to medicine. Her insistence on modern theories and practices might work in Philadelphia's clean hospitals, but here in the mountains, practicality trumped theory every time.

His gaze drifted to the small framed photograph on a shelf nearby. Rebecca Miller, his sister, stared back at him, her face forever frozen in the calm confidence of youth, unaware of what awaited her.

"I did everything right," Moses whispered to the photograph, the words hollow from repetition. "Everything by the book."

Four years had passed since Rebecca's death in childbirth, but the memory remained as sharp as a surgical blade. He'd been called to the Miller homestead on a night much like the one approaching, clear and cold, with stars piercing the darkness like ice crystals. Jake Miller, his brother-in-law and a miner who would later die under Moses's care following a mining accident, had ridden into town in a panic. Rebecca had been struggling through a difficult labor with their first child.

Moses had arrived to find Rebecca pale and exhausted. He'd done everything his training dictated: careful examination, positioning, encouragement, and when complications arose, he'd performed the necessary interventions with textbook precision.

It hadn't mattered. Rebecca had hemorrhaged suddenly and severely. Despite his frantic efforts to stop the bleeding, she had slipped away, her hand growing cold in his as Jake sobbed beside them. The baby, a perfect little girl, had followed her mother hours later despite Moses's desperate attempts to save her.

He'd prayed that night, for the first time in years, begging God for intervention. The silence that answered him had been deafening.

"Modern medicine," Moses scoffed now, the words bitter on his tongue. What good were advances and theories when they failed at the critical moment? Rebecca had died despite his careful adherence to the latest obstetrical practices he'd learned in Chicago.

After that, he'd turned increasingly to the practical, time-tested methods of frontier medicine. The remedies that didn't always have scientific explanation but had kept mountain folk alive for generations. He'd studied with Clementine Hayes, learning which herbs stopped bleeding, which poultices drew out infection, and which teas reduced fever.

A knock at the clinic door startled Moses from his dark reminiscence. He glanced at the clock again—still not quite six. Too early for Miss Smythe, and most townspeople knew better than to disturb him during a patient watch unless it was an emergency.

"Come in," he called, rising from his chair and moving toward the waiting room.

The door opened to reveal Laura Smythe, a covered basket in her hands and determination written across her face. She'd changed into a simpler dress of dark blue, practical for a night of patient monitoring, with her chestnut hair neatly braided down her back. She looked composed and far too alert for someone who'd assisted in major surgery earlier that day.

"Miss Smythe," Moses said, unable to keep the surprise from his voice. "You're early."

"I thought you might appreciate dinner," she replied, holding up the basket. The delicious aroma of beef stew wafted from beneath the cloth covering. "Mrs. Williams was concerned you hadn't eaten properly today."

Moses stared at her, momentarily disarmed by this unexpected consideration. When was the last time anyone had thought to bring him a meal during a patient watch? Usually, he subsisted on coffee and whatever stale bread he had on hand.

"I..." He cleared his throat. "That was thoughtful."

Laura stepped fully into the clinic, closing the door behind her. "How is Jonah doing?"

The familiar ground of medical discussion steadied Moses. "His vital signs are stable. No significant increase in the abdominal bruising, which suggests the internal bleeding is contained. Pulse is steady, and the leg wound looks clean so far."

Laura nodded, setting the basket on a small table near the examining room door. "Has he regained consciousness at all?"

"Briefly, about an hour ago. Coherent enough to ask about his condition. I gave him more laudanum for the pain."

"Good," Laura said, moving past Moses into the surgical room where Jonah lay. She approached the patient with quiet steps, her eyes quickly assessing his condition with professional precision.

Moses watched as she gently checked Jonah's pulse, her touch light but confident. She placed a hand on the young miner's forehead, checking for fever, then carefully lifted the bandage on his leg to examine the surgical site.

"The wound looks clean," she commented. "Your sutures are holding well."

"I've had plenty of practice," Moses replied, trying to ignore the pleasant aroma emanating from the basket she'd brought. His stomach growled traitorously.

Laura glanced up at the sound, a small smile playing at the corners of her mouth. "We should eat while he's sleeping soundly. There's enough for both of us."

Moses wanted to refuse, to maintain the professional distance he'd cultivated for years, but hunger and fatigue undermined his resistance. "I suppose we could take turns eating, keeping watch over Jonah."

"Or we could both eat here, where we can monitor him," Laura suggested, already returning to the basket. She began unpacking its contents. Two containers of stew, a cloth-wrapped loaf of bread, a small crock of butter, and apple pie wrapped in waxed paper.

Wordlessly, Moses pulled a small table closer to Jonah's bedside and brought another chair from his office. Laura arranged their meal efficiently, the domestic scene starkly incongruous in the clinical setting.

"Mrs. Williams sent more than enough for both of us," Laura said as she handed him a bowl of stew. "She seems convinced you survive primarily on coffee and determination."

A reluctant chuckle escaped Moses before he could suppress it. "Sera Williams has strong opinions about proper nutrition. She sometimes sends food with Lester, claiming medical consultations as her excuse."

"She cares about you," Laura observed, breaking off a piece of bread. "Many people in town do, from what I've gathered today."

Moses focused on his stew, uncomfortable with the personal turn in the conversation. The food was hearty and flavorful, reminding him how long it had been since breakfast—a cup of coffee and a stale biscuit consumed while reading patient notes.

"Sera's cooking is the best in the territory," he offered after several bites, hoping to steer the conversation back to safer ground.

"It's delicious," Laura agreed. "Today's emergency at the mine was quite eventful, not quite what I expected on my first day working in Aspen Hollow."

Her words reminded Moses of her performance during Jonah's surgery, a topic he found easier to address than Sera Williams's concern for his well-being.

"You handled yourself well today," he acknowledged, the admission costing him less than he'd expected. "Your training is evident in your technique."

Laura's expression brightened at the praise, however grudging. "Thank you. I had excellent instructors at the college. Dr. Emily Parker, who taught surgical nursing, was particularly influential in my training."

"A female doctor?" Moses raised an eyebrow, genuinely curious despite himself.

"Yes. The Philadelphia Medical College for Women was established specifically to train female physicians and nurses," Laura explained. "Dr. Parker was one of the first graduates and returned to teach. She's a brilliant surgeon with a particular interest in obstetrics."

Moses tensed involuntarily at the mention of obstetrics, his sister's face flashing before his eyes. He pushed the memory away, focusing instead on his stew.

"You must have dealt with far different cases in Philadelphia than what you'll encounter here," he said after a moment.

"Different in some ways, similar in others, I'm sure," Laura replied thoughtfully. "Disease and injury don't discriminate between city and country. Though I imagine mining accidents like Jonah's are more common here than in Philadelphia."

"Mining, hunting accidents, falls from horses, injuries from building or logging," Moses listed. "Frontier life is hard on the body. Not to mention the typical illnesses, pneumonia, influenza, childbed fever, diphtheria."

Laura nodded solemnly. "We had our share of those in Philadelphia as well, particularly in the poorer districts. Tenement housing breeds disease just as effectively as harsh conditions."

She paused, then added more softly, "I spent much of my final year of training in those districts. It wasn't all clean hospital wards and modern equipment, as you seemed to believe this morning."

Moses studied her across the small table, reassessing his initial judgment. The image of a sheltered city nurse he'd constructed didn't align with the woman before him, who spoke of tenements with the quiet confidence of experience.

"Why choose to come here?" he asked abruptly. "Surely, there were positions in Philadelphia that would have made better use of your training."

Laura set down her spoon, meeting his gaze directly. "I requested a frontier posting specifically. The missionary board had several openings, including two at Philadelphia hospitals and one at a city mission in Denver, but I chose Aspen Hollow."

"Why?" Moses pressed, genuinely curious now.

A shadow passed across Laura's face, brief but unmistakable. "Because I believe this is where God wants me to serve."

The mention of divine guidance almost made Moses scoff, but something in her expression stopped him. There was a depth of conviction there, and beneath it, a hint of something else—an old pain carefully controlled.

Instead, he asked, "And what does your family think of your decision to bury yourself in the mountains?"

Laura's hands stilled on her bread. "I have no family," she said quietly. "My parents and brother died when I was fifteen. Our wagon overturned, crossing a river in Kansas."

The simple statement carried the weight of profound loss, and Moses immediately regretted his cavalier question. "I'm sorry," he said, the words inadequate but sincere.

"It was a long time ago," Laura replied, though her eyes suggested otherwise. "A local pastor and his wife in Kansas took me in afterward. They supported my decision to return East for nursing training, and later, to follow this calling west again."

Moses was struck by the resilience such a journey required, orphaned on the frontier, returned to the East for education, then deliberately choosing to come back to the harsh reality of mountain life.

"That explains your familiarity with frontier conditions," he acknowledged. "I had assumed you were city-born and bred."

"A reasonable assumption based on my training," Laura conceded. "But no, I was born in Philadelphia, but my family was part of the westward migration when I was young. We were heading to Oregon when..." She trailed off, then straightened her shoulders. "When the accident happened."

Moses recognized the deliberate shift from painful memories. He used similar tactics himself when thoughts of his sister or brother-in-law threatened to surface at inopportune moments.

"And now you're back in the West," he observed. "Completing the journey in a way."

Laura looked surprised at his perception. "I hadn't thought of it that way, but perhaps you're right." She glanced at Jonah, checking that he still slept peacefully, then added, "Though my reasons for coming to Aspen Hollow aren't about completing my family's journey. They're about fulfilling a promise I made after they died."

"A promise?" Moses couldn't help asking, drawn despite himself into her story.

"To use whatever skills God gave me to prevent others from suffering, as my family did," Laura said simply. "They died from their injuries because there was no one with medical knowledge nearby. I was old enough to understand what was happening, but had no idea how to help them."

The raw honesty in her voice struck a chord with Moses. He understood all too well the helplessness of watching a loved one die despite desperate efforts to save them.

"That's why proper medical training matters so much to me," Laura continued. "Not for its own sake, but because knowledge saves lives. The right techniques, and the right preparations, can make the difference between life and death."

Her words echoed his own beliefs before disillusionment had set in, before Rebecca had hemorrhaged to death despite his textbook interventions.

"Sometimes knowledge isn't enough," Moses said, more harshly than he'd intended. "Sometimes people die, no matter what you do, no matter how well-trained you are or how carefully you follow the latest medical wisdom."

Laura studied him with unexpected perception. "You've lost patients despite doing everything right," she said softly. It wasn't a question.

Moses stiffened, uncomfortable with her insight. "Every doctor loses patients. It's part of the profession."

"Yes, but some losses mark us more deeply than others," Laura persisted gently. "I saw it in your face when we were operating on Jonah. The fear that despite your skill, it might not be enough."

Moses pushed his empty bowl away, suddenly regretting his decision to share this meal. Laura Smythe saw too much, peered past his carefully constructed walls with an ease that unnerved him.

"Jonah's going to be fine," he said curtly, deliberately changing the subject. "Based on his current condition, I expect a full recovery, assuming infection doesn't set in."

Laura accepted the redirection with grace. "The carbolic solution you used during surgery should help prevent that. Your antiseptic practices are more thorough than you led me to believe this morning."

Moses shrugged, uncomfortable with her observation. "I use what works. Lister's methods have merit, even if they're not always practical in emergency situations."

"A pragmatic approach," Laura noted with approval. "Adapting modern techniques to frontier conditions rather than rejecting them outright."

"Don't mistake practicality for endorsement of all your modern theories," Moses warned, though without the bite his words might have carried earlier. "I still maintain that many so-called advances are unproven in real-world conditions, especially outside hospital settings."

"Then we'll have to prove their value here in Aspen Hollow," Laura replied, undaunted. "Starting with Jonah's recovery."

Her quiet confidence irked and impressed Moses in equal measure. Before he could respond, Jonah stirred on the surgical table, a low moan escaping his lips as the laudanum began to wear off.

Both Moses and Laura were on their feet instantly, medical professionals once more, their personal conversation forgotten. Moses checked Jonah's pulse while Laura examined the surgical sites.

"The leg looks good," she reported. "No signs of increased swelling or infection starting."

"Abdominal wound is also unchanged," Moses confirmed. "How are you feeling, Jonah?"

The young miner's eyes fluttered open, confusion giving way to recognition. "Doc," he croaked. "Miss Smythe. Did I make it?"

"You did indeed," Laura assured him with a warm smile. "Dr. Grant performed surgery successfully on both your leg and the internal injury."

"Hurts something fierce," Jonah admitted, gritting his teeth.

"That's to be expected," Moses said, already preparing another dose of laudanum. "This will help with the pain. Try to drink some water first."

Laura supported Jonah's head as Moses held a cup of water to his lips. The young man drank greedily, then accepted the laudanum mixture.

"Is my leg still there?" Jonah asked after swallowing the medicine. "Can't feel it much."

"It's still attached," Moses assured him dryly. "Though you won't be winning any foot races for a while."

Jonah attempted a weak smile. "Didn't much care for racing, anyway." His gaze shifted to Laura. "Thank you for helping, Miss Smythe. I appreciate your being right there with Doc Grant, pulling me out and all."

"Just doing my job," Laura replied warmly. "You were very brave."

"Didn't feel brave," Jonah admitted. "Felt scared as a rabbit with that beam crushing me."

"Being afraid doesn't cancel out bravery," Laura told him. "It's what you do despite the fear that counts."

Moses watched their interaction with interest. Laura had an easy manner with patients, warm without being overly familiar. It contrasted with his own more reserved approach, yet he couldn't deny its effectiveness. Jonah visibly relaxed under her attention.

"You should rest now," Moses advised as the laudanum began to take effect. "Sleep is the best medicine for healing."

"Will you both be here?" Jonah asked, eyes already growing heavy.

"One of us will be with you throughout the night," Laura assured him. "You're not alone."

Her words seemed to satisfy Jonah, who drifted back into a drug-induced slumber. Moses found himself watching Laura as she adjusted Jonah's blanket, her movements efficient yet gentle.

"You have a way with patients," he observed, surprising himself with the admission.

Laura glanced up. "So do you, in your own fashion. Jonah clearly trusts you implicitly."

"Practical necessity," Moses dismissed. "I'm the only doctor for twenty miles."

"I think it's more than that," Laura countered. "The way people speak about you in town, there's genuine respect there, not just dependency."

Uncomfortable with her assessment, Moses gathered their dinner dishes, returning them to the basket. "We should discuss our working arrangement," he said, deliberately changing the subject again. "Assuming you still want the position after today's events."

"More than ever," Laura replied firmly. "Today confirmed that my skills can be useful here, and that we can work together effectively despite our different approaches."

Moses couldn't argue with her assessment of their surgical partnership. They had worked well together, their movements complementary rather than conflicting.

"Very well," he conceded. "I propose a trial period of one month. You'll assist with patients, maintain records, and help with treatments. In return, I'll provide guidance on frontier conditions and methods."

"And after the month?" Laura asked.

"If the arrangement proves satisfactory to both of us, we can discuss more permanent terms." Moses kept his tone professional, though part of him already doubted he would want to return to practicing alone after experiencing the efficiency of having a competent assistant.

"Agreed," Laura said promptly. "When shall I begin officially?"

"You already have," Moses pointed out, gesturing to Jonah. "Unless you'd prefer a day to settle in further?"

"No. The sooner I learn Aspen Hollow's particular needs, the better I can serve the community."

Moses nodded, respecting her dedication, even as he maintained his reservations about her methods. "I typically begin seeing patients at eight in the morning. The clinic is busiest early in the day, as miners stop in before their shifts, and again in late afternoon when they return."

"I'll be here at seven-thirty to prepare," Laura promised. "We should also discuss your record-keeping system so I can familiarize myself with your patients' histories."

The conversation shifted to practical matters, clinic procedures, common treatments, and the particular challenges of Aspen Hollow's population. As they talked, Moses was reluctantly impressed by Laura's questions. They were specific and thoughtful, focused on adapting her knowledge to local conditions rather than imposing city methods blindly.

"The altitude affects dosages," Moses explained. "Medications often work differently at this elevation, and patients with respiratory conditions struggle more severely here."

"I noticed the air is thinner," Laura acknowledged. "Are there local remedies that work particularly well for respiratory difficulties?"

"Clementine Hayes makes an effective pine and mullein infusion. I often prescribe it alongside traditional treatments."

"I'd like to meet her," Laura said with genuine interest. "Dr. Grant, would you be willing to introduce me to Mrs. Hayes? I think I could learn a great deal from her about local remedies."

The request surprised Moses. Most medical professionals he'd encountered from the East dismissed herbal treatments as superstition or, at best, placebos.

"You want to learn about herbal medicine?" he asked skeptically.

"I want to learn whatever helps patients," Laura clarified. "If local remedies are effective, especially for conditions specific to this region, I'd be foolish to ignore them out of professional pride."

Her answer was so reasonable, so aligned with his own pragmatic approach, that Moses was momentarily speechless. He'd expected to spend weeks battling her over modern versus traditional methods, yet here she was, actively seeking to incorporate local wisdom into her practice.

"I'll speak to Clementine," he said finally. "She can be... particular about whom she shares her knowledge with."

"Thank you," Laura said sincerely. "I'd appreciate that greatly."

Their discussion was interrupted by a knock at the clinic door. Moses frowned, checking his pocket watch. It was past seven in the evening, late for a non-emergency visit.

"Excuse me," he said to Laura, moving to answer the door.

Pastor Simon Lewis stood on the doorstep, his usually serene expression tight with concern. "Moses, I'm sorry to disturb you. I know you're looking after Jonah, but I've just come from the Whitman place. Young Edward has developed a high fever and a rash that his mother doesn't recognize. She's quite worried."

Moses sighed, mentally calculating the timing. The Whitman homestead was a good thirty-minute ride from town, and leaving Jonah unattended so soon after surgery was out of the question.

Before he could respond, Laura appeared behind him. "Dr. Grant, I can monitor Jonah if you need to make a house call," she offered.

Moses hesitated, caught between professional responsibility and the lingering reluctance to fully trust Laura with his patient's care.

Pastor Lewis looked between them, then smiled at Laura. "Miss Smythe, I didn't realize you were already assisting at the clinic. That's wonderful news."

"We've established a trial arrangement," Moses said before Laura could respond. He turned to her, making a quick decision. "Are you comfortable monitoring Jonah alone? The internal bleeding is my primary concern. If the abdominal bruising spreads significantly or his pulse weakens, you'll need to act quickly."

"I can handle it," Laura assured him with calm confidence. "I've managed post-operative monitoring many times."

Moses nodded curtly. "I'll check the Whitman boy. If it's something straightforward, I should be back within two hours. If you notice any concerning changes in Jonah's condition—"

"I'll send for you immediately," Laura promised.

"Good." Moses retrieved his medical bag and coat. "There's more laudanum in the cabinet if Jonah needs it for pain. No more than 15 drops per dose."

"Understood," Laura said. "I'll keep detailed notes of his condition while you're gone."

Moses paused at the door, struck by a strange reluctance to leave. It had been years since he'd entrusted a critical patient to anyone else's care, yet something about Laura's steady gaze and composed demeanor reassured him.

"I'll return as soon as I can," he told her, then followed Pastor Lewis into the evening darkness.

They walked briskly toward the pastor's waiting buggy, the older man matching Moses's longer stride with determined steps.

"She seems very capable," Pastor Lewis commented as they climbed into the vehicle. "I'm glad to see you two working together already."

Moses grunted noncommittally, unwilling to admit how quickly Laura had proven her value. "She assisted with Jonah's surgery. Did well enough."

The pastor smiled knowingly. "High praise indeed from you, Moses. I had faith she would be an asset to our community."

"You might have consulted me before requesting a nurse from the missionary board," Moses pointed out, still irked by the pastor's independent action.

"Would you have agreed?" Pastor Lewis asked mildly, flicking the reins to set the horse in motion.

"Probably not," Moses admitted grudgingly. "But that's beside the point."

"Is it?" The pastor chuckled. "You've been carrying Aspen Hollow's medical needs alone for five years, Moses. Every time I or the town council suggested finding you an assistant, you dismissed the idea outright."

"Because most 'assistants' would be more hindrance than a help in frontier conditions," Moses argued. "And I manage fine on my own."

"You exhaust yourself is what you do," Pastor Lewis corrected gently. "When was the last time you slept a full night? Or took a day for yourself? The town needs you, Moses, but we need you healthy and whole, not worked to collapse."

Moses stared straight ahead, uncomfortable with the pastor's concern. Simon Lewis had been one of the few people to break through his professional reserve over the years, offering friendship without demands or judgment. The pastor's quiet faith and genuine compassion stood in stark contrast to Moses's growing cynicism, yet somehow their friendship had endured.

"Miss Smythe seems different from what I expected," Moses admitted after a long moment. "Less... impractical than I assumed she would be."

Pastor Lewis nodded thoughtfully. "Laura has a remarkable spirit. When I corresponded with the missionary board, they spoke highly of her determination and adaptability. She specifically requested a frontier posting, you know. Quite adamant about it, apparently."

"She mentioned that," Moses said, recalling Laura's brief reference to her family's tragedy. "Did you know about her background? Losing her family in a wagon accident?"

"Yes, though she didn't share many details in her letters. Only that the experience shaped her calling to medicine." The pastor glanced at Moses. "She has a strong faith, one tested by genuine hardship. Not unlike someone else I know, though perhaps with different results."

Moses frowned at the implied comparison. "My faith is my own concern, Pastor."

"Of course," Pastor Lewis agreed easily. "I merely observe that you and Laura might have more in common than appears at first glance. Both driven by experiences, both dedicated to healing, both familiar with loss."

Moses had no response to that insight, so he changed the subject to the case at hand. "Tell me more about the Whitman boy's symptoms. When did the fever start? What kind of rash?"

The pastor accepted the redirection, detailing young Edward's condition as they drove through the darkening evening toward the Whitman homestead.

\Chapter 5

The examination of Edward Whitman took longer than Moses anticipated. The seven-year-old boy was indeed feverish, with a distinctive rash spreading across his chest and back. After careful consideration, Moses diagnosed measles, instructing Mrs. Whitman on care procedures and quarantine measures for her other children.

By the time he returned to Aspen Hollow, it was well past ten o'clock. Fatigue weighed heavily on him as he approached the clinic. The day's events, Jonah's surgery, his conversations with Laura, and now Edward Whitman's illness, blurring together in a haze of exhaustion.

Light still glowed from the clinic windows, a warm beacon in the darkness. Moses entered quietly, mindful of Jonah's need for rest.

He found Laura seated beside the surgical table, a medical journal open on her lap and a small oil lamp providing just enough light to read by. She looked up at his entrance; her face showing relief.

"How is the Whitman boy?" she asked immediately.

"Measles," Moses replied, hanging his coat. "Early stages. I've advised quarantine for the family and left instructions for care."

Laura nodded. "There were several measles cases in Philadelphia before I left."

"And Jonah?" Moses moved to examine the sleeping miner.

"Stable," Laura reported efficiently. "He woke twice, once around eight-thirty, quite lucid and in moderate pain, and again at nine-forty-five, more briefly. I administered 15 drops of laudanum after the first waking as he requested relief. His pulse has remained steady, and there's been no significant change in the abdominal bruising."

Moses checked Jonah's vital signs personally, finding them exactly as Laura had described. The wounds looked clean, with no signs of developing infection.

"You kept detailed notes," he observed, glancing at the patient chart where Laura had recorded Jonah's condition at regular intervals.

"I thought it would be helpful to track his recovery progress systematically," she explained. "I hope you don't mind that I used your patient forms."

"No, it's... thorough," Moses acknowledged, impressed despite himself.

Laura closed her medical journal. "I can continue monitoring him through the night if you'd like to rest. You've had a long day."

Moses shook his head. "I'll take the night watch. You should get some sleep."

"We could share the responsibility," Laura suggested. "Each taking half the night. That way, we'd both be fresher for clinic hours tomorrow."

The proposal was entirely sensible. Moses knew from experience that attempting to practice medicine after a sleepless night led to mistakes, yet he'd done it countless times out of necessity.

"Very well," he conceded reluctantly. "I'll take the first watch until two o'clock. You can return then and monitor until morning."

Laura studied him for a moment, then unexpectedly changed course. "Actually, if you don't mind, I'd prefer the first watch. I'm still quite alert, and this way you could get a solid block of rest before morning patients arrive."

The offer was tempting. Moses felt the bone-deep weariness that came from too many responsibilities, carried alone for too long. Still, he hesitated, uncomfortable with the idea of leaving Laura alone for hours.

"You need to rest, Dr. Grant," Laura said gently, reading his reluctance. "I promise I'll send for you immediately if there's any change in Jonah's condition."

Her directness, free from condescension or manipulation, finally swayed him. "Wake me at two, regardless," he instructed. "My quarters are upstairs. The side door and staircase lead directly up."

"I will," Laura promised. She hesitated, then added, "Thank you for trusting me with this responsibility."

Moses nodded awkwardly, unused to such straightforward appreciation. "You've earned it today," he admitted.

As he turned to leave, fatigue momentarily overwhelming his usual reserve, Moses added, "And thank you for bringing dinner. It was... thoughtful."

Laura smiled, the expression transforming her serious face in a way that caught Moses off guard. "You're welcome, Dr. Grant."

He climbed the stairs to his spartan living quarters, removing his boots and vest but leaving his shirt and trousers on in case he needed to respond quickly to a medical emergency. Stretching out on his narrow bed, Moses expected sleep to claim him immediately.

Instead, his mind raced with images from the day. Laura's competent hands during surgery, the quiet confidence in her voice as she spoke of her calling, and the resilience evident in her journey from orphaned girl to trained nurse. Most unsettling was the memory of her smile just moments ago, warm and genuine despite the exhaustion she must surely feel.

Moses rolled onto his side, irritated with himself for dwelling on such details. Laura Smythe was a professional colleague, nothing more. That he found her unexpectedly capable and occasionally pleasant to converse with was irrelevant.

Yet as sleep finally claimed him, his last thoughts were not of Jonah's surgery or Edward Whitman's measles, but of the quiet strength he'd glimpsed in Laura's blue eyes. She spoke of the promise that had guided her life since her family's death.

Maybe having an assistant wouldn't be as disruptive as he'd feared.

***

Laura checked Jonah's pulse again, satisfied with its steady rhythm beneath her fingertips. The young miner slept peacefully, the laudanum keeping pain at bay while his body began the hard work of healing.

The clinic was quiet, with only the occasional creak of the building settling and Jonah's even breathing breaking the silence. Laura used the time to study Dr. Grant's patient records, familiarizing herself with his notation system and the typical cases he treated.

His handwriting was surprisingly neat for a doctor, his notes concise but thorough. Reading between the lines, Laura could trace the patterns of illness and injury in Aspen Hollow, seasonal respiratory infections, mining accidents, childhood diseases, and the occasional serious trauma requiring surgery.

The records revealed something else, too, Moses Grant's dedication to his patients. Notes indicated numerous house calls in terrible weather, multiple-day vigils beside sickbeds, and creative adaptations of treatments when supplies ran short. The picture that emerged was of a man who had given himself completely to his calling, often at the expense of his own well-being.

That sacrifice was evident in his face, Laura reflected. Though only thirty-two, Dr. Grant carried himself with the weariness of someone much older. The lines around his eyes and the touch of gray at his temples spoke of years of heavy responsibility borne largely alone.

"He needs help, whether he admits it or not," Laura murmured to herself. The fact that he'd agreed to her trial period suggested he recognized this truth, even if reluctantly.

Her thoughts were interrupted by Jonah stirring. His eyes fluttered open, confusion giving way to recognition as he focused on her face.

"Miss Smythe," he said hoarsely. "Still here?"

"I'm keeping watch," she confirmed, bringing a cup of water to his lips. "How's your pain?"

Jonah drank gratefully, then grimaced. "Comes and goes. Leg's starting to throb something fierce."

Laura checked the clock. It had been nearly four hours since his last dose of laudanum. "I can give you something more for the pain now."

"Appreciate that," Jonah said, his face tight with discomfort. "Don't much like feeling helpless like this."

"You won't always be," Laura assured him as she measured the laudanum carefully. "With proper care and rest, you should heal well. Though it will take time and patience."

Jonah accepted the medicine, then asked, "Where's Doc Grant?"

"Resting upstairs. He'll take over watching you in a few hours." Laura adjusted Jonah's blanket. "He performed both your surgeries today and then was called to treat another patient at the Whitman homestead."

"Sounds about right," Jonah said with a weak smile. "Doc never stops. Been that way since he came to Aspen Hollow. When the fever took my ma two years back, he rode through a snowstorm to reach our cabin. Stayed three days straight, barely sleeping."

Laura adjusted the compress on Jonah's forehead. "That speaks to his dedication."

"He's a good man. Just carries too much on his shoulders." Jonah's eyes began to grow heavy as the laudanum took effect. "Folks here depend on him more than they should. But what choice is there in these mountains?"

"Now he has some help," Laura offered quietly.

Jonah's lips curved into a slight smile. "You're good for him, Miss Smythe. He needs someone who won't back down when he growls."

The young miner drifted back to sleep. She checked his pulse once more and gently examined the surgical sites. Both looked clean, with no signs of infection developing. The abdominal bruising hadn't spread further, suggesting the internal bleeding remained contained.

Laura recorded these observations in Jonah's chart, her mind turning over the young man's words. You're good for him. The comment suggested a personal connection rather than merely professional collaboration. She dismissed the notion quickly. Her purpose in Aspen Hollow was to serve, not to form attachments, especially not to a man who had made his reluctance to accept her help quite clear in the beginning.

Yet, she couldn't deny a certain fascination with Dr. Moses Grant. Beneath his gruff exterior, she'd glimpsed something compelling, a dedication to healing that matched her own, though expressed quite differently. And during surgery, they had worked together with an almost instinctive coordination that surprised her.

"Focus on your purpose here, Laura," she admonished herself softly.

To occupy her mind, she retrieved her Bible from her bag. The book in her hands brought comfort as she turned to Psalm 139, one of her favorites since childhood. The words of David spoke to God's intimate knowledge and care, a reminder that even in this remote mountain town, she remained within His loving guidance.

Time passed steadily as Laura alternated between monitoring Jonah, reading her Bible, and studying Dr. Grant's medical notes. The quiet of the night wrapped around the clinic like a blanket, the occasional sounds from the street, a distant piano from the saloon, and the night watchman's footsteps, all serving as gentle reminders of the surrounding town.

At half-past one, Laura rose and stretched, easing muscles stiff from sitting. She checked on Jonah once more, satisfied with his condition, then prepared a pot of coffee on the small stove in the corner of the office. The rich aroma filled the clinic as she tidied the surgery area and organized supplies for the coming day.

Just before two o'clock, Laura climbed the narrow staircase to Dr. Grant's quarters. She hesitated at the door, reluctant to intrude on his private space. After a moment's consideration, she knocked softly.

No response came. Laura knocked again, slightly louder, mindful of the late hour but aware of Dr. Grant's instructions to wake him at two.

When still no answer came, she cautiously turned the doorknob and peered inside. The room was sparsely furnished: a narrow bed, a small table with a lamp, a chest of drawers, and a single chair. A bookshelf held medical texts, and a few worn volumes of literature. No personal mementos or photographs adorned the walls or surfaces, giving the space an impersonal, almost monastic quality.

Dr. Grant lay on the bed, still fully clothed except for his boots and vest. His breathing was deep and even, his face relaxed in sleep in a way Laura had never seen while he was awake. Without the tension and wariness that typically marked his expression, he appeared younger, and the lines of worry temporarily smoothed away.

Laura hesitated, struck by how exhausted he must have been to fall into such a deep sleep. During their dinner conversation, he had mentioned that frontier medicine meant being constantly available, regardless of personal needs. How many nights had he sacrificed rest to tend to patients? How many meals had he missed while making house calls to distant homesteads?

"Dr. Grant," she called softly from the doorway, reluctant to enter his room further.

He stirred slightly but didn't wake.

"Dr. Grant," she repeated, louder this time. "It's two o'clock."

His eyes opened suddenly, instantly alert despite his evident fatigue. He sat up quickly, running a hand through his disheveled hair as he focused on Laura.

"Jonah?" he asked immediately, concern evident in his voice.

"Stable and resting comfortably," Laura assured him. "He woke once before midnight, in some pain. I administered another dose of laudanum, and he's been sleeping peacefully since."

Dr. Grant nodded, visibly relieved. "Any change in the abdominal bruising?"

"No, it appears unchanged. Both surgical sites look clean, with no signs of developing infection."

He swung his legs over the side of the bed, reaching for his boots. "I'll take over now. You should get some rest before morning."

"I've made coffee," Laura offered. "It should be ready by now."

Dr. Grant looked up, momentarily surprised by the gesture. "Thank you."

Laura stepped back from the doorway. "I'll wait downstairs to give you my full report before I leave."

In the clinic below, she poured two cups of coffee, placing one on the desk for Dr. Grant. She gathered her notes on Jonah's condition, ensuring they were complete and clear for the doctor to reference during his watch.

Moses descended the stairs a few minutes later, his hair combed and shirt tucked in, though the weariness remained evident in the shadows beneath his eyes. He accepted the coffee with a nod of thanks and moved immediately to check on Jonah.

"His color is good," he observed, examining the young miner carefully. "Breathing is regular, and the pulse is strong. You've done well, Miss Smythe."

The praise, though understated, warmed Laura unexpectedly.

Dr. Grant sipped his coffee, studying her over the rim of the cup. "Many would have sent for me at the first sign of discomfort rather than managing it themselves."

"There was no need to disturb your rest for something within my capabilities," Laura replied. "You were clearly exhausted, and as we agreed earlier, a doctor who hasn't slept can't provide optimal care."

A flicker of what might have been amusement crossed his face. "Are you always so practical, Miss Smythe?"

"When it comes to patient care, yes," Laura answered honestly. "Compassion and science work best in tandem, don't you think?"

Something in her words seemed to resonate with him, though he didn't directly acknowledge it. Instead, he glanced at the patient chart where she had recorded her observations.

"Your notes are thorough," he commented. "More detailed than mine tend to be."

"I was taught that careful documentation aids in tracking recovery patterns," Laura explained. "It can help identify potential complications before they become serious."

Dr. Grant nodded slowly. "A valid approach, particularly for complex cases." He hesitated, then added, "You might implement this system for our patients going forward, if you're willing."

The suggestion caught Laura by surprise.

"I'd be happy to," she replied, careful not to appear too pleased by this minor victory. "It would help me familiarize myself with the patients more quickly as well."

Moses moved to his desk, setting down his coffee cup. "You should go now. Get some sleep before clinic hours begin. I'll manage Jonah."

Laura gathered her things, aware that the moment of connection had passed. Moses had retreated behind his professional demeanor, the brief openness gone as quickly as it had appeared.

"I'll return at seven-thirty to prepare for patients," she confirmed. "Would you like me to bring breakfast?"

"That won't be necessary," he replied curtly, already turning his attention to some patient notes on his desk.

Laura nodded, accepting the dismissal without comment. At the door, she paused. "Good night, Dr. Grant. Or rather, good morning."

He glanced up, his expression unreadable in the lamplight. "Good night, Miss Smythe."

The night air was cold when Laura stepped outside, her breath forming small clouds that disappeared quickly into the darkness. Stars blazed overhead, more numerous and brilliant than she had ever seen in Philadelphia. The town was quiet now, even the saloon dark and silent.

As she walked to the boarding house, Laura reflected on the complexities of Moses Grant. One moment gruff and distant, the next revealing small glimpses of the dedicated healer beneath the harsh exterior. His resistance to her methods seemed born not of arrogance but of hard experience and perhaps some personal pain she couldn't yet identify.

"Help me understand him, Lord," she whispered to the star-filled sky. "And help me serve this community as You would have me do."

The boarding house was dark when she arrived, but Mrs. Williams had left a lamp burning low in the entryway, a thoughtful touch that made Laura feel welcome despite the late hour. She climbed the stairs quietly, mindful of the other boarders sleeping nearby.

In her room, Laura changed into her nightgown and knelt beside her bed, offering prayers of thanks for the day's events and guidance for the challenges ahead. Despite the physical fatigue of the long day, her mind remained active, processing all she had experienced since arriving in Aspen Hollow.

As she finally drifted toward sleep, Laura's last conscious thought was of the brief moment when Moses had acknowledged her contribution. It was a small beginning, but perhaps the foundation for the working relationship she hoped to build.

Chapter 6

Laura pulled her coat tighter as she stepped onto the boardwalk outside the boarding house. The bitter wind caught her breath. In the three days since Jonah's surgery, Aspen Hollow's weather had taken a dramatic turn. What had been crisp autumn air now carried winter's sharp teeth.

Laura quickly walked toward the clinic. The sudden shift in temperature had brought a flurry of patients over the past two days—children with coughs, miners with joints aching from the cold, and the elderly seeking remedies for winter ailments arriving weeks earlier than expected.

"Ah, you're here," Moses said as she entered the clinic. "Good. I'm preparing Jonah for transport home. His brother should be arriving shortly with a wagon. He'll recover faster at home, especially with what's coming."

"The storm?"

Moses nodded grimly.

Jonah was sitting up on the edge of his bed, his splinted leg extended carefully before him. His face, though still pale, had regained some color, and he offered Laura a weak smile.

"Miss Smythe! Doc says I'm being released to home arrest."

"House rest," Moses corrected dryly, though the corner of his mouth twitched slightly. "And strict house rest, at that. No weight on that leg for at least three weeks."

Laura moved to help gather Jonah's few belongings.

Moses carefully checked the bandages on Jonah's leg one final time. "The stitches are holding well. I'll come by to check on you in two days, assuming the weather allows."

Over the past three days, Laura had observed how Moses approached patient care—thorough, no-nonsense, but with an underlying concern that belied his gruff manner. Their working relationship had settled into a tentative rhythm, with Laura managing record-keeping, assisting with treatments, and sometimes seeing patients with minor ailments while Moses handled more complex cases.

"Here are some detailed instructions for your care," Laura told Jonah, handing him a folded paper. "Keeping the wounds clean is crucial, and you must take the willow bark tea for pain rather than trying to be brave and suffer through it."

"Yes, ma'am," Jonah replied with a mock salute that made Laura smile. The young miner had proven to be a good-natured patient, his resilience impressive given the severity of his injuries.

The clinic door opened, bringing another blast of cold air and, with it, Liam Crawford. Taller than his younger brother, but with the same sandy hair and open face, Liam stomped his boots to clear them of mud.

"Morning, Doc, Miss Smythe." He nodded to them both, then moved to clap his brother gently on the shoulder. "Ready to go home, little brother?"

"More than ready," Jonah affirmed. "No offense to Doc's hospitality, but I've seen enough of these four walls."

"We need to get home quickly," Liam added, his expression growing serious. "That storm's not holding off like we thought. Already starting to spit snow up on the high road, and the wind's picking up something fierce."

Moses frowned. "Then let's get him loaded up. I don't want him caught in a blizzard between here and your place."

Working together, Moses and Liam carefully lifted Jonah, supporting him between them, while Laura gathered his things and followed them outside to where Liam's wagon waited. Sophia Crawford, Liam's wife, had lined the wagon bed with quilts and blankets, creating a nest of sorts to cushion Jonah during the journey.

"Sophia's been fussing all morning getting things ready," Liam explained as they settled Jonah into the makeshift bed. "She's made enough bone broth and stew to feed the whole mining camp."

"Make sure he takes these drops for pain if needed," Moses instructed, handing Liam a small brown bottle. "No more than fifteen drops, and only every six hours. And this powder can be mixed with water for fever if it returns."

The wind whipped around them as they spoke, catching at clothes and hair, its mournful howl growing louder between the buildings. Laura looked up at the sky, noting how the clouds had darkened. A few scattered snowflakes drifted down, dancing erratically in the gusting wind.

"You'd best hurry," Moses told Liam, his eyes also tracking the increasingly threatening sky. "This weather feels wrong for October. Too cold, too fast."

Liam nodded, pulling his coat tighter. "We're only ten minutes from town. Should beat the worst of it." He climbed up to the driver's seat and gathered the reins. "Thanks for saving this fool's life, Doc. You too, Miss Smythe."

"Just doing our job," Moses replied with characteristic understatement. "Stop by the clinic if his condition changes."

As Liam's wagon pulled away, Moses continued to study the approaching storm, his brow furrowed with concern. "In all my years in these mountains, I've rarely seen a blizzard form this quickly or this early in the season."

"Do you think the town is prepared?" Laura asked, watching as people hurried along the street, clearly sensing the impending weather.

"Aspen Hollow folk know how to weather a storm," Moses answered. "But this one's catching us before the full winter preparations are complete. It could be problematic if it lasts more than a day or two."

A commotion from across the street caught their attention. Twila Abernathy burst through the door of the mercantile, her usually composed face tight with worry as she spotted them.

"Dr. Grant!" she called, hurrying across the muddy street without regard for her skirts. "It's Tommy. His fever's worse, not better, and now Felix is down with it, too."

Moses's entire demeanor shifted, alert and focused. "How high is the fever? Any coughing, rash?"

"Both burning up something terrible," Twila replied, wringing her hands. "Tommy's been coughing all night, and Felix started early this morning. No rash that I can see, but they're both so weak they can barely lift their heads."

"We'll come right away," Moses assured her.

Moses retrieved his medical bag from inside the clinic. He and Laura hurried to the general store.

Silas Abernathy was handling customers with distracted efficiency, his concern for his sons evident in the tight lines around his eyes as they entered. He nodded gratefully to Moses and Laura as they passed.

"Millie's with the boys now," Twila explained as they climbed the stairs to the family's living quarters above the store.

The Abernathy home was modest but comfortable, with hand-made quilts brightening the walls and the scent of fresh coffee lingering in the air. Twila led them to a bedroom, where Tommy and Felix lay in adjacent beds, both flushed with fever. Millie sat between them, applying cool compresses to their foreheads.

"Dr. Grant, Miss Smythe," Millie said, rising from her chair. The usually cheerful schoolteacher looked drawn with worry. "Tommy seemed to be improving, then suddenly worsened last night. And Felix was fine yesterday."

Moses moved immediately to Tommy's bedside, placing a hand on the boy's forehead. Even from where she stood, Laura could see the sixteen-year-old was in distress. His breathing labored and his skin alarmingly flushed.

"How long has the cough been this severe?" Moses asked as he listened to Tommy's chest with his stethoscope.

"Since late last night," Twila answered. "It woke both Silas and me up, sounded like he couldn't catch his breath."

Laura approached Felix, who at eighteen was less visibly ill than his younger brother, but clearly suffering. His eyes opened as she placed her hand on his wrist to check his pulse.

"Miss Smythe," he mumbled, voice rough. "Sorry... not very good company today."

"Don't worry about that," Laura soothed, noting his rapid pulse and the heat radiating from his skin. "When did you first start feeling ill?"

"Last night... after supper. Thought I was just tired from unloading freight."

Laura checked his throat and lymph nodes, which were swollen and tender. "Any pain when you breathe deeply?"

Felix nodded weakly. "Like someone's sitting on my chest."

Moses moved to examine Felix after finishing with Tommy, his expression growing more concerned as he did so. When both examinations were complete, he beckoned Laura to follow him to the corner of the room, speaking in low tones.

"This isn't a typical seasonal complaint," he said grimly. "The fever's too high, onset too rapid, and the respiratory symptoms concern me. Tommy's lungs sound congested, and Felix's are beginning to show the same pattern."

Laura nodded. "Could it be influenza? The symptoms match, though it's early in the season."

"Possibly, or pneumonia developing secondary to another infection." Moses ran a hand through his hair, a gesture Laura had come to recognize as a sign of deep concern. "Either way, we need to act quickly. The combination of high fever and respiratory distress can turn deadly fast, especially in this climate."

They returned to the worried family, Moses speaking with the calm authority that seemed to reassure even the most frightened patients and families.

"Both boys have a serious respiratory infection," he explained to Twila and Silas, who had come upstairs to check on his sons. "We need to bring those fevers down immediately and loosen the congestion in their lungs."

"What can we do?" Silas asked, his arm around his wife's shoulders.

"First, steam treatments," Moses directed. "Boil water and have them breathe the steam, and add a few drops of pine oil if you have it. It will help loosen the congestion. Keep cool cloths on their foreheads to combat the fever, and make sure they drink plenty of fluids, willow bark tea for the fever and pain."

Laura added, "Change their position every few hours to prevent the fluid from settling in one part of the lungs. And ventilate the room well, despite the cold, fresh air is important."

"Miss Smythe will prepare a mustard plaster for each of them," Moses continued. "Applied to the chest. It will help with the congestion. And I'll leave medicine for the fever."

Twila nodded, already moving to begin heating water. "What about Millie? Could she get sick too?"

Moses exchanged a glance with Laura. "It's possible. This appears to be contagious. Has Millie been showing any symptoms?"

"Just tired," Millie answered. "But I thought that was from the extra schoolwork with the harvest festival coming up."

"Monitor yourself closely," Laura advised her. "At the first sign of fever or cough, you should rest and send word to us."

While Moses mixed fever powders and gave further instructions to the parents, Laura went to the kitchen to prepare the mustard plasters. She worked efficiently, remembering how Moses had shown her just yesterday the proper way to mix the ground mustard seed with flour and enough water to form a paste, and then spread the mixture on clean cloths.

"This will feel warm, then hot," she explained when she returned to apply the plasters to the boys' chests. "It draws blood to the surface and helps clear the congestion, but we must remove it after fifteen minutes to prevent burns."

As she worked, Laura noticed Twila watching her with a mixture of worry and gratitude.

"I'm so glad you're here, Miss Smythe," Twila said quietly. "The way you and Dr. Grant work together, it gives me hope for my boys."

Laura smiled reassuringly. "Dr. Grant is an excellent physician, and we'll do everything possible to help Tommy and Felix recover quickly."

Once the treatments were administered and detailed instructions given, Moses and Laura prepared to leave. The wind had picked up considerably during their time in the Abernathy home, and the scattered snowflakes had given way to a steady fall that was already beginning to dust the boardwalks.

"I'll return this evening to check on them," Moses promised, packing his medical bag. "In the meantime, if either boy has trouble breathing or the fever spikes higher, send for me immediately."

Outside, the wind hit them with alarming force, cutting through Laura's coat despite its thickness. Main Street was largely deserted now, most townspeople having sought refuge indoors as the storm intensified.

"This is developing fast," Moses shouted over the wind as they made their way toward the clinic. "We should prepare for the possibility of being unable to make rounds tomorrow."

Laura tucked her chin against the biting cold. "Do you think this illness has spread throughout the town?"

"It's a strong possibility," Moses admitted. "Respiratory infections can move quickly through tight-knit communities like Aspen Hollow, especially when people are confined indoors during storms."

They struggled against the wind, heads bent, as they moved along the nearly empty boardwalk. Suddenly, Moses stopped, looking down the street past the row of businesses to where a small cabin stood slightly apart from the others. Smoke curled from its chimney, disappearing almost immediately in the gusting wind.

"Miss Smythe," he said, turning to Laura with sudden decision in his eyes. "I think it's time you met Clementine Hayes."

Laura followed his gaze to the cabin. "The herbalist?"

Moses nodded. "If this storm is bad, and this illness spreads, we'll need every remedy at our disposal. Clementine's knowledge of medicinal plants has saved lives when conventional medicines failed or ran out."

"Now's the perfect time, then," Laura agreed, eager to meet the woman Moses had spoken of with such respect.

Moses adjusted his course, heading toward the cabin instead of the clinic. "Clementine is… particular," he cautioned as they walked. "She doesn't share her knowledge freely, and she can be wary of outsiders, especially those with formal medical training."

"You seem to have earned her trust," Laura observed, raising her voice to be heard over the wind.

"It took time," Moses admitted. "When I first arrived in Aspen Hollow, I dismissed her remedies as folk superstition. A harsh winter and dwindling medical supplies taught me humility. She knew which plants could reduce fever when my quinine ran out, which poultices could draw infection from wounds when I had no carbolic acid."

"How did she learn her craft?" Laura asked, genuinely curious.

"Her grandmother was Cherokee, taught her the traditional uses of plants from these mountains. Her father was a trapper who married her mother against her family's wishes." Moses paused, choosing his words carefully. "Clementine stands between worlds, not fully accepted by either. It's made her cautious with strangers, but fiercely dedicated to healing."

"What advice can you give me for meeting her?" Laura asked.

"Be honest. Clementine has an uncanny ability to sense insincerity," Moses said. "Don't pretend to know more than you do about her methods, but don't discount them either. Show respect for her knowledge without condescension. Furthermore, whatever she tells you or possibly shows you... memorize it... ingrain her shared knowledge into your mind."

They approached the small cabin. Unlike most buildings in Aspen Hollow, it wasn't situated square to the street but angled slightly, as if in subtle defiance of town planning. A well-tended garden stretched behind it, though most plants were now withered by frost. The scent of something pungent yet pleasant, pine, sage, and something Laura couldn't identify, mingled with the smoke from the chimney.

"Will she welcome us in such weather?" Laura asked, noting the closed curtains.

"Clementine expects visitors when they're most in need. She has an uncanny sense of when her skills are required," Moses replied cryptically. As if to confirm his words, the cabin door opened before they reached it.

A woman stood in the doorway, tall and straight-backed despite her years, which Laura guessed to be mid-fifties. Her dark hair, streaked with silver, was pulled back in a simple braid. Her face, striking rather than conventionally beautiful, held eyes that seemed to evaluate everything they saw with remarkable clarity.

"Took you long enough, Doctor," Clementine called. "I've been watching the sky all morning. This storm isn't natural." Her gaze shifted to Laura, assessing but not unwelcoming. "And you've brought the new nurse. Good. We'll need all hands before this is over."

Moses stepped onto the porch, gesturing for Laura to follow. "Laura Smythe, this is Clementine Hayes. She knows more about healing plants than any three medical textbooks combined."

"You flatter me, Doctor, which means you need something," Clementine replied with a hint of amusement. She extended her hand to Laura. "Welcome to Aspen Hollow, Miss Smythe. I hope you're ready for what's coming."

Laura took the offered hand, surprised by its strength and warmth. "It's an honor to meet you, Mrs. Hayes. Dr. Grant speaks very highly of your knowledge."

"It's Miss Hayes," Clementine corrected without rancor. "And the doctor's praise is born of necessity. These mountains don't care for medical degrees when the passes are snowed in and supplies run low." She stepped back from the doorway. "Come inside, both of you. This snow has teeth, and I've got a pot of tea that might help us think clearly about what's brewing in Aspen Hollow."

As they followed Clementine into the cabin, Laura glanced at Moses, who gave her a slight nod of encouragement. The wind howled behind them as Clementine closed the door, shutting out the gathering storm.

Chapter 7

The interior of Clementine's cabin enveloped Laura like a warm embrace after the biting wind outside. A fire crackled in a stone hearth, casting dancing shadows across walls hung with bundles of dried plants. The single room was meticulously organized. Shelves lined with glass jars containing powders, leaves, roots, and liquids of varying colors. A wooden table covered with mortar and pestles of different sizes, and a small bed tucked into one corner beneath a colorful quilt.

"Sit," Clementine instructed, gesturing to a pair of wooden chairs near the hearth. "That storm's only beginning, and you both look half-frozen already."

Moses removed his hat and sat in one of the offered seats. Laura followed suit, grateful for the fire's warmth as it began to thaw her chilled fingers.

"We've come about the Abernathy boys," Moses began without preamble. "Tommy and Felix have fallen ill with a severe respiratory infection. High fever, congestion, rapid onset."

Clementine nodded as she moved to the stove, where a kettle simmered. "They're not the only ones. Willis Holcomb stopped by hours before dawn for a cough remedy for his family. And I've seen three miners since yesterday with similar complaints."

Laura exchanged a concerned glance with Moses. "That suggests we're dealing with something contagious that's spreading quickly."

"It's moving faster than it should," Clementine remarked, pouring steaming liquid from the kettle into three earthenware mugs. "Natural sickness has a rhythm to it, a pattern that follows the seasons and the movements of people. This feels... different."

"Different?" Moses questioned, his brow furrowing.

Clementine handed each of them a mug before sitting in a third chair across from them. "I'm suggesting that not all sickness comes from things we can immediately pinpoint, doctor."

The herbalist's words sent an unsettling chill through Laura. The fragrant steam rising from her mug smelled of pine, mint, and something unfamiliar, slightly bitter but not unpleasant.

"What's in this tea?" Laura asked, partly out of professional curiosity and partly to redirect the conversation from Clementine's ominous statement.

"Pine needle for the lungs, mint to clear the head, elderberry to strengthen the body's defenses, and a touch of wild honey to make it palatable," Clementine explained. "Drink. It will help keep you both strong while you tend to the sick."

Laura sipped cautiously. The flavor was complex, earthy, and aromatic with a subtle sweetness that balanced the bitter notes. "It's good," she said with genuine surprise.

"Medicine doesn't have to taste terrible to be effective, despite what some doctors believe," Clementine replied with a pointed look at Moses.

A slight smile tugged at Moses' mouth. "A lesson you've taught me more than once." He sobered quickly, returning to their purpose. "Clementine, if this illness continues to spread, my standard treatments may not be enough. I may run out of supplies, especially if the storm isolates us for days. What remedies would you recommend?"

Clementine studied Moses over the rim of her mug. "You've come a long way from the arrogant young doctor who arrived here five years ago, dismissing my 'mountain superstitions.'"

"Necessity is an effective teacher," Moses acknowledged. "As is watching your tinctures work when my medical supplies ran out during that first winter."

The herbalist nodded, satisfied with his response. Her sharp gaze shifted to Laura. "And you, Miss Smythe? What do you think of 'folk remedies' alongside your modern medical training?"

Laura considered her answer carefully, aware that this was a test of sorts. "I believe healing comes in many forms," she replied honestly. "God has provided medicines in nature long before we learned to create them in laboratories. I'd be foolish to dismiss knowledge that has sustained communities for generations, especially when I've witnessed the limits of modern medicine firsthand."

Clementine's expression remained neutral, but Laura sensed approval in the slight relaxation of her shoulders. "Good answer," she said finally. "Too many come from those fancy schools thinking science has replaced God's wisdom rather than helped us understand it better."

The herbalist rose and moved to her shelves, selecting several jars. "For the fever and congestion, pine and elderberry syrup will help, taken three times daily." She placed a blue glass bottle on the table. "This tincture of boneset and yarrow will reduce the fever better than your willow bark in these cases."

Moses nodded. "I've seen its effectiveness."

"For the chest congestion," Clementine continued, selecting another jar containing a thick, dark substance, "this pine resin salve with mullein and wild cherry bark should be applied warm to the chest and covered with flannel. It draws the infection upward better than a mustard plaster and doesn't risk burning the skin."

Laura listened intently, noting the precise measurements and applications Clementine described. The herbalist's knowledge was clearly systematic and specific, not the vague folk wisdom some might dismiss it as.

"I'll prepare more of each," Clementine said, "but I'll need fresh pine resin. The storm will make collecting difficult."

"I can help gather supplies if you tell me what to look for," Laura offered, earning another appraising look from the herbalist.

"Perhaps," Clementine replied noncommittally. She returned to her chair, her expression growing more serious. "But there's something else troubling me about this illness. The timing, alongside this unnatural storm... it feels wrong."

Moses leaned forward, elbows on his knees. "What do you mean by 'unnatural'?"

"The animals knew three days ago," Clementine said, gesturing toward the window where snow now fell in thick, swirling sheets. "The deer moved down from the high meadows too early. Birds that normally stay through early winter suddenly disappeared. And there's a taste in the air, a metallic bitterness that doesn't belong."

Laura found herself drawn into Clementine's words. There was something compelling about the herbalist's certainty, rooted not in superstition but in deep observation of the natural world.

As if to emphasize her point, a fierce gust of wind rattled the cabin windows, driving snow against the glass with a sound like thrown sand. The fire in the hearth flickered wildly for a moment before steadying again.

"We should return to the clinic," Moses said, glancing at the window with concern.

"Take these with you," Clementine said, quickly wrapping several bottles and jars in cloth. "Enough to start treating a few patients. I'll prepare more and get them to you."

Laura accepted the bundle, carefully placing it in her medical bag. "Thank you, Miss Hayes. I hope we can speak more when circumstances allow. I'd like to learn from your knowledge."

A hint of a smile softened Clementine's stern features. "You're more open-minded than most, Miss Smythe. Perhaps there's hope for modern medicine yet." She turned to Moses. "Watch for other symptoms—skin rashes, tremors, confusion."

Moses nodded, donning his hat once more. "Yes ma'am. Stay safe, Clementine."

The herbalist handed them each a small pouch of dried leaves. "Pine needle tea. Drink it three times daily. Whatever is making others sick, it won't do for the healers to fall ill as well."

Clementine placed a weathered hand on Laura's arm, her voice dropping so only Laura could hear. "You have a gift for healing that goes beyond your training, Miss Smythe. Trust that gift, especially when science and medicine reach their limits."

Before Laura could respond, Clementine opened the door.

"God be with you both," Clementine called as they stepped into the brewing storm. "This town will need His mercy before this passes."

The wind nearly knocked Laura off her feet as they left the shelter of the porch. Moses grabbed her arm, steadying her against the force of the gale.

"Stay close!" he shouted over the howling wind.

Laura nodded, clutching her medical bag tightly with one hand while gripping Moses' arm with the other. They leaned into the wind, heads bent low, as they fought their way down the street.

They had almost reached the clinic when the sound of a wagon approaching drew their attention. Laura made out Mr. Willis Holcomb, driving with uncharacteristic speed, his horse struggling against the wind.

"That's unusual," Moses remarked. "Willis doesn't usually come to town on trading days, let alone twice in one day. Perhaps the cough medicine Clementine gave him isn't working?"

Chapter 8

illis pulled his team to a stop near the clinic, his weathered face tight with anxiety. He jumped down from the wagon seat, nearly losing his footing.

"Doc Grant!" he called, spotting them approaching. "Thank God. It's Angela and the boys—all three down with a fever. Virgie's beside herself trying to care for them."

"Fever and cough?" Moses asked sharply.

Holcomb nodded. "Coughing fit to burst their lungs, and burning up despite the cold. Jeb's the worst. He can barely get a full breath. The cough medicine I fetched from Miss Hayes earlier doesn't seem to be working."

Moses and Laura exchanged a concerned glance. "How many other people have you been in contact with since yesterday, Willis?" Moses asked.

"Just the men I work with and Miss Hayes." Holcomb ran a hand over his face with worry.

Deputy Marshal Hank Diamond walked their way, his normally stoic face creased with worry.

"Doc, Miss Smythe," he called, "you'd better come quick. Just got word from the mining camp. They've got at least six men down with high fevers, and Jasper McCoy says three of his regulars left the saloon early last night with the same symptoms."

Laura felt a chill that had nothing to do with the howling wind and incoming snow. One or two cases of severe respiratory illness might be a coincidence, but this many appearing simultaneously throughout Aspen Hollow suggested something far more concerning.

Moses's expression darkened as he took in the implications. "How many total cases are we aware of now?"

"The Abernathy boys, the three Holcomb children," Laura counted quickly. "Plus six miners and three men from the saloon. That's at least fourteen cases, all except for Tommy, presenting within the last twenty-four hours."

"Tommy Abernathy has been sick for a few days, but now he's worse. Whatever this is has spread across different parts of town," Moses added grimly. "This might not be a simple outbreak of seasonal illness."

Willis looked between them, his worry deepening. "What could it be then, Doc? Some kind of influenza?"

Moses shook his head, his jaw tightening as he surveyed the rapidly deteriorating weather and considered the equally rapidly emerging health crisis.

"I don't know yet," he admitted. "But with a blizzard bearing down on us and multiple serious cases appearing simultaneously, we need to act quickly. Miss Smythe, gather whatever supplies you can carry and dress in layers. Willis, Miss Smythe, will go with you to your homestead and I will see to the mining camp men."

The wind howled louder between the buildings, spitting sporadic bits of snow into their faces with stinging force.

Willis looked desperately toward the road leading out of town. "My family, Doc—I need to get back to them."

Laura met Moses's gaze, reading the gravity of the situation in his eyes.

"I'll gather supplies for multiple locations," she said decisively. "Fever reducers, carbolic acid, bandages, laudanum for severe cases."

Moses nodded at Laura's quick understanding. "Deputy, we need to organize this systematically. Send someone to notify Pastor Lewis. The church may have to serve as an auxiliary treatment area if this spreads further."

"I'll handle it," Deputy Diamond replied, already turning to head toward the church.

"And Marshal," Moses called after him, "have someone stop by Clementine Hayes' home and let her know of the other people who have come down with this sickness."

Laura hurried into the clinic, her mind racing. She grabbed as many bottles of quinine and carbolic acid as she could fit into her medical bag, among other things. The clinic's supply cabinet revealed their limitations. They had medicines for perhaps thirty patients with severe symptoms, but if this illness continued to spread throughout the town, they would quickly run short.

Moses entered behind her. "Pack as much as you can, and we'll spit the remedies Clementine just gave us."

"What do you think this is?" Laura asked as she worked.

Moses's face was grim as he packed his own medical bag. "The rapid onset and widespread nature suggest an infectious agent affecting the respiratory system. The fever, coughing, and breathing difficulty match several possibilities—influenza, pneumonia, or perhaps something transmitted through the air."

"Could it be related to the mine?" Laura proposed.

Moses paused, considering. "It's possible. Mining operations can release minerals and contaminants. But that wouldn't explain the sudden onset across different parts of town simultaneously." He closed his bag with a decisive snap. "Whatever it is, we need to contain it while treating those already infected."

Within minutes, Moses helped Laura onto the seat beside Willis on his wagon, then mounted his horse.

"I'll meet you at the Holcomb residence after I see to the men at the mining camp," Moses called to her over the wind.

"Be careful," she called back.

Willis cracked the reins, and the wagon lurched forward. Laura braced herself against the jolting ride. The wind whipped mercilessly at her face despite the scarf she'd wrapped tightly around her neck and lower face.

"How far is your homestead, Mr. Holcomb?" she shouted over the storm's roar.

"Three miles east!" Willis said, hunching against the weather. "Usually a short trip, but in this blow..." He left the sentence unfinished, focusing instead on urging the struggling horses forward.

The town quickly fell behind them. The road was beginning to disappear beneath a white blanket. Laura gripped the seat with white knuckles as the wagon swayed precariously.

"Virgie's been up all night with the children," Willis said, his voice tight with worry. "Angela started first—she's sixteen, our oldest. Jeb and Donnie were burning up not long after."

"How old are your sons?" Laura asked, trying to prepare mentally for the cases she would face.

"Jeb's fourteen, Donnie's twelve," Willis replied. "Strong boys normally, but this has laid them out something fierce."

The wagon crested a small rise, and the wind hit them with renewed fury, nearly tearing Laura's hat from her head. She clutched it with one hand while maintaining her grip on her medical bag with the other. The temperature seemed to be dropping by the minute, the cold seeping through her layers of clothing despite their thickness.

After what felt like an eternity of jolting progress, a small homestead appeared. A log cabin with smoke streaming horizontally from the chimney, a barn, and a few outbuildings huddled against the elements.

Willis pulled the wagon as close to the cabin door as possible. Before he could climb down to help her, Laura was already jumping to the ground, medical bag in hand.

"Get the horses in the barn," she called to Willis. "I'll see to your family."

The cabin door burst open as she approached, revealing Virgie Holcomb, her face haggard with exhaustion and worry.

"Oh, thank the Lord," she cried. "Come in quick, Miss Smythe. The children are worse, especially Jeb."

The interior of the cabin was stifling hot, the air thick with steam from pots of water boiling on the stove, an attempt to ease the children's breathing. Three pallets had been arranged near the hearth, each occupied by a feverish child. The two boys shared similar features, sandy hair like their father's and freckles across their noses, while Angela, despite her illness, showed signs of becoming a beauty like her mother.

Laura moved immediately to Jeb, who seemed to be struggling the most for breath. His skin was alarmingly hot to the touch, his lips tinged slightly blue around the edges.

"How long has his breathing been this labored?" Laura asked, opening her medical bag.

"Since just before dawn," Virgie replied, wringing her hands in her apron. "It keeps getting worse. I've been giving them willow bark tea like Dr. Grant showed us for fevers, but it barely seems to touch it. The cough medicine that Willis fetched from Clementine doesn't seem to be helping."

Laura examined each child in turn. All three presented with high fevers, chest congestion, and varying degrees of respiratory distress. Jeb's condition was indeed critical. The infection had settled deep in his lungs, producing an ominous rattling sound with each labored breath.

"We need to act quickly," Laura said, removing bottles and packages from her bag. She handed Virgie one of Clementine's remedies. "This is a tincture for fever. Three drops in water for Angela and Donnie, five for Jeb, every four hours. It's stronger than willow bark."

While Virgie prepared the medicine, Laura created a steam treatment using pine needles from Clementine's supplies. The pungent aroma filled the cabin as she positioned Jeb to breathe the medicated vapor.

"The steam will help loosen the congestion," she explained. "We'll do this for each child, but Jeb needs it first and most frequently."

Willis entered, bringing a blast of cold air that momentarily cleared the stuffy atmosphere. His face fell as he saw his children's condition.

"What can I do?" he asked, voice thick with emotion.

"Keep the fire steady, and in about twenty minutes, help me turn Jeb onto his side. We need to clear the fluid from his lungs," Laura instructed. She turned to Virgie. "I need clean cloths soaked in cool water for their foreheads, and if you have any pine resin, I can make a chest plaster that will help draw out the infection."

For the next hour, Laura worked steadily, applying treatments and monitoring each child's response. Donnie seemed to respond most quickly to the medications, his fever dropping slightly and his breathing becoming less strained. Angela's condition improved marginally, but Jeb remained critical.

"I don't understand," Virgie whispered as they worked together to apply a chest plaster to Jeb. "They were all perfectly healthy just a day ago."

"This illness is moving unusually fast," Laura confirmed, recalling Clementine's ominous words about the "unnatural" quality of the sickness. "Have you noticed anything unusual before they fell ill? Something they ate or drank, or some place they visited?"

Virgie thought for a moment. "Nothing out of the ordinary. They went to school yesterday. They've been drinking from our well, and I'm sure the school's well, same as always. The boys helped their father with the animals yesterday, and Angela helped me preserve the last of the garden harvest yesterday evening."

Laura frowned, wondering what connection might exist between these three children, the Abernathy boys, and the miners who had fallen ill. There must be some common factor, some exposure they all shared.

After the initial treatments were administered, Laura prepared a basin of water mixed with carbolic acid.

"We need to be vigilant about hygiene," she told the Holcomb's. "Wash your hands in this solution frequently, especially after caring for the children. Cover your mouth and nose with a cloth when near them, and don't share cups or utensils."

Virgie looked alarmed. "You think it's that catching?"

"I think we need to be careful," Laura replied diplomatically. "Multiple cases have appeared in town almost simultaneously. Until we understand what we're dealing with, caution is essential."

As if to underscore the seriousness of the situation, Jeb suddenly began coughing violently, his thin body convulsing with the effort. Laura quickly moved to elevate his upper body, supporting him through the spasm. When it finally subsided, his breathing seemed slightly easier, but he remained frighteningly hot to the touch.

"The medicine will take time to work," Laura reassured the worried parents. "The important thing now is to keep him hydrated and try to bring down the fever."

Outside, the storm had intensified; the wind howling through every crack in the cabin walls. Laura glanced anxiously at the door, wondering how Moses was faring at the mining camp and when he would be able to join her.

"This storm's settling in for the long haul," Willis observed, following her gaze.

The implications were sobering. If the illness continued to spread, and the storm isolated different parts of the community, their ability to coordinate care would be severely hampered.

"In that case," Laura said decisively, "I need to teach you both as much as I can about treating illness. Dr. Grant may not be able to reach us, and I may need to borrow a horse and return to town to help others."

She spent the next hour instructing Virgie and Willis on proper techniques for the steam treatments, chest plasters, and fever management. She wrote clear instructions for medication dosages and timing, emphasizing the importance of consistent care.

"Every four hours, without fail, even through the night," she stressed. "And if Jeb's breathing worsens or if any of them develop new symptoms, confusion, rash, or seizures, you must find a way to get word to Dr. Grant or me immediately."

By late afternoon, the snow outside had accumulated. The temperature in the cabin fluctuated between stifling when the fire was built up for steam treatments and chilly when the door was briefly opened for fresh air. Laura's worry grew as the hours passed with no sign of Moses.

Finally, as she was preparing another round of medications, a heavy knock came at the door. Willis opened it to reveal Moses, his face reddened from the biting wind.

"Dr. Grant!" Virgie exclaimed. "We weren't sure you'd make it in this storm."

Moses stomped his boots and brushed snow from his coat. "Almost didn't." His eyes immediately sought Laura, then moved to the three patients by the hearth. "How are they?"

Laura gave him a detailed report on each child's condition and the treatments she'd administered. "Donnie is responding well, Angela moderately so, but Jeb remains serious. I've used Clementine's tincture for the fever and the pine resin plaster for the chest congestion."

Moses nodded approvingly as he hung his coat to dry. "Good work." He moved to examine Jeb first, his expression growing grave as he listened to the boy's chest.

"Significant fluid in the lungs," he confirmed softly. "We need to be aggressive with the treatments." He looked up at Laura. "The situation at the mining camp is deteriorating rapidly. Eight men now, not six, all with similar symptoms. Two are in serious condition."

"What about treatment facilities?" Laura asked.

"I've arranged for the mining company's office to serve as a temporary infirmary," Moses replied. "Jasper McCoy is working with Pastor Lewis to prepare the church as well."

The grim arithmetic was inescapable. At least seventeen cases now, possibly more that hadn't yet been reported, and a blizzard that made coordination and treatment increasingly difficult.

"I'm concerned about the spread of infection," Laura said quietly. "Perhaps we should consider implementing quarantine measures for the town, at least until we better understand the nature of this illness."

Moses nodded, his expression somber. "I've already discussed it with Deputy Diamond. He's arranging for messengers to spread word that people should remain in their homes except for emergencies." He paused, running a hand through his snow-dampened hair. "But the mining camp presents a particular challenge. Men are housed in close quarters, perfect conditions for rapid spread."

"What about water?" Laura asked suddenly, a thought occurring to her. "Could the water supply be contaminated somehow?"

Moses considered this. "It's possible, though Aspen Hollow draws from several sources. The town well, Aspen Creek for those closer to it, and individual wells for homesteads farther out." He turned to Willis. "Has your family been drinking exclusively from your own well?"

Willis nodded. "We've got a good well, never given us trouble. The children probably drank from the school's well yesterday."

"The Abernathy's use the town well," Moses mused. "And the miners draw from Aspen Creek upstream from town." His brow furrowed in concentration. "If it's waterborne, it would have to affect multiple water sources simultaneously."

"Unless there's contamination upstream that's affecting all the water in the area," Laura suggested.

The possibilities were disturbing, but with night falling and the storm intensifying, there was little they could do to investigate further at the moment.

"We need to focus on the patients we have now," Moses decided. "Miss Smythe, I need you to return to town with me and help establish the church as a central treatment area."

Laura hesitated, looking at Jeb's labored breathing. "We should leave soon if we hope to make it back to town before visibility becomes impossible."

Moses nodded. "We'll depart as soon as I've examined all three children again, just to be sure, and you review the treatment plan with the Holcombs and make sure they understand everything."

While Moses completed his examinations, Laura reviewed the detailed written instructions for Virgie and Willis again, including all the techniques she had taught them.

"I've left enough tincture for twelve more doses," she told Moses quietly when she was finished. "If Jeb doesn't improve by morning..."

"I understand," he replied, his voice equally low. "I've seen this pattern before in severe respiratory infections. The next twelve hours will be critical for him."

The gravity of the situation hung between them, neither needing to articulate the potential consequences if their treatments failed. For a brief moment, Laura felt the weight of it all, the spreading illness, the storm, and the lives, depending on their decisions.

As if sensing her thoughts, Moses briefly touched her arm. "You've done everything possible for these children, Miss Smythe. Now we need to extend that care to the rest of Aspen Hollow."

Laura nodded, drawing strength from his confidence in her abilities.

Outside, the world had transformed into a swirling wall of white, the snowfall now so thick that the barn was barely visible from the cabin door. The journey back to town would be perilous, but every hour that passed meant more people potentially falling ill without access to treatment.

Chapter 9

Moses leaned forward against the relentless wind, his body serving as a shield for Laura, who clung tightly to his back. The blizzard had transformed the familiar three-mile stretch between the Holcomb homestead and Aspen Hollow into an alien landscape of swirling white fury. His horse struggled forward, head lowered against the onslaught, hooves punching through the rapidly accumulating snow.

"Are you okay?" Moses shouted over his shoulder, his words immediately swallowed by the howling gale. He felt Laura's nod against his back, her arms tightening around his waist as the horse stumbled slightly before regaining its footing.

The bitter cold sliced through his layers of clothing, numbing his exposed face despite the scarf pulled high over his nose. He blinked rapidly, fighting to keep his eyes open against the stinging particles of ice that pelted them like tiny needles. Visibility had deteriorated to mere feet in front of them, the world beyond reduced to a chaotic blur of white.

Laura pressed closer, seeking what little warmth and protection his body offered. Moses adjusted his position, trying to block more of the wind from her smaller frame. Her medical training might have prepared her for many challenges, but he doubted Philadelphia had equipped her for a Rocky Mountain blizzard in full rage.

"How much farther?" Laura's voice reached him in fragments between gusts.

"Hard to say," Moses admitted, straining to identify any landmark in the swirling whiteness. "Maybe a mile. The church steeple should be visible soon."

The horse whinnied in protest as another violent gust threatened to push them sideways. Moses tightened his grip on the reins, guiding the animal back toward what he hoped was still the road. Without visible markers, they were navigating by instinct and memory.

"I've never seen a storm form this quickly," Laura observed, her breath warm against his ear as she leaned closer to be heard.

"Neither have I," Moses replied grimly. "In these mountains, the weather can change fast, but this..." He let the sentence hang, focusing instead on keeping them moving forward.

Ten agonizing minutes passed before the vague outline of Aspen Hollow's church steeple emerged through the snow. Relief surged through Moses at the sight of that familiar silhouette.

"There!" he pointed, feeling Laura shift behind him to look. "We're almost there."

The streets of Aspen Hollow were deserted, doors and windows tightly shuttered against the storm. The only movement came from swirling eddies of snow driven by the relentless wind. As they approached the church, however, Moses spotted several horses and wagons huddled near the hitching posts, partially buried under growing drifts.

"Others have already arrived," Laura noted, her voice tight with concern.

"Let's hope it's help rather than more patients," Moses replied, guiding his horse alongside the others.

He dismounted first, his boots sinking deep into the snow as he reached up to help Laura down. Her hands gripped his shoulders as he lifted her from the saddle, setting her gently beside him. For a brief moment, they stood close; her face inches from his, snowflakes catching in her eyelashes and dusting her cheeks with white.

"The supplies," she said, breaking the moment as she turned to retrieve her medical bag from the saddle.

Moses secured his horse quickly, knowing the animal would need proper care soon but prioritizing the immediate crisis. With their bags in hand, they pushed through the mounting snowdrifts toward the church entrance.

Pastor Lewis opened the heavy wooden door before they could knock, his normally serene face etched with worry.

"Dr. Grant, Miss Smythe—thank the Lord you've made it back safely." He ushered them inside, quickly closing the door against the howling wind. "We've started bringing in the sick, as Deputy Diamond suggested."

Moses stamped snow from his boots, taking in the transformed interior of Aspen Hollow's house of worship. The familiar rows of pews had been pushed against the walls, creating an open space in the center of the church. Several pallets had already been arranged on the floor, four of them occupied by patients in various states of distress.

"How many so far?" Moses asked, shedding his snow-crusted coat.

"Eight here," Pastor Lewis replied. "Six miners brought in by their foreman, Mrs. Bellweather, and one of the Abernathy children.

Deputy Diamond reports at least nine more cases across town, but the storm is making it difficult to transport them."

Laura had already moved toward the patients, kneeling beside a young miner whose cheeks burned with fever. She placed a hand on his forehead, her expression grave.

"We need to establish some order here," Moses declared, surveying the makeshift infirmary. "This storm could last days. We need clean water, firewood, and more bedding."

"Several townspeople have volunteered to help," Pastor Lewis explained, gesturing toward the back of the church, where Sera Williams and Marybeth Flanagan were sorting through a pile of blankets and linens. "Mrs. Williams has brought food from the boarding house, and Jasper McCoy delivered firewood before the worst of the storm hit."

"Excellent," Moses nodded. "But we need more organization if we're going to effectively treat—"

"Dr. Grant," Laura interrupted, her voice calm but urgent. "This miner's fever is dangerously high, and Mrs. Bellweather's breathing is severely compromised. We need to begin treatment immediately."

Moses moved to her side, bending to examine the miner. The young man's skin burned beneath his touch, his breathing rapid and shallow.

"Same presentation as the Holcomb boy," Moses confirmed quietly. He glanced at Laura. "We'll need to divide responsibilities. I suggest you manage the initial assessments while I prepare the medications."

Laura nodded, already rolling up her sleeves. "We should establish a handwashing station immediately. And we'll need to separate the patients by severity."

Moses watched as she moved with purposeful efficiency, directing Marybeth to bring water and soap near the entrance.

"Everyone who assists must wash their hands between patients," she instructed firmly. "And we need clean cloths for each individual. No sharing of linens or utensils."

Sera Williams approached, wiping her hands on her apron. "What can I do to help, Miss Smythe?"

"We need cool water for compresses," Laura replied. "And if you could organize a rotation of people to constantly refill the kettle for steam treatments, that would be invaluable."

Moses unpacked his medical bag, arranging bottles of medicine and herbal remedies on a small table near the church altar. As he worked, he continued to observe Laura's interactions with the volunteers. She spoke with quiet authority, her instructions clear and concise, yet delivered with a gentle confidence that inspired cooperation rather than resistance.

"Dr. Grant," Pastor Lewis said, approaching with a worried expression. "I've been wondering—should we attempt to evacuate those not yet ill? Perhaps send them to neighboring communities before the storm makes travel impossible?"

Moses shook his head grimly. "It's already too late for that. The roads will be impassable within hours if they aren't already. And we don't know who might be incubating the illness without showing symptoms yet. We could spread it further." He measured powder into small paper packages, creating individual doses. "Our best strategy is to treat the sick and implement strict hygiene measures to slow the spread."

The church door burst open, bringing a swirl of snow and bitter cold. Deputy Diamond stepped inside, supporting a middle-aged man who coughed violently against his shoulder.

"Another one, Doc," the deputy announced grimly. "Found Arthur Bellweather collapsed halfway between his cabin and town. He was trying to reach his wife."

Laura immediately moved to assist, helping guide the man to an empty pallet near his wife. "Mr. Bellweather, we're going to take care of you," she assured him, her voice steady and warm despite the chaos surrounding them. "Your wife is here too. You're both in good hands."

Moses approached, medical bag in hand. "How many more cases have you encountered, Deputy?"

Diamond's weathered face was grim beneath his snow-dusted hat. "Hard to say for certain. Reports are coming in piecemeal through this storm. At least three more at the mining camp, too ill to transport. Jasper says two of his regulars didn't show up for their usual evening drinks and might be sick at home."

"We need to establish a more systematic approach," Moses decided, looking around at the rapidly filling church. "Miss Smythe!"

Laura looked up from where she was examining Arthur Bellweather's chest.

"Could you direct the setup of treatment stations and patient records?"

"Of course. We'll need to categorize patients by severity, establish dedicated treatment areas, and set up a consistent documentation system."

Within twenty minutes, Laura had transformed the church's chaotic interior into an organized infirmary. Patients with the most severe symptoms were placed nearest the stove for warmth, those with moderate illness grouped separately, and a small area near the altar was designated for preparing treatments. Marybeth Flanagan was instructed to record each patient's name, symptoms, and treatments in a ledger borrowed from Pastor Lewis's study.

"Everyone who assists must wash their hands here," Laura demonstrated at the basin she had established near the entrance, scrubbing her hands vigorously with soap. "Before and after touching each patient, without exception."

Moses moved between patients, assessing symptoms and administering treatments.

"The Bellweathers are both presenting with the same pattern we saw at the Holcomb homestead," Laura reported quietly as they briefly conferred near the medicine table. "Rapid onset, high fever, progressive respiratory distress."

Moses nodded, mixing a tincture of Clementine's herbs with water. "I'm seeing identical presentations across all patients, regardless of age or location within town. It supports your theory about a common source."

"But not necessarily waterborne," Laura mused, preparing a chest plaster. "The timing is too simultaneous, and the sources too diverse."

"Airborne, then?" Moses suggested, lowering his voice to avoid alarming nearby volunteers. "But that doesn't explain the rapid spread across physically separated locations."

"Unless there was a gathering recently where everyone was exposed," Laura suggested. "Or perhaps—"

Her theory was interrupted by a violent coughing fit from one of the miners. They both rushed to his side, finding him struggling for breath, his lips taking on an alarming bluish tinge.

"Elevate his upper body," Moses instructed, reaching for his stethoscope. "We need to clear his airways."

Laura quickly positioned herself behind the miner, supporting his torso at an angle that would ease his breathing. "Easy now," she soothed, her voice calm despite the urgency of the situation. "Try to take slow breaths if you can."

Moses listened to the miner's chest, his expression growing graver at the congested sounds within. "Significant fluid in both lungs," he reported quietly. "Similar to young Jeb Holcomb's condition."

Working together, they administered a stronger dose of medicine, applied mustard plasters to the miner's chest, and positioned him to help drain the fluid. Moses noticed how seamlessly they coordinated their efforts, anticipating each other's needs with minimal verbal communication.

As the miner's breathing gradually eased, Laura wiped her brow with her sleeve, fatigue evident in the slight slump of her shoulders. They had been working non-stop since morning, traveling through a blizzard between patients, with no opportunity for rest or food.

"You should take a brief break," Moses suggested, surprising himself with the concern in his voice. "You've been going since dawn."

Laura shook her head, already moving toward Mrs. Bellweather. "So have you. And there's too much to be done."

Moses watched her go, noting the determined set of her shoulders despite her obvious fatigue. The Laura Smythe, who had stepped off the stagecoach days ago, whom he had dismissed as a city-trained nurse out of her depth, was proving to be something quite different. She was demonstrating a resilience and practical competence he hadn't expected.

The next hours passed in a blur of activity. More patients arrived, brought through the howling storm by increasingly desperate family members. Each new arrival presented with the same alarming pattern: high fever, severe coughing, rapidly developing congestion, and in the worst cases, labored breathing that suggested pneumonia was setting in.

By early evening, sixteen patients filled the church floor, their coughing and occasional moans creating a somber backdrop to the hushed activity of the caregivers. Pastor Lewis moved quietly among them, offering prayers and comfort alongside physical assistance. Deputy Diamond had departed to check on homesteads close to town and those that lived in town above business and behind their stores, promising to return with any additional cases he discovered.

Moses paused near the altar, taking a rare moment to assess their situation. The medicine table was already looking depleted, despite their efforts to conserve supplies. If the illness continued to spread at its current rate, they would exhaust their resources long before the storm released its grip on Aspen Hollow.

"Dr. Grant." Laura's voice pulled him from his grim calculations. She approached, her face showing signs of strain despite her composed demeanor. "Two more patients are developing the blue tinge around their lips, suggesting oxygen deprivation. We need more of the stronger tincture."

Moses nodded, mentally reviewing their supplies. "We have enough for perhaps eight more strong doses. After that..."

"After that, we'll need to replenish from the clinic," Laura finished for him. She glanced toward the church windows, where snow still pelted against the glass with undiminished fury. "I was planning to make a quick trip there while you covered things here."

"Alone? In this weather?" Moses raised his eyebrows, surprised by the suggestion. "It's gotten worse, not better."

"I can follow the boardwalk most of the way. We need those supplies, Dr. Grant, especially if more patients arrive overnight."

Moses studied her face, noting the determination in her eyes despite the fatigue evident in the shadows beneath them. The logical part of him acknowledged the necessity of her plan. They did indeed need additional medicine, and splitting their efforts made practical sense. Yet, he was reluctant to let her venture out into the storm alone.

"I'll go," he decided abruptly.

Laura shook her head firmly. "With respect, Dr. Grant, that's inefficient. You're the physician. The critical patients need your expertise here. I can gather supplies and return quickly."

Pastor Lewis approached with a steaming mug in each hand. "I insist you both take a moment for some hot broth," he said, offering the mugs. "Mrs. Williams prepared it, and neither of you has eaten since you arrived."

The rich aroma of the broth reminded Moses how long it had been since their last meal. He accepted the mug gratefully, noting that Laura did the same.

"Thank you, Pastor," Laura said, cradling the warm mug in her hands. "This is exactly what we needed."

"How are the patients responding to treatment?" Pastor Lewis asked, his kind face showing the strain of the day's events.

"Some improvement in the less severe cases," Moses reported after a sip of the nourishing broth. "But those with advanced symptoms are still in serious condition. We're doing everything possible with the resources available."

"Which is why I need to retrieve additional supplies from the clinic," Laura added, her tone brooking no argument. "We're likely to receive more patients through the night, and our current stock of medicine won't suffice."

Moses found himself outmaneuvered by her practical logic. "Very well," he conceded reluctantly. "But not alone. I'll ask Mr. Williams to accompany you."

"I can manage a four-block journey, Dr. Grant. I grew up in Philadelphia. We had snowstorms there too."

"Not like this, you didn't," Moses muttered, but he recognized the determination in her expression. She would go with or without his approval.

Pastor Lewis, seeming to sense the tension, smiled gently. "The Lord watches over His servants, especially those engaged in works of mercy. I'll pray for Miss Smythe's safe journey."

Laura finished her broth and handed the empty mug back to Pastor Lewis. "I'll prepare a list of exactly what we need. Dr. Grant, perhaps you could review it to ensure I don't miss anything essential?"

Moses nodded, accepting the diplomatic compromise.

They moved to a small table near the altar, where Laura produced paper and pencil from her medical bag. As they worked together on the list, heads bent close in concentration, Moses was acutely aware of her presence beside him. The faint scent of lavender that somehow persisted despite the day's arduous work, the graceful efficiency of her handwriting, and the way she anticipated items he would want before he mentioned them.

"I believe that covers the essentials," Laura said finally, reviewing the completed list. "I should be able to carry everything in two bags."

"Take my scarf," Moses said suddenly, removing the woolen garment from around his neck. "It's thicker than yours, and the wind is vicious out there."

Laura looked up, surprise flickering across her face at the unexpected gesture. "That's very kind, but—"

"It's practical," Moses interrupted, avoiding her gaze as he handed her the scarf.

A small smile touched Laura's lips as she accepted the offering. "Very practical indeed, Dr. Grant."

As Laura prepared to depart, donning her coat and wrapping Moses's scarf securely around her neck and lower face, he began struggling with an unfamiliar sense of concern. Why did Laura's journey into the blizzard provoke this uncomfortable twist in his gut?

"Be extremely cautious," he instructed, as she buttoned her coat. "Follow the boardwalk exactly."

"I will exercise all due caution," Laura promised, pulling on her gloves. "And I'll return as quickly as possible. Please check Mrs. Bellweather's breathing while I'm gone. I'm concerned about the increasing congestion in her right lung."

"I'll monitor her closely."

Pastor Lewis opened the church door, revealing the undiminished fury of the storm outside. The wind howled through the opening, bringing a swirl of snow across the threshold.

Laura turned to Moses one last time, her blue eyes meeting his with calm determination. "I'll be back soon with what we need, Dr. Grant."

She stepped out into the swirling whiteness; her figure immediately obscured by the driving snow. Pastor Lewis quickly closed the door against the bitter cold, turning to Moses with a reassuring smile.

"She's a remarkably capable young woman," the pastor observed. "The Lord sent her to Aspen Hollow at exactly the right time, wouldn't you say?"

Moses was unable to disagree. In the midst of what was rapidly becoming the worst health crisis he had witnessed in Aspen Hollow, Laura Smythe's arrival seemed providential. Her organizational skills, medical knowledge, and unflagging energy had already made a significant difference in their ability to manage the growing number of patients.

"She has proven... unexpectedly valuable," he admitted, his gaze still fixed on the door through which she had disappeared.

"More than valuable, I'd say," Pastor Lewis remarked with gentle insight. "In times of trial, God often sends precisely the help we need."

Moses turned back toward the patients, uncomfortable with the direction of the conversation.

As he moved among the patients, Moses' thoughts repeatedly returned to Laura, out alone in the raging storm. Had he been too quick to acquiesce to her plan? Should he have insisted on accompanying her or sending someone else? The rational part of his mind recognized she was right, his medical skills were needed here with the critical patients, yet he couldn't shake the growing concern for her safety.

He bent to examine young Tommy Abernathy, forcing his attention back to the task at hand. The boy's fever remained high despite the treatments they had administered, his small chest rising and falling rapidly with each labored breath.

"How is he, Doc?" Mrs. Williams asked, approaching with fresh cool cloths for the child's forehead.

"Fighting hard," Moses replied, placing his stethoscope against Tommy's chest. "The congestion is still significant, but the medicine is beginning to work. We need to keep him cool and continue the steam treatments."

The next patient was Arthur Bellweather, whose condition had deteriorated since his arrival. Moses administered another dose of Clementine's strongest tincture, noting with concern the rapidly dwindling supply. They desperately needed the additional medicines Laura had gone to retrieve, and more of Clementine's herbal remedies.

"How long has Miss Smythe been gone?" he asked Marybeth, who was recording treatment information in the ledger.

The young woman glanced at the church clock. "About twenty minutes, Dr. Grant."

Moses nodded, calculating that Laura should have reached the clinic by now, even accounting for the harsh conditions outside. The journey back, laden with supplies, would take longer.

"Let me know when she returns," he instructed, moving on to check Mrs. Bellweather.

The matron's condition closely mirrored her husband's, with the concerning addition of more pronounced congestion in her right lung, just as Laura had noted. Moses administered treatment, his movements automatic, while his mind continued to track the minutes of Laura's absence.

After completing his circuit of patients, Moses stood near the church windows, peering out into the swirling darkness. The snow fell with unrelenting intensity, driven nearly horizontal by the powerful wind. Visibility was virtually non-existent, the familiar buildings of Main Street completely obscured by the white fury.

"She'll be fine, Doc," Pastor Lewis said quietly, joining him at the window. "Miss Smythe strikes me as a woman who knows her capabilities very well."

Moses nodded without speaking, his eyes still searching the impenetrable curtain of snow for any sign of movement.

"While we wait," Pastor Lewis continued, "perhaps you could tell me more about what we're facing with this illness. How concerned should we be?"

The question drew Moses's focus back to their immediate crisis. "Very concerned," he admitted grimly. "The rapid onset and progression suggest a particularly virulent infection. If it continues to spread at this rate, we could see dozens more cases before the storm passes."

"And our supplies?"

"Limited," Moses acknowledged. "Even with what Miss Smythe is bringing from the clinic, we'll be stretched thin if the numbers increase significantly. And some patients will likely require care for days, not hours."

Pastor Lewis absorbed this sobering assessment with the calm dignity that had earned him the respect of even the roughest miners in Aspen Hollow. "Then we must pray for wisdom and guidance. And for Miss Smythe's safe return."

Moses had never been one for public prayer, keeping his complicated relationship with faith largely private, but he nodded in agreement. In the face of this growing crisis, with limited resources and mounting cases, they needed all the help they could get, divine or otherwise.

Chapter 10

The church door slammed shut against the blizzard's shriek, plunging Laura into a sudden, relative hush, though the wind still howled in the eaves like a hungry wolf. Her body fought a violent tremor, her teeth chattering so hard she could barely control them. Every breath was a painful rasp in her lungs, tasting of ice and snow. She was vaguely aware of dropping the heavy medicine bags on the table. Then, strong hands were on her arms, steadying her, guiding her.

"Laura!"

It was Dr. Grant's voice, laced with a note she hadn't heard before—something beyond his usual gruff concern, something... softer. His hands felt surprisingly warm through her thick coat. He didn't say anything more, simply propelled her forward, away from the biting draft by the door, deeper into the church.

She stumbled, her legs feeling like lead, and Moses' arm wrapped firmly around her waist, supporting her weight. The air inside the church was thick with the smells of sickness and herbs, overlaid with the faint, comforting aroma of wood smoke from the stove. Lanterns cast long, flickering shadows across the makeshift infirmary, illuminating the rows of pallets where the sick lay, their breaths ragged and uneven.

He guided her toward the large wood stove, its iron belly radiating blessed heat. "Here," he commanded gently, easing her into a sturdy wooden chair that had been pulled close to the warmth. Only then did he release her, his hands lingering on her shoulders.

"You're chilled to the bone," he stated, his voice regaining its characteristic practical edge, though the underlying softness remained. He knelt beside her, swiftly unfastening the thick woolen scarf that obscured the lower half of her face.

He unwound the scarf, revealing her numb cheeks, flushed red by the biting wind, and her eyes, which were watering and rimmed with cold. He didn't comment on her appearance, for which she was grateful.

"The medicine?" she managed to ask, her voice still shaky despite the chair's solid support. Her teeth continued their relentless chatter.

"Safe," Moses replied, already lifting the heavy bags, his movements efficient and strong. "Pastor Lewis and Mr. Williams are sorting it now." He gestured towards the back of the church, where Pastor Lewis and Mr. Williams were indeed carefully unpacking bottles and boxes, their expressions relieved as they inventoried the precious supplies.

Moses turned back to her, his deep blue eyes usually so guarded, now holding a clear, undisguised concern. "Are you hurt? Did you fall?"

Laura managed a weak shake of her head. "Just... cold. Very cold." The heat from the stove was slowly seeping into her frozen limbs, a painful thawing sensation.

"Stay here, by the fire," he instructed, his tone leaving no room for argument.

He hesitated for a moment, then reached out, his large hand hovering near her cheek before gently cupping her jaw. His touch sent a surprising warmth through her. "You're trembling," he observed, his thumb lightly stroking her cheekbone. His gaze lingered on her face, searching, assessing.

Laura held her breath, momentarily lost in the intensity of his blue eyes, so close, so focused on her.

He withdrew his hand as quickly as he'd offered it. A flicker of something unreadable crossed his face, before his usually guarded expression settled back into place. He stepped back, breaking the close proximity, and busied himself with adjusting the damper on the stove, his movements brisk, almost abrupt.

And then he was gone, striding purposefully toward the medicine table.

Laura leaned back in the chair, letting the heat from the stove penetrate her chilled body. She watched Moses as he conferred with Pastor Lewis and Mr. Williams, his head bent in concentration, his instructions clear and concise.

She closed her eyes for a moment, offering a silent prayer of gratitude for her safe return, for the medicines they so desperately needed, and for the unexpected warmth... both from the stove and from Moses' unexpected tenderness. She pushed the latter thought aside. Now was not the time for such musings. There were patients to tend to, a community to care for. But the warmth of his hand lingered, a small, persistent ember in the vast, cold landscape of their shared ordeal.

After a few minutes, the trembling subsided, replaced by a dull ache in her muscles and a profound weariness that threatened to pull her under. She knew she couldn't succumb to it. Taking a deep breath, she pushed herself to her feet; her legs were still a little unsteady, but her resolve was firm.

She moved through the infirmary, her nurse's instincts kicking in. The church was quieter now. Many patients were resting, their breathing still labored, but perhaps a little less frantic than before. Sera Williams and Marybeth were moving quietly between the pallets, offering sips of water and adjusting blankets, their faces etched with concern but their movements efficient and comforting.

Laura checked on Mrs. Bellweather first, her heart sinking slightly at the shallow, rattling breaths. The older woman's face was pale, her lips still tinged with blue despite the oxygenating steam treatments. She adjusted the cool cloth on Mrs. Bellweather's forehead, noting the clammy skin, a sign of the fever still raging beneath. There was little more she could do now but ensure comfort and administer the medications regularly.

Moving on, she checked on one of the young miners who had been struggling so fiercely before she'd left for the clinic. His breathing was marginally improved, the rattling in his chest was slightly less pronounced.

"Nurse?" he whispered, his voice hoarse.

"Just checking on you," Laura replied softly, offering a gentle smile. "How are you feeling?"

"Better... I think," he managed, his breathing still shallow.

"Rest now," she urged, tucking the blanket more securely around his shoulders. "You need your strength."

She continued her rounds, offering quiet words of reassurance, adjusting pillows, and ensuring each patient was as comfortable as possible.

Pausing near the side wall, amidst the pushed-aside pews, Laura found a moment of relative solitude. A simple wooden pew offered a quiet space, removed from the immediate activity yet still within sight of the patients. She sank onto the hard seat, her body aching with exhaustion, and closed her eyes again, this time in prayer.

Father God, she began silently, her heart overflowing with a mixture of weariness and fervent hope. We are in the midst of a storm, a storm both outside and within these walls. We are small, Lord, and this illness is vast and frightening. Grant us strength, grant us wisdom, grant us your healing grace to see us through this dark night.

She prayed for each patient by name, for the Holcomb children, for the Abernathy's, for the miners, for Mrs. Bellweather and her husband, for all those who were suffering in Aspen Hollow. She prayed for Moses, for his strength and wisdom, for his weary heart to find solace and renewal. She prayed for the volunteers, for their tireless service and their unwavering compassion. And she prayed for herself, for the strength to continue, for the unwavering faith to be a beacon of hope amidst despair.

Her prayer was not a recitation of words, but a pouring out of her soul, a communion with the divine that had sustained her through every trial in her life. It was in these moments of quiet communion that she found her deepest strength, her unwavering optimism, her capacity for compassion that seemed to stretch beyond her own human limitations. Her faith was not a passive belief, but an active force, a wellspring of resilience that flowed through her actions, her words, her touch.

After a time, she felt Moses' presence settling beside her on the pew. She didn't open her eyes immediately, finishing her silent prayer before acknowledging him.

"You should rest," Moses said quietly, his voice husky with fatigue. "What you did—going out in that storm alone—was remarkably brave. And foolish."

Laura opened her eyes, finding his gaze fixed on her profile. "It was necessary. You would have done the same," she replied simply. "How are the patients?"

"Holding steady." He leaned back against the pew, his shoulders sagging slightly. "We've done everything we can for now. They need rest, and so do we."

Laura nodded, noting the dark circles beneath his eyes, the strain etched into the lines of his face. "When did you last sleep, Dr. Grant?"

A ghost of a smile touched his lips. "I believe you've earned the right to call me Moses, after nearly freezing to death to retrieve our supplies."

"I was nowhere near freezing to death," she protested, though she couldn't help returning his slight smile. "And you're avoiding my question... Moses."

His name felt intimate on her lips. A small boundary crossed between them.

"Sleep is a luxury during a crisis," he replied, rubbing a hand across his stubbled jaw. "One I've learned to do without when necessary."

"Even the most skilled physician needs rest to function effectively," Laura countered. "We have competent volunteers monitoring the patients. We should take advantage of this quiet moment."

Moses looked out across the church floor, where patients slept fitfully under the watchful eyes of Sera and Marybeth. Pastor Lewis moved quietly among them, stopping occasionally to offer a prayer or a comforting word.

"Perhaps you're right," he conceded. "A short rest while we can."

They sat in weary companionship. The wind continued to howl outside, rattling the windows with occasional fierce gusts.

"May I ask you something?" Laura ventured after a moment.

Moses turned toward her. "Go ahead."

"Why did you become a doctor?" The question had been on her mind since she first met him, this contradiction of a man, so skilled yet so cynical, and so dedicated yet so weary of his calling.

Moses was quiet for so long that Laura thought he might not answer. When he finally spoke, his voice was low, almost contemplative.

"My father was a physician in a small town in eastern Colorado. Not unlike Aspen Hollow, though less isolated. I grew up watching him care for everyone, from miners to ranchers' wives. He was... devoted to his patients." Moses paused, his gaze distant. "When I was twelve, there was an outbreak of diphtheria. My father worked day and night, barely sleeping, barely eating. He saved many lives."

Laura sensed the approaching shadow in his narrative. "And then?"

"And then he contracted it himself." Moses' voice remained steady, but his hands tightened imperceptibly on his knees. "He died within days. My mother followed him a week later, leaving my sister Rebecca and me alone."

"I'm so sorry," Laura said, resisting the urge to place her hand over his.

Moses shrugged, the gesture dismissive yet somehow vulnerable. "It was a long time ago. We went to live with our aunt in Denver. She was... strict, but fair. Made sure we were educated."

"And you chose to follow in your father's footsteps, despite what happened to him," Laura observed. "That takes courage."

"Or stubbornness," Moses replied with a trace of his usual dry humor. "Rebecca always said I had more than my share of that."

Laura smiled at that. "I believe I've noticed that quality in you."

A brief chuckle escaped him, the sound surprising in its warmth. "I apprenticed with a doctor in Denver first, then completed more formal training further east. Medicine was... different then. Changing rapidly. New theories about germs and infection were just beginning to be accepted."

"You learned traditional methods but kept up with modern advancements," Laura noted, impressed.

"I tried." His voice took on a harder edge. "But there's often a vast gulf between what we learn in medical texts and what works in places like this." He gestured toward the frontier community represented by the sick lying before them.

"Is that why you came to Aspen Hollow? To bridge that gulf?"

Moses was quiet again, considering. "Initially, I came because no one else would. The town had no doctor, and the mining company was willing to subsidize one. I thought I'd stay a year, perhaps two." A wry smile twisted his lips. "That was five years ago."

"You stayed because they needed you," Laura said, understanding dawning.

"I stayed because..." He hesitated, searching for words. "Because despite everything, the isolation, the limited resources, the heartbreaking cases where I could do nothing, there was purpose here. Real purpose. Not the prestige of a Denver practice or the comfort of a city life, but the knowledge that without me, many of these people would have no medical care at all."

Laura nodded, deeply moved by his honesty. "That's a calling, Moses. A true vocation."

He glanced at her sharply. "You sound like Pastor Lewis."

"Is that a bad thing?"

"No," he admitted after a pause. "Just unexpected."

They fell silent again, listening to the storm outside and the soft sounds of the sick within. A patient coughed, the harsh sound breaking the quiet, and both of them tensed, ready to rise if needed. But the coughing subsided, and they remained seated, their bodies heavy with fatigue.

"What about you?" Moses asked unexpectedly. "Why nursing? You mentioned your family's tragedy, but there must be more to it."

Laura drew a deep breath, grateful for his interest, yet finding the memories painful to revisit. "After my parents and brother died in the accident, I was lost. Just... completely adrift. The pastor and his wife who took me in, they gave me shelter and love, but the grief was... overwhelming."

Moses nodded, his eyes reflecting understanding. He knew grief intimately.

"I was angry with God for a long time," Laura continued, her voice low. "I couldn't understand why He would take my family. Why He would leave me so utterly alone. Why He gave me no way to help them as they suffered."

"Many would have abandoned their faith entirely," Moses observed.

"I nearly did," Laura admitted. "But Mrs. Prichard, the pastor's wife, she had a way of allowing me my anger while gently reminding me of God's presence, even in the darkest moments." She smiled faintly at the memory. "She never pushed or preached. She simply... loved me through it. And slowly, I began to see that while God hadn't prevented my family's deaths, He had provided refuge afterward."

"And nursing?"

"That came later. When I was seventeen, there was a train accident near our town. Many were injured. The local doctor was overwhelmed, and Mrs. Prichard volunteered to help. She took me with her." Laura's eyes grew distant from the memory. "I expected to be terrified, to be reminded of my family's suffering. Instead, I found... purpose. I could do something. I could ease pain, bring comfort. I couldn't stop death from coming eventually, but I could make the journey more gentle."

Moses watched her face as she spoke, his expression intent.

"After that, I knew," Laura continued. "I saved every penny from working at the general store. Mrs. Pritchard helped me apply to nursing school in Philadelphia. It was... challenging. Not just the training, but being a young woman alone in a big city. But I never doubted my path after that day at the train accident."

"And your faith returned alongside your calling," Moses observed.

Laura nodded. "Not all at once. It was gradual, like a tide coming back in. I began to see God's hand not in the prevention of suffering because suffering comes to all of us in this fallen world, but in the healing that follows. In the hands that reach out to help, in the hearts that open to comfort."

Moses was quiet, digesting her words. "That's... a generous view of faith, considering what you experienced."

"It's not always easy to maintain," Laura admitted with a small smile. "Some days, doubt creeps back in. But then I see a patient recover, or I witness a moment of unexpected kindness, and I'm reminded that hope persists, even in the darkest times."

"Like tonight," Moses said softly, his gaze sweeping across the church floor where the sick rested under watchful care.

"Yes, exactly like tonight," Laura agreed. "Look at how this community has come together. Pastor Lewis opening the church, Mrs. Williams bringing food, Mr. Diamond braving the storm to bring in the sick, Marybeth working tirelessly. Even Jasper McCoy from the saloon contributed. That's no coincidence, Moses. That's the better angels of our nature, as President Lincoln once said. And I believe those better angels are inspired by something greater than ourselves."

Moses studied her face in the lantern light, his expression thoughtful. "You make faith sound almost... reasonable," he said finally.

Laura laughed softly, the sound like a clear bell in the somber atmosphere. "High praise from a man of science."

He smiled in response, a genuine smile that transformed his features, softening the lines of weariness and worry that had marked his face all day. "I'm not entirely lost to reason, despite what you might think."

"I've never thought that," Laura countered gently. "From the moment I saw you working on Jonah Crawford, I recognized your skill and dedication. Your methods might differ from mine in some ways, but your commitment to healing has never been in question."

Moses looked momentarily taken aback by her frank assessment. "I... thank you for that."

The conversation lulled, both of them feeling the weight of the day pressing down. Laura fought to keep her eyes open, exhaustion threatening to overwhelm her now that the immediate crisis had stabilized.

"You should rest properly," Moses said, noting her struggle. "There's a small anteroom off the main church where Pastor Lewis keeps extra supplies. He's cleared a space with some blankets. You could lie down for a few hours."

Laura shook her head. "I shouldn't leave the patients. What if someone takes a turn for the worse?"

"I'll wake you immediately if needed," Moses promised. "And I'll rest after you. We're no good to anyone if we collapse from exhaustion."

Laura hesitated, torn between her duty and her body's desperate need for sleep.

"Please, Laura," Moses added, his voice dropping lower, the concern in it unmistakable. "You've done more than enough today."

The use of her given name, spoken with such gentle insistence, made the decision for her. "Alright," she conceded. "But only for a few hours, and you must promise to wake me if there's any change in the patients."

"You have my word," Moses assured her, rising from the pew and extending his hand to help her up.

Laura accepted his assistance, her smaller hand enveloped in his larger one. He didn't immediately release her after she stood, and for a brief moment, they remained connected, hands clasped between them.

"Your journey through the storm was truly brave." Moses said quietly, his blue eyes holding hers. "Foolhardy, perhaps, but brave nonetheless."

Laura felt warmth spread through her at his words, at the genuine admiration in his voice. "I only did what was necessary."

"That's precisely what makes it brave," he countered, finally releasing her hand. "Few people do what's necessary when it's difficult or dangerous. You didn't hesitate."

A bout of harsh coughing drew their attention to one of the patients. Moses turned immediately, his professional focus returning.

"Get some rest," he instructed over his shoulder. "I'll handle this."

Laura watched him stride purposefully toward the ailing patient, his movements sure despite his fatigue. She made her way to the small anteroom, finding it simply furnished but clean and quiet.

A makeshift pallet had been prepared on the floor, with several thick blankets and what appeared to be Pastor Lewis's spare coat, rolled up as a pillow. The thoughtful gesture brought tears to Laura's eyes, a testament to the kindness that seemed to flourish even amidst the crisis.

She removed her shoes and sank onto the pallet. Her body protested the hard floor, but compared to the biting cold of her journey through the blizzard, it felt like a luxury. She pulled the blankets over herself, their weight comforting.

Her last conscious thought before sleep claimed her was of Moses, not the gruff, cynical doctor who had first greeted her in Aspen Hollow, but the man she had glimpsed tonight. The man who had guided her to the warmth with gentle hands, who had shared his deeply personal history, who had looked at her with genuine concern and admiration.

In that moment between wakefulness and sleep, she acknowledged what she had been trying to deny, that something was growing between them, something unexpected but undeniable. Something that both thrilled and frightened her.

Then exhaustion won, and she surrendered to a deep, dreamless sleep.

Chapter 11

Laura woke with a start, disoriented by the unfamiliar surroundings. For a moment, she couldn't place where she was—not the boarding house, not the clinic. Then memory flooded back: the church, the blizzard, and the illness sweeping through Aspen Hollow.

Pale gray light filtered through the small window of the anteroom, suggesting early morning. She had slept longer than intended. Concern propelled her upright, hastily smoothing her rumpled dress and reaching for her shoes.

A soft knock at the door preceded Marybeth's appearance, the young woman's face showing signs of a sleepless night but still managing a smile.

"You're awake," Marybeth observed. "Dr. Grant said not to disturb you, but I heard a movement in here and thought I'd check on you."

"How are the patients?" Laura asked immediately, pulling on her boots.

"Stable, mostly," Marybeth reported. "Mrs. Bellweather had a difficult night, but Dr. Grant managed to ease her breathing somewhat.

The others are about the same, not worse, but not much better, either."

Laura stood, quickly pinning her hair back into its practical style. "And Dr. Grant? Did he rest at all?"

Marybeth shook her head. "Not that I saw. He's been checking patients all night, adjusting treatments. Pastor Lewis tried to convince him to lie down for a while, but he refused."

"Stubborn man," Laura muttered, though her tone held more concern than criticism.

Marybeth handed her a basin of water. "I thought you might want to freshen up. There's bread and coffee in the main room when you're ready."

"Thank you, Marybeth," Laura said gratefully, accepting the basin. "I'll be out shortly."

After washing her face and hands and straightening her appearance as best she could, Laura made her way back into the main church. The scene that greeted her was both heartening and sobering.

The patients lay in their makeshift beds, some sleeping fitfully, others awake and being tended to by the volunteers. Sera moved among them, offering sips of broth to those who could manage it. Pastor Lewis sat beside Tommy Abernathy, reading quietly from a small Bible. And Moses—Laura spotted him kneeling beside Mrs. Bellweather's pallet, his stethoscope pressed to the older woman's chest, his face a study in concentration. Even from a distance, she could see the exhaustion in the slump of his shoulders, and the shadows under his eyes more pronounced than ever.

As if sensing her presence, he looked up, their eyes meeting across the church floor. A flash of relief crossed his face before his professional mask returned. He said something quietly to Mrs. Bellweather, patting her hand reassuringly, then rose and made his way toward Laura.

"You should have wakened me sooner," she chided gently as he approached. "You look exhausted."

"You needed the rest," he replied simply. "And I'm accustomed to long nights."

Laura studied him critically. The stubble on his jaw was heavier now, his eyes bloodshot, his movements betraying his fatigue despite his attempts to hide it. "My turn to insist now—you need sleep, Moses."

He shook his head. "There's too much to do. Deputy Diamond returned an hour ago with reports of more cases in town, though the storm is making it impossible to transport them here. The entire Abernathy family is ill now."

"All the more reason for you to rest while you can," Laura argued. "If there are more patients coming, we need you at your best."

Before he could protest further, she placed a firm hand on his arm. "Doctor's orders," she said with a small smile. "Or nurse's orders, in this case."

A spark of amusement flickered in his tired eyes. "Are you pulling rank on me, Miss Smythe?"

"If that's what it takes to get you to rest, yes," she replied. "I'm fully capable of monitoring the patients for a few hours. And I'll wake you immediately if there's any significant change."

Moses appeared ready to argue, but then seemed to reconsider, his body's demands perhaps finally overriding his stubborn will. "Very well," he conceded with a sigh. "But no more than three hours. And—"

"And I'll wake you if there's any change," Laura finished for him. "I promise."

He nodded, retrieving his medical bag from near the medicine table. "Mrs. Bellweather needs another steam treatment in an hour. The young miner, Davis, is doing some better. And Tommy's fever—"

"Moses," Laura interrupted gently. "I know what needs to be done."

He looked momentarily surprised, then a weary smile softened his features. "Of course you do."

"Go," she urged, gently steering him toward the anteroom. "The sooner you rest, the sooner you'll be able to return with a clear head."

With visible reluctance, Moses finally headed toward the small room Laura had just vacated, pausing at the doorway to look back once more, as if ensuring she was truly capable of handling things in his absence. Laura met his gaze steadily, projecting a confidence she mostly felt. After a moment, he nodded and disappeared into the anteroom.

Laura took a deep breath, surveying the church-turned-infirmary. She spotted a pot of coffee on a small table near the back and headed toward it, knowing she would need its fortification for the hours ahead.

Cup in hand, she began a methodical circuit of the patients, checking temperatures, adjusting blankets, offering water where needed. She spoke softly to each one, providing reassurance along with medical care.

"How is Dr. Grant holding up?" Pastor Lewis asked, joining her as she recorded notes in the ledger Marybeth had established.

"Exhausted, but refusing to acknowledge it," Laura replied with a small smile. "I finally convinced him to rest for a few hours."

Pastor Lewis nodded approvingly. "A minor miracle, I'd say. He's not a man who easily steps away from his responsibilities, even when his own health is at stake."

"I've noticed," Laura agreed, her tone gently disapproving yet underlain with admiration.

"He's been different since you arrived," Pastor Lewis observed, his kind eyes studying her face. "More... engaged. Less solitary."

Laura felt her cheeks warm slightly under his perceptive gaze. "We've simply found a way to work together effectively," she demurred.

"Perhaps," the pastor replied, a subtle smile playing at his lips. "But I believe it's more than that. You challenge him, not just professionally, but personally as well. It's good for him."

Before Laura could formulate a response that wouldn't reveal too much of her own confused feelings, the church door opened, admitting a blast of cold air and a snow-covered figure.

Deputy Diamond stomped his boots at the threshold, his typically stoic expression troubled. "Miss Smythe," he called, spotting her. "Got more sick folks needing attention. The storm's let up just enough that I might be able to bring some in by sled."

Laura moved quickly to meet him. "How many, Deputy?"

"Eight that I know of," he replied grimly. "The Johnson family, father and daughter, two more miners from the camp and the rest of the Abernathy family. Mrs. Abernathy requested they all be brought here as soon as possible. She wants to be near Tommy. I can't get to the outlying homesteads yet. The drifts are too deep."

"Bring them all as safely as you can," Laura instructed. "We'll prepare space for them."

As the deputy departed, Laura turned to Pastor Lewis. "We'll need to rearrange some patients to make room. And prepare more of the fever tincture. And we need fresh broth."

The pastor nodded, already moving to help. "I'll have Sera and Marybeth assist me with the arrangements."

For the next hour, Laura worked steadily, preparing treatments, administering medicine to the current patients, and organizing space for the new arrivals. She performed the steam treatment on Mrs. Bellweather, noting with cautious optimism that the older woman's breathing seemed slightly less labored than before.

"That a girl," Laura encouraged as Mrs. Bellweather managed a few deeper breaths. "This helps clear your lungs."

Mrs. Bellweather reached for Laura's hand, her grip weak but determined. "Thank you," she whispered hoarsely.

Laura squeezed her hand gently. "Rest now. Save your strength."

As she moved to check on Tommy, she noticed Marybeth staring out the window, her young face creased with worry.

"Marybeth? Is everything alright?"

The young woman turned, blinking rapidly. "It's just... this storm. It's not natural, Miss Smythe. I've lived here all my life, and I've never seen anything like it so early in the season. And this sickness coming so sudden-like..."

Laura moved to stand beside her, looking out at the swirling white landscape. The wind had abated somewhat, but snow still fell steadily, building drifts that nearly obscured the lower windows of buildings across the street.

"We're doing everything we can to weather both storms—the one outside and the one afflicting so many."

"Miss Hayes said something similar happens when the balance is upset," Marybeth continued, her voice low. "When something isn't right with the land or the water."

Laura glanced at her sharply. "When did you speak with Miss Hayes?"

"This past summer, when I had that terrible rash from gathering berries," Marybeth explained. "She talked about how everything in nature is connected, how one disturbance can cause ripples that affect everything else."

Laura considered this, recalling Clementine's ominous words about the metallic taste in the air, the unusual behavior of the animals before the storm. Was there something to the herbalist's concerns? Some environmental factor they hadn't considered?

Her contemplation was interrupted by the church door opening again, admitting Deputy Diamond and several men carrying makeshift stretchers.

For the next several hours, Laura was too busy to dwell on Marybeth's words or Clementine's warnings. The Johnson and Abernathy families were in serious condition, their symptoms matching the pattern they'd seen in the other patients. The miners were slightly less affected, but still requiring immediate care.

Laura worked methodically. She directed the volunteers, administered medications, and monitored the most critical patients with unwavering focus.

It was nearly midday when she finally paused, realizing that Moses had slept far longer than the three hours they had agreed upon. Concerned, she approached the anteroom, knocking softly before opening the door.

Moses lay on the pallet, still fully clothed except for his boots, his face relaxed in sleep. The perpetual furrow between his brows had smoothed out, making him appear younger, less careworn. His chest rose and fell in the deep, steady rhythm of profound exhaustion.

Laura quietly closed the door, unable to bring herself to wake him. Deputy Diamond had reported that the storm was finally beginning to ease, the wind dropping to manageable levels. Perhaps by evening, they might be able to check on other households, assess the full extent of the illness throughout Aspen Hollow.

She returned to the main floor, accepting a bowl of hot stew from Mrs. Williams with grateful thanks.

"You should sit and eat properly," the older woman advised kindly. "You've been on your feet for hours."

"I will, in a moment," Laura promised, her gaze sweeping over the patients once more.

Mrs. Williams followed her glance, nodding in understanding. "Dr. Grant still sleeping?"

"Yes, and I didn't have the heart to wake him," Laura admitted. "He was beyond exhausted."

"He pushes himself too hard," Mrs. Williams observed. "Always has. Works himself to the bone caring for others, barely spares a thought for his own needs."

"He sees it as his duty," Laura said.

"Maybe so," Mrs. Williams agreed. "But even the strongest man has his limits. He's lucky to have someone looking out for him now."

"It's only natural that we support each other in a crisis."

Mrs. Williams gave her a knowing smile, but didn't press the issue. "Eat your stew before it gets cold. Doctor's orders—or nurse's orders, as the case may be."

Laura found a quiet corner to sit and eat, grateful for the hot food and the momentary respite. As she ate, she observed the church with fresh eyes, noting the remarkable transformation that had occurred in less than twenty-four hours.

What had begun as a chaotic emergency response had evolved into an organized system of care. Volunteers moved purposefully between patients, Marybeth maintained the detailed treatment ledger, and Pastor Lewis provided spiritual comfort with practical assistance. Despite the grave circumstances, there was a beautiful harmony to their collective efforts, a testament to the strength of a community in crisis.

Laura was just finishing her stew when the anteroom door opened, and Moses emerged. His hair was rumpled, his clothes creased from sleep, but his eyes were clearer, the worst of his exhaustion seemingly addressed by the solid hours of rest.

He immediately scanned the room, his gaze finding her with what appeared to be relief. He crossed to join her, frowning slightly as he neared.

"You let me sleep far too long," he accused, though there was no real heat in his words.

"You needed it," Laura replied simply. "And we managed well enough."

Moses glanced around, noting the additional patients. "New arrivals?"

Laura nodded and quickly updated him. "Their symptoms match the pattern we've seen. High fever, respiratory distress, rapid progression."

Moses listened intently, his professional focus fully restored. "Any improvement in our earlier patients?"

"Some," Laura reported. "Mrs. Bellweather's breathing is slightly better after the steam treatments. Tommy's fever has reduced somewhat. The miners are holding steady."

Moses nodded, clearly pleased with her thorough assessment. "You've done well," he said, the simple praise warming her more than it should have.

"We've worked as a team," Laura corrected gently, gesturing toward the volunteers. "Everyone has contributed."

"True," Moses acknowledged. "But your organization and knowledge have been instrumental." He hesitated, then added more quietly, "Thank you for letting me rest. I needed it more than I realized."

The admission clearly cost him something, this proud, self-sufficient man acknowledging his limitations. Laura smiled, touched by his honesty.

"You're welcome. Partners in healing, remember?"

The phrase seemed to resonate with him, bringing a slight smile to his face. "Partners," he agreed, the word carrying a weight beyond their professional alliance.

Their moment of connection was interrupted by a commotion at the church door. Deputy Diamond entered, supporting a snow-covered Clementine Hayes.

"Look who I found making her way through the drifts," Deputy Diamond announced, helping the herbalist shake off the worst of the snow.

Clementine's stern face was set in lines of determination. She carried a large basket covered with a thick cloth, which she promptly handed to Laura as she approached.

"More remedies," she explained briskly. "Stronger than before."

"Thank you for braving the storm to bring these," Laura said sincerely, accepting the heavy basket.

Clementine's sharp eyes surveyed the church interior, taking in the rows of patients with a practiced healer's assessment. "How many now?"

"Twenty-seven in total here," Moses replied. "Unknown numbers are still in their homes that we haven't been able to reach."

Clementine nodded grimly. "As I feared. It's spreading rapidly." She turned to Laura, her expression intense. "Have you considered what might be causing it?"

Laura recalled Marybeth's earlier remark about Clementine's views. "Marybeth mentioned you spoke of balance in nature, how disturbances can have far-reaching effects."

"The girl remembers well," Clementine approved. "This isn't just any illness. The timing, the spread, the symptoms, they speak of something introduced, something that doesn't belong."

Moses frowned skeptically. "What exactly are you suggesting, Clementine?"

The herbalist met his gaze steadily. "I'm suggesting that you look beyond your medical texts, Doctor. This sickness moves too quickly, appears too suddenly in too many places at once. It suggests a common source—perhaps the water, or food."

Laura exchanged a glance with Moses. "I had similar thoughts about the water," she admitted. "But as Moses pointed out, different areas of Aspen Hollow draw from different sources."

"Unless those sources are all connected beneath the surface," Clementine countered. "Or unless something has been deliberately introduced."

The suggestion hung in the air, disturbing in its implications. Moses's frown deepened.

"That's a serious allegation, Clementine," he said carefully.

"It's not an allegation, it's a possibility," she corrected sharply. "One you should consider if you want to truly address this crisis rather than merely treat its symptoms."

Before Moses could respond, a cry from one of the patients drew their attention. Tommy was seized by a violent coughing fit, his small body convulsing with the effort.

Moses and Laura moved instantly to the child's side, their discussion with Clementine temporarily set aside in favor of the immediate crisis. Together, they worked to ease the boy's breathing, administering medicine and supporting his frail body through the spasm.

When Tommy finally settled back, exhausted but breathing more easily, Laura looked up to find Clementine watching them with an approving expression.

"You work well together," the herbalist observed quietly. "Different approaches, complementary strengths."

Neither Laura nor Moses disputed the assessment, perhaps because they had both come to recognize its truth.

"I'll help you prepare these new remedies," Laura offered, gesturing to Clementine's basket. "If they're stronger, we should be precise in their administration."

Clementine nodded, following Laura to the medicine table. As they worked side by side, measuring and mixing the herbal preparations, the older woman spoke in a low voice.

"Moses is yours. You know this, right? The spirits have told me so. You have been called her for much more than your nursing skills," she observed without preamble.

Laura nearly dropped the bottle she was holding. "I don't know what you mean."

Clementine's weathered face creased in a rare smile. "Yes, you do."

Laura focused intently on measuring the correct dose, avoiding Clementine's perceptive gaze. "We've simply found a way to work effectively together, despite our different approaches."

"Hmm," Clementine hummed noncommittally. "You are good for him. He's carried his burdens alone for too long."

Before Laura could formulate a response, Moses joined them, his expression serious.

"Deputy Diamond says the storm is abating," he reported. "If it continues to improve, we might be able to check on the outlying homesteads by tomorrow morning."

"Good," Clementine nodded. "The sooner we understand the full extent of this illness, the better."

"In the meantime," Moses continued, "I've been thinking about what you said, about a common source."

Clementine looked mildly surprised at his openness to her theory. "There's hope for you yet, Doctor."

A hint of his dry humor surfaced. "Don't sound so astonished, Clementine. I can be reasonable when evidence warrants it."

"And what evidence has convinced you?" the herbalist challenged.

"The pattern of infection," Moses admitted. "Laura and I have been tracking it, and there are anomalies that don't match typical contagion spread." He glanced at Laura. "Your suggestion about the water or food may have merit after all, despite the different sources."

Laura felt a small thrill at his acknowledgment. "If it is waterborne, we need to advise everyone to boil water before consumption or use for washing."

"I'll spread the word," Deputy Diamond offered, having approached in time to hear their discussion.

As the deputy departed with their warning, Laura stood between Moses and Clementine. Two very different healers united in purpose despite their divergent approaches. There was something powerful in this moment, this bridging of traditional wisdom and modern medicine, of faith and science, of different paths converging on a shared goal.

Chapter 12

Tommy's small hand suddenly gripped Laura's wrist with surprising strength.

"Miss Laura," he rasped, "is my ma here?"

Laura nearly dropped the cup of water she'd been about to offer him. The boy was not only awake but coherent, yet still appeared feverish. She quickly set down the cup and knelt beside his pallet.

"Yes, Tommy. Your mother is right over there," she said softly, pointing to where Mrs. Abernathy lay sleeping a few beds away. "She's been ill too, but she's resting now."

Tommy's eyes, still bright with fever but now focused and aware, followed her gesture. "Pa?"

"He's here too. Your whole family was brought in yesterday." Laura smoothed back the damp hair from his forehead, marveling at how much cooler it felt than the night before. "How are you feeling?"

"Thirsty," the boy admitted. "My chest hurts when I breathe deep."

Laura reached for the cup again. "Small sips," she instructed, supporting his head as he drank. "That's it. Not too much at once."

Moses appeared beside her, drawn by the sound of coherent conversation where there had previously been only fevered murmuring. His eyes widened slightly at the sight of Tommy awake and drinking.

"Well now," he said, kneeling beside Laura, "this is an improvement, young man."

Tommy managed a weak smile. "Hello, Dr. Grant."

Moses placed a gentle hand on the boy's forehead, then reached for his stethoscope. "Let's have a listen to those lungs of yours."

Laura moved back slightly, giving Moses room to work while she watched Tommy's face. The improvement was remarkable. Though still weak and ill, he showed the first real signs of recovery.

After completing his examination, Moses replaced his stethoscope around his neck. "The congestion is lessening," he reported, a note of cautious optimism in his voice. "And his fever has dropped considerably."

"Does that mean I can go home soon?" Tommy asked hopefully.

Moses shook his head. "Not quite yet. You still need rest and medicine. But you're definitely on the mend."

After ensuring Tommy was comfortable again, Moses gestured for Laura to join him a few steps away. "This is significant," he said quietly. "He's the first patient to show substantial improvement."

Laura nodded, hope warming her chest. "Do you think the others will follow the same pattern?"

"It's too early to tell, but it's encouraging." Moses surveyed the church floor, where the other patients lay in various states of illness. "If Tommy's improvement continues, it suggests the illness runs its course in approximately three to four days, at least in younger, healthier individuals."

"Mrs. Bellweather's breathing seems easier this morning as well," Laura noted. "And two of the miners are showing reduced fevers."

A ghost of a smile touched Moses' lips. "Perhaps we're seeing the tide turn."

Laura matched his cautious optimism. "If the treatments are working-"

The church door swung open, cutting off her thought as Deputy Diamond stepped inside, bringing with him a gust of cold air and the scent of fresh snow. He removed his hat, shaking off the white powder that clung to it.

"Morning, Doc, Miss Smythe," he greeted, approaching them. "Thought you'd want to know the storm's let up for now. We've got a window of maybe six to eight hours before the next band hits us, according to old Jim Hatcher's knee. Says it aches something fierce when more snow's coming."

Moses considered this information. "Is travel possible?"

"Difficult but doable," Diamond replied. "The drifts are high, but the wind's died down enough that visibility's decent. I managed to check on the Miller homestead. They're all healthy so far, thank the Lord."

"What about the mining camp?" Laura asked. "Have you had any word from there?"

The deputy shook his head. "Not since before the storm worsened. Last report was eight men down, but that was nearly thirty-six hours ago."

Clementine Hayes approached, having overheard their conversation. She had spent the night at the church, helping tend to patients and prepare remedies.

"The mining camp needs checking," she stated matter-of-factly. "If you want to understand this sickness, that's where you should look."

Moses frowned. "What makes you say that?"

The herbalist's weathered face was impassive. "Call it instinct. The miners were among the first affected, weren't they?"

"Yes," Laura confirmed, "along with the Abernathy boys."

"And the Holcomb children," Moses added. "All within a short time of each other."

Clementine nodded. "This weather break won't last long. If you're going to go, it should be now."

Moses looked torn, his gaze moving from the patients to the window, where weak winter sunlight struggled through the clouds.

Laura touched his arm lightly. "I could go," she offered. "You could stay with the patients here."

"Absolutely not," Moses replied immediately, his tone brooking no argument. "If anyone goes to the mining camp, we go together."

The firmness of his response surprised Laura, though she found herself oddly touched by his protectiveness.

"The patients here are stable," Pastor Lewis interjected, having silently joined their group. "Mrs. Williams, Marybeth, and I can manage them for a few hours."

"I'll accompany you," Clementine announced.

Moses ran a hand through his hair, clearly weighing the decision. Finally, he nodded. "Very well. We'll ride to the mining camp, assess the situation there, and return before the next storm arrives."

"I'll have horses saddled for you," Deputy Diamond offered. "They'll be ready in twenty minutes at the livery."

As the deputy departed, Moses turned to Laura. "Pack whatever medical supplies you think we might need. I'll prepare doses of Clementine's remedies to take with us."

Laura nodded and moved toward the medicine table. Pastor Lewis followed, helping her gather clothes, carbolic acid, and other essentials.

"The mining camp is rough territory," he warned gently. "Especially in winter."

"I'll be fine," Laura assured him, wrapping bottles carefully in cloth to prevent freezing or breakage.

Pastor Lewis smiled, his kind eyes crinkling. "Your courage continues to impress Miss Smythe. I believe God knew exactly what He was doing when He sent you to Aspen Hollow."

Laura's hands stilled for a moment. "I hope so," she admitted. "Sometimes I wonder if I'm making any difference at all."

"You are," the pastor assured her with gentle certainty. "Not just to the patients, but to others as well."

Moses approached, medical bag in hand. "Ready?"

She nodded, shouldering her bag. "Yes."

They bundled up in their warmest clothes, Laura borrowing an extra woolen scarf from Mrs. Williams, and headed out into the crisp morning air. The temperature had risen slightly with the sun, making the cold bearable. The streets of Aspen Hollow were buried under impressive drifts of snow, with narrow paths carved between buildings by the hardy souls who had ventured out during the brief respite in the weather.

At the livery, three horses stood saddled and waiting. Laura approached a sturdy chestnut mare, running a gloved hand along her neck. The animal nickered softly, warm breath forming clouds in the cold air.

"Can you ride?" Moses asked, adjusting the girth on his mount.

"Since childhood," Laura confirmed, smoothly mounting despite her layers of clothing. "My father believed every child should learn."

Moses nodded approvingly and swung into his saddle with ease. Clementine mounted her horse with surprising agility, settling into the saddle like someone born to it.

They set off single file, Moses breaking the trail through the deep snow, with Laura following and Clementine bringing up the rear. The world around them was transformed, a pristine white landscape under a pearl-gray sky. The silence was profound, broken only by the crunch of their horses' hooves and the occasional distant crack of a snow-laden branch giving way.

As they climbed higher, the trail narrowed, hugging the mountainside. To their right, the ground fell away steeply, offering breathtaking views of Aspen Hollow nestled in the valley below. The church steeple rose above the other buildings, a beacon of hope in the white wilderness.

"Beautiful, isn't it?" Moses called back, noticing Laura's gaze.

"Magnificent," she agreed. "Even in the midst of hardship, God's creation takes one's breath away."

They rode in silence for a time, each lost in their thoughts as they navigated the challenging terrain. When the trail widened slightly, Clementine urged her horse forward until she was riding alongside Laura.

"You feel it too, don't you?" the herbalist asked abruptly.

Laura glanced at her, puzzled. "Feel what?"

"The wrongness." Clementine gestured vaguely at the surrounding forest. "It's more than just the illness or the storm. Something fundamental is out of balance."

Laura considered the herbalist's words. There was indeed something unsettling about the rapid spread of the illness, its simultaneous appearance in different parts of town, the unusual severity of the storm. Yet, she hesitated to attribute supernatural significance to what might simply be a particularly virulent outbreak coupled with harsh winter weather.

"I believe there's a natural explanation," she said carefully. "Though perhaps one we haven't discovered yet."

Clementine made a noncommittal sound. "Natural doesn't mean simple, girl. Everything in Creation is connected, from the smallest drop of water to the tallest mountain. Disturb one thing, and ripples spread outward, affecting everything they touch."

"You sound like you suspect something specific," Laura observed.

"I have my suspicions," Clementine admitted.

Moses had slowed his horse to listen to their conversation. "Are you suggesting someone deliberately caused this illness?" he asked, his tone skeptical.

"Not necessarily deliberate," Clementine replied. "But careless, perhaps. Disrespectful of the natural order."

Moses shook his head slightly. "I prefer to focus on what we can observe and verify."

"As do I," Clementine retorted.

Further discussion was forestalled as they rounded a bend and the mining camp came into view. Unlike the relatively orderly layout of Aspen Hollow, the camp was a haphazard collection of structures clinging to the mountainside. Canvas tents, rough wooden shacks, and a few more substantial buildings huddled together near the dark mouth of the mine entrance. Smoke rose from several chimneys, the only sign of life in the otherwise still encampment.

"It's quiet," Laura remarked.

Moses nodded grimly. "Many miners may be too sick to work."

They rode into the camp, drawing curious stares from the few people visible outside. A gaunt-faced woman hanging wash on a line near an outdoor campfire between two shacks watched them warily, pulling a young child closer to her skirts as they passed.

Moses led them toward the largest building, a two-story structure with the words "Flint Mining Company" painted on a weather-beaten sign above the door. He dismounted, tying his horse to a post, then helped Laura down from her saddle.

"This is the company office," he explained. "When I was here before, they'd converted the first floor into a makeshift infirmary for the sick miners."

A harried-looking man with a thick beard emerged from the building, his expression brightening at the sight of them.

"Doc Grant! Thank the Lord you've come," he exclaimed. "We've got fourteen men down now, and three of the women and children as well."

"Fourteen?" Moses repeated, clearly dismayed by the number.

The man, who introduced himself as Melvin MacTavish, a mine foreman, nodded grimly. "It's spreading fast. Even Mr. Flint himself has taken ill."

This news clearly surprised Moses. "Barnaby Flint is here? I thought he usually stayed in Denver."

"Came in on the last stage before the storm," Melvin explained. "Wanted to check on operations. Fell ill just yesterday, and he's in a bad way."

They followed Melvin into the building, where the company's main office had indeed been transformed into an infirmary, similar to their setup at the church. Pallets covered the floor, each occupied by a miner showing the now-familiar symptoms of high fever, coughing, and respiratory distress.

In the far corner, somewhat separated from the others, lay a middle-aged man whose gray-streaked beard and finer clothes marked him as someone of importance. Even in illness, there was something imposing about him, an aura of authority that persisted despite his weakened state.

"That's Mr. Flint," Melvin murmured. "He's been out of his head with fever since early this morning. Keeps muttering words I cannot comprehend."

Laura exchanged a quick glance with Moses.

"Who's been caring for everyone?" Laura asked, noting the rudimentary organization of the infirmary.

"Mrs. Normand and Mrs. Clark have been doing their best," MacTavish replied, gesturing toward two exhausted-looking women moving among the patients. "They've given them water and whatever medicines we had on hand."

"You've done admirably under difficult circumstances," Moses assured the women as they approached. "We've brought additional medicines and supplies."

Laura immediately began assessing the patients, moving from one to the next, checking temperatures and lung sounds. Moses did the same on the opposite side of the room, while Clementine observed silently, occasionally sniffing the air or touching a patient's forehead with her weathered hand.

The severity of the cases varied, but all showed the same basic pattern they'd observed in town. Laura noted with concern that several of the miners exhibited more advanced symptoms, their breathing shallow and labored, lips tinged with blue.

"These men need immediate treatment," she called to Moses. "Particularly those three by the wall."

Moses nodded, already preparing doses of Clementine's strongest fever tincture. They worked side by side, administering medications, positioning patients to ease breathing, and instructing Mrs. Normand and Mrs. Clark on proper care techniques.

"He's burning up," Laura murmured as they reached Barnaby Flint. The mine owner's skin was hot to the touch, his breathing rapid and shallow. "His fever is dangerously high."

"Same presentation as the others, but more advanced," Moses confirmed, listening to Flint's chest with his stethoscope. "Significant congestion in both lungs."

They administered medicine and placed cool cloths on Flint's forehead. The mine owner stirred restlessly, his eyes opening briefly but unfocused.

"Runoff," he muttered, grasping weakly at Moses's sleeve. "Didn't know... the creek."

Moses and Laura exchanged a significant look over the delirious man.

"Mr. Flint," Moses said clearly, leaning closer. "What about the runoff? What about the creek?"

But Flint had already slipped back into fevered sleep, his grip on Moses's sleeve going slack.

After they had treated all the patients and organized a system of care, Clementine announced her intention to check on other ill miners in the camp's outlying shacks.

"People need my remedies," she stated matter-of-factly.

With Clementine gone and the two women tending to the patients following their instructions, Moses and Laura moved to a small office adjacent to the main room, where a desk and a few chairs offered a space for private conversation.

"What do you make of Flint's ramblings?" Laura asked, sinking gratefully into a wooden chair.

Moses leaned against the desk, arms folded across his chest. "It could be nothing but fever dreams. Or it could be significant."

"He mentioned runoff and the creek," Laura noted. "Mining operations can release minerals and chemicals that might contaminate water sources, couldn't they?"

"Yes," Moses agreed, his expression troubled. "Though most mine operators take precautions to prevent such contamination."

"Most, but perhaps not all," Laura suggested carefully.

Moses nodded slowly. "It's a possibility we should investigate. If there is mine runoff contaminating Aspen Creek, and if that's the source of the illness..."

"It would explain the pattern of infection," Laura finished for him. "The miners drawing water directly from the creek would be affected first, followed by others who use that water source further downstream."

They fell silent, each contemplating the implications. Outside the small window, snow had begun to fall again, light flurries dancing in the air.

"I hope Clementine returns soon," Laura remarked, watching the snowflakes.

"She knows these mountains better than most," Moses reassured her.

Another silence fell between them, comfortable rather than awkward. Laura studied Moses's profile as he gazed out the window, noting the strong line of his jaw, the slight furrow between his brows that never quite disappeared, and the way the winter light accentuated the silver threading through his dark hair at the temples.

He must have sensed her gaze, for he turned toward her, a question in his eyes.

"You're tired," she observed softly.

A small smile touched his lips. "As are you."

"Yes," she admitted. "But it's a good kind of tired. The kind that comes from doing meaningful work."

Moses nodded in understanding. "Though I wonder sometimes... what meaning can be found in so much suffering? What purpose does it serve?"

The question hung in the air between them, weighty with implications. Laura recognized it wasn't merely philosophical—it was deeply personal for him.

"I don't believe suffering itself has meaning," she said carefully. "I believe we bring meaning to it through our response."

Moses tilted his head slightly, considering her words. "And what meaning have you found in your own suffering, Laura?"

The directness of the question took her breath away.

"Connection," she answered honestly after a moment. "I've found that suffering deepens our capacity to connect with others, with ourselves, with God. My family's death left a hole in my heart that nothing could fill. But in that emptiness, I discovered room for greater compassion, greater understanding of others' pain."

Moses watched her intently, his blue eyes searching her face as if looking for something specific.

"And God?" he asked quietly. "How does He fit into your understanding of suffering?"

Laura chose her words with care, sensing the importance of this moment. "Faith isn't about expecting God to prevent all suffering. It's about finding His strength when suffering comes. I don't believe God caused my family's deaths, Moses. But I do believe He helped me find purpose through that pain."

"That's a generous view," Moses observed.

"Not generous," Laura corrected gently. "Necessary. I couldn't continue believing in a God who deliberately caused such pain. But

I could believe in One who wept alongside me and then helped me rebuild from the ashes."

Moses turned back toward the window.

"You mentioned previously you had a sister," Laura said. "Tell me about her."

His shoulders tensed visibly. For a moment, she thought he might refuse to respond, might close off as he had so many times before when conversation veered toward personal matters.

"Rebecca," he said finally, his voice tight.

Laura waited, not pushing, allowing him the space to continue or not, as he chose.

"She was twenty-two," Moses continued after a long pause, his voice lowering. "Married to a good man, Jake Miller. They were so happy when they discovered she was expecting. Rebecca wanted me to deliver her baby, trusted me completely." His voice caught slightly on the last word.

Laura remained silent, her heart aching for the pain evident in his every word.

"The pregnancy progressed normally. No complications, no concerns. But then the labor..." He trailed off, staring unseeingly out the window. "It went on too long. She grew exhausted. The baby was positioned wrong—breech and unable to turn. I tried everything, every technique I'd learned, everything the textbooks recommended."

He turned to face her, his eyes haunted. "I did everything right. Everything the textbooks taught. And I still lost her and the baby."

The raw anguish in his voice brought tears to Laura's eyes. She rose from her chair, moving closer to him, drawn by an instinctive need to offer comfort.

"Moses," she said softly, "you know as well as I do that sometimes, despite everything we know, despite our best efforts, we cannot change the outcome."

"I was her brother," he said, his voice rough with emotion. "I was her doctor. She trusted me with her life and the life of her child, and I failed them both."

"You didn't fail," Laura insisted gently. "You fought for them with everything you had. That's not failure, it's love."

Moses shook his head, turning away again. "Jake never blamed me. That was almost worse than if he had. He just... accepted it, said it was God's will." Bitterness tinged his voice. "What kind of God wills the death of a young mother and her innocent child?"

The question hung in the air, not rhetorical but genuinely anguished. Laura could see now the source of his cynicism, his distrust of both medicine and faith. He had lost not only his sister, but his belief in the systems that should have saved her.

"I don't think God willed Rebecca's death," Laura said quietly. "I think He grieved it, just as you did. Just as Jake did."

"Then why allow it?" Moses demanded, turning to face her again. "If He's all-powerful, why not prevent such pointless suffering? Why did he allow Jake to be in a mine accident shortly after Rebecca died? Why did he allow me to amputate Jake's leg because of the accident? Why did he allow infection to set in, which killed him?"

"I don't know," Laura admitted honestly. "I don't pretend to understand God's ways fully. But I do know that blaming Him hasn't healed your heart, Moses. It's only kept the wound open."

Her words seemed to strike something deep within him. He stared at her, his blue eyes bright with unshed tears.

"How could I keep believing in a God who let all that happen?" he asked, his voice barely above a whisper. "Or in medicine that failed when I needed it most?"

Laura took a step closer, close enough that she could have reached out to touch him. "Some wounds don't heal because we keep them open, checking them, making sure they still hurt."

"And if letting them heal feels like betrayal?" His voice was hoarse, vulnerable in a way she had never heard from him before.

"Then we honor those we've lost by living fully rather than by continuing to bleed," she said gently. "Do you think Rebecca or Jake would want you to carry this burden forever? To close yourself off from faith, from connection, from hope?"

Something broke in Moses's expression. He turned abruptly toward the window, but not before Laura saw a tear escape and track down his cheek.

Without thinking, she reached out, touching his arm. He didn't pull away.

"After my family died," she said, "I was so angry. At God, at the world, at myself for not being able to save them. I thought my anger was loyalty... that if I stopped being angry, stopped hurting, I would somehow be betraying their memory."

Moses remained silent, but she could feel he was listening intently.

"A wise woman told me something I've never forgotten," Laura continued. "She said, 'Grief is love with nowhere to go.' All that love you had for Rebecca and Jake, all those hopes and dreams, they didn't die with either of them. They're still part of you, looking for somewhere to belong."

A shudder passed through Moses. Slowly, he turned to face her, no longer hiding the tears that glistened in his eyes.

"I miss her," he said simply. "Every day. I miss Jake too. He was like the brother I never had."

"Of course you do," Laura whispered, her own eyes filling with tears of compassion.

A barrier dissolved between them. Moses looked down at Laura's hand still resting on his arm, then back to her face. The vulnerability in his expression took her breath away.

Without conscious thought, Laura moved closer, opening her arms in silent invitation. For a heartbeat, Moses hesitated, years of carefully maintained emotional distance warring with the raw need for comfort. Then, with a nearly imperceptible sigh, he stepped into her embrace.

It was not a passionate gesture, but one of profound human connection. Moses's arms encircled her waist, his head bowing to rest lightly against her hair. Laura held him, one hand moving soothingly across his back, offering wordless comfort as his body trembled slightly with suppressed emotion.

They stood like that for several moments; the silence broken only by the soft sound of their breathing and the gentle whisper of snowflakes against the window. Laura closed her eyes, acutely aware of Moses's heartbeat against her chest, the solid warmth of him, the faint scent of pine and soap that clung to his clothing.

When they separated, it was slowly, almost reluctantly. Moses didn't step fully away, maintaining a closeness that would have been improper in any other context. His hand came up to touch her cheek briefly, a gesture of such tenderness that Laura felt her heart constrict.

"You are an angel," he murmured, his voice low and intimate.

Laura nodded, not trusting her voice. A connection had formed between that transcended their professional partnership or emerging friendship.

The spell was broken by the office door swinging open. They stepped apart quickly as Clementine entered, snow dusting her shoulders and hat.

If the herbalist noticed their unusual proximity or the emotion lingering in the air, she gave no sign of it. "The storm's picking up again," she announced without preamble. "We should go."

She fixed them with a penetrating stare. "But first, you need to see something."

Moses cleared his throat, visibly pulling himself back into his professional role. "Did you find something?"

"The well behind the company office," Clementine confirmed grimly. "The water's not right. There's a scent to it... metallic, and harsh. Something's not right."

Laura exchanged a concerned glance with Moses. "Added deliberately, you think?"

"Perhaps not," Clementine replied. "But it's contaminated, no doubt about that. And the creek that feeds it runs right past the mine drainage point."

"Mine runoff," Moses said quietly, his eyes meeting Laura's.

"Let's examine it," Laura suggested, already reaching for her shawl and coat.

They followed Clementine outside, where the snowfall had indeed intensified, large flakes swirling down from a leaden sky. The herbalist led them around the back of the building to a stone well. She lowered the bucket, then brought it up filled with water.

"Smell it," she instructed, holding the bucket toward them.

Laura leaned forward, inhaling cautiously. An unmistakable metallic odor rose from the water, sharp and unnatural. Moses did the same, his frown deepening.

"This isn't normal," he agreed. "There's definitely contamination."

"And if this is the miners' drinking water…" Laura began.

"It would explain why they were among the first affected," Moses finished. "But how does this connect to cases in town? The Abernathy boys don't drink from this well."

Clementine beckoned them to follow her a short distance from the building to where a small stream trickled down the mountainside. Even with snow covering most of the ground, they could see the watercourse cutting through white banks.

"This feeds the well," she explained. "But look where it goes."

They followed the stream's path with their eyes as it wound down the mountain, eventually joining a larger creek that passed near the edge of the mining camp.

"That's a tributary of Aspen Creek," Moses realized aloud. "Which flows right past the edge of town, where the Abernathy boys often play."

"And provides water for the town well," Laura added, the pieces falling into place. "If there's mine runoff contaminating this stream…"

"Then it's flowing directly into Aspen Creek and contaminating the town's water supply," Moses concluded grimly.

Clementine nodded, her expression somber. "Nature doesn't poison itself this way. This was done, whether by carelessness or design."

They watched the contaminated water flow inexorably downstream, carrying its invisible poison toward the town.

"We need to take samples," Moses decided, reaching for his medical bag. "And return to town immediately. People need to be warned not to use water from the creek or the town well."

Laura nodded in agreement. "And we need to determine what specific contaminants we're dealing with. If we know that, we might be able to develop more targeted treatments."

Moses found an empty bottle in his bag and carefully filled it with water from both the well and the stream. "This should be enough for testing," he said, stoppering the bottle securely.

They returned to the company office to check on the patients one last time before departing. Laura gave final instructions to Mrs. Normand and Mrs. Clark on continuing treatments, promising to send more medicine as soon as possible.

As they prepared to leave, Laura paused beside Barnaby Flint's pallet. The mine owner still burned with fever, his breathing harsh and labored. She applied a cool cloth to his forehead, her mind troubled by the implications of their discovery.

"The water..." Flint muttered, his eyes fluttering open briefly. "Tell Pastor Lewis... my fault..."

Laura leaned closer. "Mr. Flint, what about the water? What's your fault?"

But his eyes closed again, consciousness slipping away before he could respond.

Outside, the snowfall was heavier now; the wind beginning to pick up. They mounted their horses quickly, aware that their window of good weather was rapidly closing.

As they prepared to ride out, Moses maneuvered his horse alongside Laura's, their knees nearly touching.

"Laura," he said quietly, his voice pitched for her ears alone, "what happened in there—what I shared with you..."

"Stays between us," she assured him gently, understanding his concern. "Always."

Relief flickered across his face, followed by something warmer. "Thank you," he said simply. But the look in his eyes conveyed much more gratitude, yes, but also a new openness, a connection that hadn't existed before.

They rode out of the mining camp single file, Clementine leading the way this time, her knowledge of the mountain trails invaluable in the deteriorating weather. The journey down would be more treacherous than the climb up had been, with fresh snow obscuring the path and the wind growing stronger with each passing minute.

Laura urged her horse forward, following Clementine's tracks. Behind her, Moses rode steadily, a reassuring presence at her back. Despite the danger of their situation and the gravity of their discovery, Laura felt an undeniable sense of hope blooming within her. Not just hope for understanding and eventually controlling the illness affecting Aspen Hollow, but hope of a more personal nature.

The walls around Moses Grant's heart had begun to crumble today. He had allowed her to see his pain, to offer comfort, to touch the wounded places he had kept hidden for so long. It was a profound gift of trust, one she would honor with the same care and devotion she brought to her nursing.

As they descended the mountain, the snow swirling around them and Aspen Hollow waiting in the valley below, Laura sent up a silent prayer of gratitude. For safety in the storm, for progress in their understanding of the illness, and for the precious, fragile connection that had formed between her and the man she was coming to care for deeply.

Chapter 13

The wind howled with renewed fury, driving needles of ice against any exposed skin. Laura hunched lower over her horse's neck, eyes narrowed against the onslaught. What had begun as light snowfall at the mining camp had transformed into a raging blizzard again. The path, barely visible when they'd ascended, now disappeared entirely beneath fresh drifts that reached past the horses' knees.

"Keep close!" Moses called from behind her, his voice nearly lost in the roar of the storm.

Laura followed Clementine's dark shape ahead, the herbalist somehow finding their way despite the whiteout conditions. The chestnut mare beneath her stumbled suddenly, front hoof plunging into a hidden depression. Laura pitched forward, clutching desperately at the saddle horn as the horse struggled to regain its footing.

Strong hands suddenly gripped her arm, steadying her. Moses had maneuvered his mount alongside hers with remarkable speed.

"I've got you," he said, close enough that she could hear him clearly despite the wind. His eyes, intense with concern, searched her face. "Are you hurt?"

"No," Laura assured him, regaining her balance. "Thank you."

He didn't immediately release her arm, his gloved hand lingering in what seemed like reluctance to break contact. Finally, he nodded and guided his horse back into position, though he remained closer than before.

Clementine had stopped ahead, waiting for them. The older woman's eyes missed nothing, flicking between Laura and Moses with a knowing assessment before she turned her mount forward again.

"We need to make better time," Clementine called back to them. "This storm is worsening fast."

They pushed on; the horses laboring through deepening snow. Laura's face burned from the cold. Her fingers, though gloved, had grown numb, making it difficult to maintain a proper grip on the reins. She couldn't imagine how Moses was faring, as he'd insisted she wear his thicker gloves while he made do with a spare pair from his saddlebag.

"Moses," she called when he drew alongside her again at a wider section of trail. "Do you think Barnaby Flint knew about the contamination?"

Moses's expression was grim beneath the snow collecting on his hat brim. "His delirium suggests guilt. 'Tell Pastor Lewis... my fault.' Those aren't the words of an innocent man."

"But did he cause it deliberately or through negligence?" Laura wondered aloud.

"Either way, the poison flows downstream, and the innocent suffer."

They fell silent again, conserving energy for the arduous journey. The afternoon light was fading rapidly, darkness gathering beneath the storm clouds. Laura estimated they had perhaps an hour of daylight remaining, if they could even call the murky gray illumination "daylight."

"We're nearly there," he said, voice rough from the cold. "Look."

Through gaps in the swirling snow, Laura could make out the valley below, and the scattered lights of Aspen Hollow flickering like earthbound stars. The church steeple rose above the other buildings, a beacon guiding them home.

"Thank God," she murmured, the words escaping as a prayer rather than a mere expression.

Moses glanced at her. "Indeed."

The descent into town proved treacherous. The horses picked their way carefully down the snow-covered trail, hooves occasionally sliding on hidden ice beneath the fresh powder. Laura's back ached with tension, every muscle taut with concentration.

As they finally reached the outskirts of Aspen Hollow, the familiar buildings emerged like phantoms through the curtain of white.

Light from every window of the church cast golden rectangles onto the surrounding snow. As they approached, the door opened, spilling more light into the gathering darkness. Deputy Diamond's broad silhouette appeared in the doorway.

Clementine dismounted first. She took the reins of Laura's horse as Moses swung down from his saddle and stepped to Laura's side.

"Allow me," he said, reaching up to help her dismount.

Laura placed her hands on his shoulders as his hands encircled her waist. Even through layers of winter clothing, she felt the strength in his grip as he lifted her down. When her feet touched the ground, his hands remained at her waist, their faces close in the gathering darkness.

"Thank you," she said softly, meeting his gaze.

"Dr. Grant! Miss Smythe!" Deputy Diamond called. "Thank the Lord you've made it back safely."

Moses's hands dropped from Laura's waist as they turned toward the deputy. "We've made some concerning discoveries," Moses replied, retrieving his medical bag from his saddle. "Is Pastor Lewis still inside?"

"Yes, sir. He's been waiting anxiously for your return."

Clementine had already led the horses toward a small stable beside the church. "Go inside," she called to them over her shoulder. "I'll see to the animals."

Laura and Moses entered the church quickly, grateful for the wave of warmth that greeted them. The interior was much as they had left it, though with more patients than before. Every available space on the floor was occupied with pallets, and the air hung heavy with the sounds of labored breathing and occasional coughing.

Pastor Lewis approached immediately, relief clear on his weary face. "You're back, praise be. We've been most concerned."

"How are the patients?" Laura asked, already unwrapping her scarf and removing her outer layers.

"Tommy continues to improve," Pastor Lewis reported, "but several others have taken turns for the worse."

"And we've had three new cases since you left," Deputy Diamond added. "The Peterson's' youngest boy and two of Jenkins's farm hands."

Moses frowned as he removed his snow-covered coat. "Pastor, we need to speak with you privately. We've made a discovery that may explain the outbreak."

Laura moved to a basin of water, washing her hands thoroughly before approaching the nearest patients. "And Mr. Flint asked specifically for you, Pastor. He's gravely ill at the mining camp, but he seemed intent on confessing something to you."

Pastor Lewis's expression grew troubled. "Confessing? Did he say what about?"

"Only that it was 'his fault,'" Moses replied quietly. "We believe the mine runoff has contaminated the town's water supply."

Laura joined them again. "The contamination flows directly into Aspen Creek, which feeds the town well."

"And explains why those who draw water directly from the creek, like the miners and the Abernathy boys, were among the first affected," Moses continued, naturally picking up her train of thought.

"We also need to implement immediate water protocols," Laura added. "All water must be boiled before use, and—"

"—and people should avoid using creek water entirely if possible," Moses finished.

They both paused, suddenly aware of how they'd fallen into a rhythm of completing each other's thoughts. Moses's expression flickered, something like self-consciousness crossing his features before he straightened, putting a slight but noticeable distance between them.

Laura felt the subtle withdrawal like a physical chill but respected the boundary he seemed to be establishing. After the vulnerability he'd shown at the mining camp, she understood his instinct to retreat, to protect himself from further exposure.

"I'll organize the boiling protocols," she said instead, turning toward Sera, who was tending to a miner near the stove.

Pastor Lewis looked between them with perceptive eyes. "Deputy Diamond can begin spreading word about the boiling water."

"We need those water tests," Laura called over her shoulder as she knelt beside a patient. "And quick access to clean water sources—perhaps springs higher up the mountain that wouldn't be affected by the mine runoff?"

"There's a spring about two miles west," Deputy Diamond offered. "It will be very difficult to reach in this weather, but it might be our best option."

As they discussed logistics, Laura moved methodically among the patients, checking temperatures and lung sounds. When she reached Millie Abernathy's pallet, she frowned in concern. The young schoolteacher's face was flushed with fever, her breathing more labored than when Laura had left.

"Millie?" Laura touched her friend's cheek gently.

Millie's eyes fluttered open, glassy with fever. "Laura," she whispered. "You're back."

"Yes, and I'm going to help you feel better," Laura promised, reaching for a cool cloth to place on Millie's forehead.

"My brother—" Millie began, but a harsh cough interrupted her words.

"Felix and Tommy are both here too," Laura assured her, supporting Millie's head as the coughing subsided. "Dr. Grant is checking on Felix right now."

Across the room, Moses kneeled beside Felix's pallet, his stethoscope pressed to the boy's chest, his expression grave. Laura caught his eye, and a wordless communication passed between them—both Abernathy's were in serious condition.

For the next several hours, Laura and Moses worked tirelessly among the patients. Moses maintained a professional demeanor, his instructions clear but impersonal. Only occasionally did Laura catch him watching her with an expression that suggested his thoughts were far from clinical.

When they met at the medicine table to prepare fresh tinctures, Laura reached for a bottle of willow bark at the same moment Moses did. Their fingers brushed, a simple touch that shouldn't have meant anything, yet Moses jerked his hand back as if burned, then looked immediately apologetic.

"I'm sorry," he said, his voice low. "You take it."

"It's all right," Laura replied evenly, pretending not to notice his overreaction. "There's plenty for both treatments."

Moses nodded, not meeting her eyes as he measured a dose for Felix. The slight but deliberate distance he maintained throughout the evening was both frustrating and understandable. Laura had glimpsed the depths of his pain and had been allowed into places he likely hadn't shared with anyone. It was natural that he might need to regain his footing.

Still, it stung more than she cared to admit.

As the evening wore on, Laura threw herself into organizing the water protocols. Under her direction, volunteers set up large pots for boiling water, and established a rotation for maintaining the supply.

"Some folks are saying it's nonsense," Deputy Diamond reported when he returned from another circuit of the town. "Old Man Jenkins says he's been drinking from the creek for twenty years and ain't never been sick a day."

"People often resist change, especially when it inconveniences them," Laura replied, handing him a cup of hot coffee. "But we need to convince them. Lives may depend on it."

"We need proof," Moses said, joining their conversation. "The water tests should provide that, but they'll take time we don't have."

The hours passed in a blur of activity. Patients were tended to, water was boiled, medicines were administered. Midnight came and went, the storm continuing to rage outside, rattling the church windows with occasional fierce gusts.

Shortly after two in the morning, Laura realized she hadn't seen Moses for over an hour. She found Marybeth dutifully maintaining the treatment ledger and asked if she'd seen him.

"I believe he went toward the back of the church," Marybeth replied, stifling a yawn. "Near Pastor Lewis's study."

Laura nodded her thanks and made her way through the rows of patients toward the rear of the building. The area was quieter, set apart from the main floor, where most of the activity centered. As she approached Pastor Lewis's small study, she noticed the door was ajar, a thin line of lamplight spilling into the darkened corridor.

She hesitated, not wanting to intrude if Moses was conferring privately with the pastor. Then she heard a sound that made her heart constrict, a muffled, ragged breath that might have been a suppressed sob.

Laura moved closer, peering carefully through the gap in the door. What she saw stopped her in her tracks.

Moses sat alone in the small study, his head bowed, hands clasped together, so tightly his knuckles were white. His shoulders trembled slightly with the effort of contained emotion. He wasn't exactly praying, not in any formal sense, but the posture, the concentrated stillness, suggested a man reaching desperately for something beyond himself.

Laura was about to withdraw, feeling like an intruder on a profoundly private moment, when Moses spoke in a whisper so faint she barely caught the words.

"I don't even know if You're listening anymore."

The raw honesty in those words, the naked vulnerability they revealed, held Laura motionless. Moses continued, unaware of her presence.

"I've been so angry for so long. But these people need... something I can't give them alone." He drew a shuddering breath. "If You're there... if You ever were... help us."

Laura must have made some small sound, for Moses's head jerked up, his eyes finding her in the doorway. For a heartbeat, she saw naked emotion on his face, grief, fear, and shame at being caught in such a vulnerable state.

"I'm sorry," she said immediately. "I didn't mean to intrude."

Moses straightened, composing himself with visible effort. "It's all right," he said, his voice rough. "I was just..."

"Trying to pray," Laura finished softly when he trailed off.

He nodded, surprised by her understanding. "Rather poorly, I'm afraid."

Instead of the pity or judgment he perhaps expected, Laura simply moved into the room and sat in the chair opposite him, leaving the door partially open as propriety demanded, but creating a small pocket of privacy.

"There's no wrong way to reach out to God," she said gently.

Moses studied her face in the lamplight. "You're not going to tell me that faith requires proper forms and rituals?"

A small smile touched Laura's lips. "God isn't particularly concerned with proper forms when a heart is seeking Him honestly."

"Even a heart that's been angry with Him for years?"

"Especially that kind of heart," Laura replied. "Anger at least acknowledges relationship. Indifference would be far worse."

Moses looked down at his hands, now resting on his knees. "I don't know what I'm doing," he admitted quietly. "I just... Millie and Felix

Abernathy are so ill. They are so young, in their prime. They remind me of Rebecca, of—" He broke off, unable to complete the thought.

Laura understood without him saying more.

He nodded, unable to speak for a moment. "I've seen this illness progress now, watched its pattern." He shook his head. "Felix has had breathing troubles since childhood. And Millie's fever is dangerously high, as well as Mrs. Bellweather."

"You're afraid of failing them, as you believe you failed Rebecca," Laura said gently.

Moses looked up sharply. "I know I failed her."

"You did everything humanly possible."

"It wasn't enough."

"It never feels like enough when we lose someone we love," Laura agreed. "But that doesn't make it your fault."

Moses was silent for a long moment, weighing her words. "How do you maintain such faith? After everything you've seen, everything you've lost?"

Laura considered her answer carefully. "I don't claim to understand why God allows suffering. I only know that when suffering comes, as it will in this fallen world, faith gives me the strength to face it rather than be consumed by it."

"And when others suffer? When children are gasping for breath and burning with fever?"

"Then faith gives me courage to stand beside them in their pain, to offer what comfort and healing I can, and to trust that even when I can't see purpose in suffering, it doesn't mean there is none." Laura leaned forward slightly. "Moses, doubting is human. Questioning is natural. God isn't fragile. He can handle your anger and your questions."

"We should return to the patients," he said, though without urgency.

"In a moment," Laura agreed. She hesitated, then added, "Moses, whatever you're feeling—about Rebecca, about the Abernathy's, about...us—it's all right to take time to sort through it. I understand."

His eyes met hers, surprise evident in their blue depths. "Us?" he repeated, the single syllable carrying a weight of questions.

Laura felt heat rise to her cheeks but didn't look away. "I value our partnership, professional and...otherwise. What you shared with me at the mining camp—that was a gift of trust I don't take lightly."

"I don't regret telling you about Rebecca and Jake," he said slowly. "But I'm not used to being... seen that way. It's uncomfortable."

"Vulnerability often is," Laura acknowledged. "But it's also how genuine connection forms."

A ghost of a smile touched his lips. "You're very wise for someone so young."

"Not wise," Laura demurred. "Just experienced in grief and its aftermath."

Moses stood, extending a hand to help Laura from her chair.

"We should check on the Abernathy's," he said, but his tone was warmer than it had been earlier, the deliberate distance diminished if not entirely gone.

Laura accepted his hand, rising to her feet.

They returned to the main floor, moving first to Millie's pallet. Laura checked her temperature while Moses listened to her lungs. They exchanged concerned glances over their patient. Millie's condition remained serious, though perhaps marginally improved from earlier.

They repeated the process with Felix, finding him also stable but still critically ill. Laura prepared fresh compresses while Moses mixed medicines, their movements synchronizing naturally despite the earlier awkwardness.

"The next few hours will be crucial for both of them," Moses observed as they moved away from the Abernathy's.

Laura nodded, surveying the room. Many patients slept fitfully, while volunteers moved quietly among them, adjusting blankets and offering sips of water. Deputy Diamond was speaking in low tones with Pastor Lewis near the door. Clementine sat cross-legged beside a young miner's pallet, grinding herbs in a small mortar.

"You should rest," Moses said, noting Laura's exhaustion despite her efforts to hide it. "It's been an extraordinarily long day."

"As should you," she countered.

"I'm fine," he insisted, though the shadows beneath his eyes belied his words.

"At least sit down while you work," Laura suggested. "We can prepare the next round of medicines together."

Moses agreed, and they moved to the small table that served as their medicine preparation area. Laura set about measuring tinctures while Moses wrote notes in the treatment ledger, their shoulders occasionally brushing as they worked side by side.

The quieter hours before dawn settled around them, creating a pocket of calm in the midst of crisis. Most patients slept, their breathing creating a symphony of uneven rhythms. Pastor Lewis had dozed off in a chair near the altar, his Bible open on his lap. Even Deputy Diamond had succumbed to exhaustion, snoring softly from a pew in the corner.

Laura reached for the herbs Clementine had prepared, her hands steady despite her fatigue. "Do you think the water situation can be resolved quickly once the storm passes?" she asked, keeping her voice low.

"It depends on what's contaminating it and how extensive the pollution is," Moses replied, equally quiet. "But with proper precautions in the meantime, we should be able to prevent new cases."

He stood, moving to where a fresh pot of coffee simmered near the stove. Laura continued her work, assuming he was getting a cup for himself. To her surprise, when he returned, he placed a steaming cup beside her, prepared exactly as she preferred it, with a touch of milk and no sugar.

"You remembered how I take my coffee," she said, unable to hide her surprise.

"I notice things," Moses replied simply, though his eyes held a warmth that made her heart beat faster.

Laura accepted the cup gratefully, their fingers brushing briefly during the exchange. "Thank you."

Laura sipped her coffee, watching Moses's hands as he carefully measured doses of willow bark tincture. His fingers were long and capable, moving with the precision born of years of medical practice.

"How many doses should we prepare for the morning?" she asked, perhaps a bit too brightly.

Moses glanced up. "Enough for twenty-five patients, I think. Some are improving enough to need less frequent doses."

Their eyes met over her coffee cup, and something electric passed between them. A shared awareness, a mutual recognition of the connection growing despite their attempts to contain it within professional boundaries. Neither spoke, neither needed to. The understanding was implicit, hovering in the air between them like a physical presence.

The moment stretched, taut with possibility. Laura found herself holding her breath, wondering if Moses might say something, might acknowledge what they both clearly felt.

The church door burst open with a crash, shattering the moment. Cold air and swirling snow swept in, along with three figures struggling under the weight of a stretcher.

"Doc Grant!" a familiar voice called—Jasper McCoy from the saloon. "We've got Barnaby Flint here! Found him half-frozen trying to reach town!"

Moses was on his feet instantly, moving toward the newcomers. Without thinking, he reached back, grabbing Laura's hand to pull her with him. The reflex, seeking her partnership in this emergency, was instinctive and telling.

The men were lowering Barnaby Flint onto an empty pallet near the door. The mine owner looked worse than when they'd left him at the mining camp, his face gray, his breathing labored, and his lips tinged with alarming blue.

"He insisted on coming," Jasper explained, brushing snow from his coat. "Said he had to speak with Pastor Lewis. Wouldn't take no for an answer, so we bundled him up best we could and brought him by sled."

Moses knelt beside Flint, medical instincts taking over as he quickly assessed the man's condition. His hand still held Laura's, seemingly forgotten by the urgency of the moment.

"Pulse is weak and rapid," he reported as Laura knelt opposite him. "Respiration severely compromised. Temperature—" He placed a hand on Flint's forehead. "Dangerously high."

Flint's eyes fluttered open, clouded with fever but fixed with desperate intensity. "Pastor," he gasped, his voice barely audible. "Need... Pastor Lewis... confession..."

"Fetch Pastor Lewis," Laura instructed one of the men who'd brought Flint in. "Quickly!"

As the man hurried off, Flint's hand shot out, grasping weakly at Moses's coat. "My fault," he wheezed. "All... my fault. The water... tell them..."

"Save your strength, Mr. Flint," Moses urged, reaching for his stethoscope. "We'll get Pastor Lewis for you."

Laura prepared a dose of Clementine's strongest fever tincture, her movements swift and practiced.

Pastor Lewis arrived, bleary-eyed but instantly alert at the sight of Barnaby Flint's condition. "Mr. Flint," he said gently, kneeling beside the sick man. "I'm here."

Flint turned his head with obvious effort, focusing on the pastor's face. "Confession," he repeated. "Private. Please."

Pastor Lewis nodded, glancing at Moses and Laura. "Can he be moved to my study?"

Moses shook his head. "He's too weak. But we can give you privacy here."

Chapter 14

Moses handed Laura a cup of water, his fingers briefly brushing against hers as she accepted it. The small contact sent warmth through her exhausted body. He sat down beside her on the church pew.

"Drink," he instructed, his voice rough from fatigue. "You're dehydrated."

Laura nodded, lifting the cup to her lips. In the lantern-lit dimness of the church, Moses couldn't help but notice the slight flush across her cheeks. She shivered subtly, despite the relative warmth of the sanctuary.

"Are you cold?" he asked, brow furrowing with concern.

"I think I'm just tired," Laura replied. "As I'm sure you are." She attempted a smile that didn't quite reach her eyes.

Moses studied her face more carefully. Dark circles shadowed her eyes, and tendrils of chestnut hair had escaped her usually neat arrangement, curling damply against her temples. Yet even in her exhaustion, there was something compellingly beautiful about her—a quiet strength that moved him in ways he wasn't entirely comfortable acknowledging.

Their shoulders touched as Laura shifted slightly, sending another jolt of awareness through him. He cleared his throat, deliberately creating a small space between them.

"Pastor Lewis has been with Barnaby for nearly an hour," he observed, glancing to where the mining magnate lay. "I wonder what's being said."

Laura's gaze followed his. "Whatever sins Mr. Flint is confessing, I hope he finds peace."

Pastor Lewis looked up and nodded to Deputy Diamond, who had been sitting nearby. The deputy stood and walked toward a pew that held stacks of clean linens. He grabbed a folded sheet and walked to where Barnaby laid and gently unfolded the linen and spread the sheet over the man's body, covering his face.

"He's gone," Laura whispered, her voice catching.

Moses felt a heaviness settle in his chest, not the sharp pain of unexpected loss, but the weight of death that accompanied his profession. Yet something was different this time. Instead of shutting himself away from the emotion as he typically did, he found himself watching Laura as she bowed her head.

"May God have mercy on your soul, Barnaby Flint," she murmured, her eyes closed in prayer. "And grant comfort to those who mourn you."

Moses bowed his head as well. "Amen," he whispered.

Pastor Lewis approached them. The lines in his face seemed deeper than they had been days earlier, etched by fatigue and the burden of carried confidences.

"He's with God now," the pastor said, lowering himself onto the pew across from them.

"Did he—" Moses began.

"He made his confession, yes," Pastor Lewis confirmed, rubbing his palms together slowly. "And I believe he died at peace, though greatly troubled by what he'd done and what he'd failed to do."

Laura leaned forward slightly. "What exactly did he tell you, Pastor? About the water?"

Pastor Lewis sighed deeply. "It wasn't deliberate malice. More a terrible negligence born of profit-seeking and willful blindness." He glanced toward the shrouded form. "Barnaby arrived from Denver only recently, having received reports of decreased production at the mine. When he arrived, he noticed an unusual metallic smell around the mining camp but dismissed it as normal for mining operations."

Moses nodded grimly. "The contamination."

"Yes," Pastor Lewis continued. "Several miners had already fallen ill, but Barnaby assumed it was the usual winter coughs and fever. He didn't connect it to what was happening in town until he himself fell sick."

"Did he understand the source?" Laura asked, her voice slightly hoarse. She cleared her throat and Moses noticed her shift uncomfortably on the pew.

"He admitted that about a month ago, he authorized a change in how the mine drainage was handled," Pastor Lewis explained. "The previous method was more costly but properly directed runoff away from water sources. The new approach saved money but allowed contaminated water to flow into the tributary that eventually feeds our creek and town well."

Moses felt anger rising in his chest. "People are dying because he wanted to save money?"

"He claimed he didn't realize the runoff would reach the town's water," Pastor Lewis replied, though his tone suggested he didn't entirely believe this excuse. "When he recognized the potential connection between the water and the illness, he was already too sick to take action. That's why he was so desperate to reach town—to confess and warn everyone."

Moses stood abruptly, pacing in the narrow space before the pew. "All this suffering because of one man's carelessness." His hands clenched into fists at his sides.

"Moses," Laura said softly, and something in her tone made him turn to look at her. The flush on her cheeks had deepened, and she pressed a hand against her temple briefly before dropping it to her lap.

His physician's instincts immediately sharpened. Abandoning his anger for the moment, he moved closer, studying her with a critical eye.

"Laura?" The single word carried a weight of concern.

"I'm fine," she insisted, but her voice lacked conviction. "Please, continue. What else did Mr. Flint say?"

Pastor Lewis had noticed the exchange and was now watching Laura with growing concern. "He left instructions for his company to pay for all medical expenses related to the illness, and to implement proper drainage systems immediately." The pastor paused. "He also asked for my assurance that God might forgive him."

"And what did you tell him?" Moses asked, his attention divided between the pastor's words and Laura's concerning appearance.

"That God's mercy exceeds our understanding, and that true repentance is never rejected," Pastor Lewis replied. "Judgment belongs to God alone, not to us."

Moses's jaw tightened. "Easy to speak of forgiveness when you haven't watched children gasping for breath because of his neglect."

"Moses," Laura admonished gently, reaching out to touch his arm. "The pastor is right. Judgment isn't ours to mete out. Mr. Flint will answer to God for his actions, as will we all for ours."

Her touch and words quelled some of his anger, though resentment still simmered beneath the surface. "You're too generous, Laura."

"Not generous," she countered, echoing their earlier conversation. "Just aware of my own need for mercy." She attempted to smile but winced instead, pressing her fingers to her temple again.

Moses stepped closer, no longer bothering to hide his concern. Without asking permission, he placed his palm against her forehead.

"You don't feel fevered," he said.

Laura tried to shake her head, but stopped, as if the movement caused pain. "I'm just tired. We're all exhausted."

Moses took her wrist, his fingers finding her pulse. "How long have you felt this way?" The steady thrum beneath his fingertips was too rapid, too weak.

"I've been a bit off since we returned from the mining camp," she admitted reluctantly.

"You need food, water, and rest," Moses interrupted, all thought of Barnaby Flint forgotten in the face of this new, more immediate concern. He turned to Pastor Lewis. "Is there any broth left from dinner?"

The pastor nodded, rising quickly. "I'll fetch some, and some tea as well."

As Pastor Lewis moved away, Moses sat beside Laura, close enough that their shoulders touched again. This time, he didn't pull away.

"Why didn't you say something earlier?" he asked quietly, his voice a mixture of professional concern and something deeper, more personal.

"There are so many patients. I didn't want to—"

"To be a burden?" Moses finished for her.

She closed her eyes briefly. "I think I do need to rest, but there's too much to be done, too many people needing care for me to be—"

"Human?" Moses interrupted again, his tone gentler now. "You've been reminding me for days that we all have limits, that even the most dedicated physician needs rest. Perhaps you should heed your own advice."

A ghost of a smile touched her lips. "Using my words against me, Doctor?"

"If that's what it takes to make you rest, then yes," he replied, surprised by the wave of tenderness that swept through him.

Pastor Lewis returned with a steaming mug of broth and another of tea. "Here we are," he said, handing them to Moses. "Mrs. Williams just made a fresh pot of both."

Moses helped Laura hold the mug of broth steady as she took small sips. Her hands trembled slightly, confirming his assessment. Without thinking, his free hand moved to rest lightly against her back, supporting her.

"Where do you feel discomfort?" he asked, slipping into his professional demeanor even as his heart raced with personal concern.

"My head aches terribly, and I feel extremely tired," Laura admitted.

Moses exchanged a worried glance with Pastor Lewis.

"You need to eat and then rest," Moses stated flatly.

Pastor Lewis cleared his throat. "I'll prepare a pallet in my study. It will be quieter there."

Moses nodded his head.

"I've been stupid," Laura murmured, her voice barely audible. "So focused on caring for others that I've compromised my ability to help anyone."

"That's not stupidity," Moses countered gently. "It's dedication. Perhaps excessive dedication, but the motive was pure."

She looked up at him, her blue eyes looking exhausted. "Thank you for noticing. I might have pushed myself a bit too much."

Moses felt something tighten in his chest. "I notice everything about you, Laura," he said.

Laura's lips parted slightly in surprise, and Moses found his gaze drawn to them before he hastily looked away, suddenly conscious of their proximity.

"I should check on Millie before I rest," Laura said, attempting to stand. Moses placed a hand on her arm, restraining her.

"I'll check on Millie shortly," he said firmly.

Moses helped Laura to her feet, his arm around her waist providing both support and an anchor against the dizziness she was clearly experiencing. Her body leaned into his as they walked the short distance to the pallet, and he was acutely aware of her warmth, her fragility, and her strength—somehow all present simultaneously.

She sank onto the makeshift bed with a poorly concealed wince that didn't escape Moses's notice.

"Your muscles ache," he observed, not a question but a statement.

Laura nodded slightly. "Everything feels heavy. I've never felt this exhausted before."

Pastor Lewis returned to check on them. "How is our nurse faring?" he asked kindly.

"Not well," Laura admitted with a weak smile. "I make a terrible patient. Always have."

"She's already plotting ways to escape bed rest," Moses commented dryly, measuring Clementine's tincture into a cup.

"I am not," Laura protested.

Pastor Lewis looked between them, a slight smile playing at his lips despite the seriousness of the situation. "I have every confidence that Dr. Grant will keep you in line, Miss Smythe. He can be quite... determined."

"Stubborn, you mean," Laura corrected, accepting the medicine Moses handed her.

"I prefer 'persistent,'" Moses countered, watching to ensure she drank every drop.

Their easy banter belied the gravity of Laura's condition, but Moses was grateful for it, nonetheless. If she could still joke, she wasn't critically ill.

"I'll pray for peaceful sleep for you," Pastor Lewis said, patting Laura's hand.

As the pastor moved away, Moses knelt beside Laura's pallet, medical bag open beside him. "I need to listen to your lungs," he said, his professional tone firmly in place despite the intimate nature of the examination.

Laura nodded, sitting up. He hesitated momentarily, aware of the impropriety of placing the instrument against her chest, even over her clothing.

"Perhaps Mrs. Williams could—" he began, but Laura shook her head.

"Don't be ridiculous, Moses. You've examined dozens of patients this way, and I trust you completely. There's nothing improper about medical care."

Her matter-of-fact approach steadied him. Moses nodded, placing the stethoscope against her back first, instructing her to breathe deeply.

Despite his professional demeanor, he couldn't ignore the rapid beating of his heart as he listened to hers.

"Everything sounds good. I do not detect any congestion," he reported, removing the stethoscope and returning it to his bag. "Now, lay back and rest."

"You're very authoritative when you're worried," Laura observed, a hint of teasing in her tired voice.

Moses felt the corner of his mouth lift slightly. "Only when my patients are stubborn."

"I'm not stubborn," Laura protested weakly. "Just dedicated."

"Both, I think," Moses countered, adjusting the blanket around her shoulders.

Laura's eyes drifted closed, her exhaustion finally claiming her. Moses remained beside her pallet, watching the rise and fall of her chest as she succumbed to sleep.

The protective instinct that surged through him was overwhelming in its intensity. This woman, who had arrived in Aspen Hollow barely two weeks ago, had somehow become essential to him in ways he couldn't fully articulate, even to himself.

Pastor Lewis approached quietly, standing beside Moses as they both gazed down at the sleeping nurse.

"She's a remarkable woman," the pastor observed softly.

"Yes," Moses agreed simply, unable to find more adequate words.

"And she matters to you," Pastor Lewis continued, the statement gentle but direct.

Moses didn't immediately respond. Did Laura matter to him? The answer was undeniable, though the implications were complicated and, frankly, frightening.

"She's an excellent nurse," he said finally. "The town is fortunate to have her services."

Pastor Lewis's knowing smile suggested he wasn't fooled by Moses's professional assessment. "Indeed. And perhaps certain individuals are particularly fortunate."

Moses shifted uncomfortably under the pastor's perceptive gaze. "I should check on the Abernathy's," he said, clearly changing the subject.

Pastor Lewis nodded, allowing the deflection. "Of course. I'll sit with Miss Smythe until you return."

Reluctantly, Moses moved away from Laura's bedside, forcing himself to focus on his duties to the other patients. He checked Millie first, finding her fever slightly reduced and her breathing marginally improved. Felix showed similar modest improvement, though both still required careful monitoring.

Mrs. Bellweather's condition was more concerning. Her breathing remained labored despite the treatments, and her fever was stubbornly high. Moses adjusted her medications, adding a stronger dose of Clementine's lung-clearing tincture.

As he worked his way through the patients, Moses found his thoughts continually returning to Laura.

Chapter 15

Moses watched Laura as she slept. Her breathing had steadied in the hours since she'd collapsed, but the shadows beneath her eyes remained, testament to days of exhaustion and self-neglect. A lock of chestnut hair had fallen across her cheek. Without thinking, he reached to brush it away, his fingers hovering just above her skin before he pulled back, suddenly conscious of the intimacy of the gesture.

Instead, he straightened the blanket covering her, tucking it more securely around her shoulders. The small office that served as Pastor Lewis's study was mercifully quiet compared to the main sanctuary where patients lay in various stages of illness. Only the occasional pop from the small fire in the hearth and Laura's soft breathing broke the silence.

"Don't you dare get sick," Moses whispered, the words barely audible even to himself.

He had lost track of how long he'd been sitting beside her pallet, medical bag open nearby, stethoscope around his neck. Every twenty minutes, he checked her pulse, reassuring himself. Merely exhaustion, not the contamination sickness—that's what all the signs indicated. But Moses had seen too many seemingly simple conditions worsen without warning to take comfort in initial assessments.

Laura shifted slightly in her sleep, her brow briefly furrowing before relaxing again. Without conscious thought, Moses reached for her hand, his larger one enveloping hers. Her skin felt cool but not cold, a good sign. He should have released her hand immediately; professional detachment demanded it. Instead, he found himself studying the contrast. Her smaller, feminine hand with its capable fingers that had so deftly bandaged wounds and mixed medicines, now lying trustingly within his own.

The door opened quietly behind him. Moses quickly withdrew his hand, straightening as Pastor Lewis entered carrying a steaming cup.

"Fresh tea," the pastor explained softly, setting the cup on the small table beside Laura's pallet. "Clementine's special blend. For when she wakes."

Moses nodded his thanks, hoping the dim lamplight concealed the heat he felt rising to his face.

Pastor Lewis settled on the opposite Moses, studying him with kind but perceptive eyes. "You should rest too, Doctor."

"I'm fine," Moses replied automatically.

"You've been awake for hours. You need proper rest as well," Pastor Lewis observed gently.

Moses ran a hand through his hair, suddenly aware of how disheveled he must look. "As do you, Pastor. Laura pushed herself beyond reasonable limits."

"Indeed, she did," Pastor Lewis agreed, glancing at the sleeping nurse's face. "Reminds me of someone else I know."

Moses shot him a look that the pastor met with a mild smile.

"Your dedication to your patients is admirable, Moses," Pastor Lewis continued. "But I wonder if it's purely professional concern I see in your eyes when you look at Miss Smythe."

Moses stiffened, his jaw tightening as he looked away. "She's an excellent nurse. The community needs her skills."

"Of course," Pastor Lewis nodded, allowing a brief silence to settle between them before adding, "And what about you, Moses? Do you need her as well?"

The directness of the question struck Moses like a physical blow. He opened his mouth to deliver a swift denial, but found the words wouldn't come.

"I..." he began, then stopped, uncertain how to continue.

Pastor Lewis didn't press, simply waited with the patience of a man accustomed to allowing others the space to find their own truths.

"She's disrupted everything," Moses finally admitted, his voice so low Pastor Lewis had to lean forward to hear. "My practice, my routines, my..." he hesitated, "my carefully maintained distance."

"And that disturbs you?"

Moses exhaled slowly. "I've grown accustomed to a certain... solitude. It's safer that way."

"Safer," Pastor Lewis repeated thoughtfully. "Yet perhaps not fuller."

Moses glanced down at Laura, watching the gentle rise and fall of her chest. "I don't know how to care for someone again without fear of failing them," he confessed, the words breaking free before he could reconsider them.

The pastor nodded, understanding dawning in his eyes. "Ah. And there it is."

"There what is?" Moses asked, defensiveness creeping into his tone.

"The heart of it all." Pastor Lewis leaned forward, his voice gentle but direct. "Your fear of failing Miss Smythe is connected to your fear of failing Rebecca, isn't it? And perhaps to your fear of faith itself."

Moses looked up sharply. "What do you mean?"

"I mean that faith and love share a common foundation: trust despite uncertainty." Pastor Lewis's gaze was kind but unflinching. "When Rebecca died, you lost trust in both your medical abilities and in God's goodness. It was easier to close yourself off than to risk that kind of loss again."

Moses felt exposed, as if the pastor had opened a door in his mind that he'd long kept locked. "She told you about our conversation," he said, a note of accusation in his voice.

"No," Pastor Lewis shook his head firmly. "Laura has shared nothing of your private discussions. But I've known you for years, Moses. I've watched you hold everyone at arm's length, including God."

Moses looked away, uncomfortable with the pastor's insight.

"I saw you in my study earlier," Pastor Lewis continued softly. "Trying to pray."

"A moment of weakness," Moses muttered, embarrassed.

"No," Pastor Lewis corrected gently. "A moment of tremendous strength. It takes courage to reach out when you're uncertain of being received."

Moses was silent, his eyes fixed on Laura's sleeping form.

"You know," Pastor Lewis said after a moment, "faith isn't about certainty. It's about trusting even when the path is unclear. Rather like medicine in that way."

Moses raised an eyebrow. "Medicine is based on observable facts and evidence."

"Is it?" Pastor Lewis smiled slightly. "Yet, even with all your knowledge and training, you can't predict with absolute certainty how a patient will respond to treatment. You must make your best judgment and then... trust."

The comparison struck closer to home than Moses cared to admit. He'd made similar arguments to Laura about faith during their conversation at the mining camp, yet when she'd turned those same points back toward him, he'd deflected.

"It's not that simple," he protested.

"Actually, it is often that simple," Pastor Lewis countered gently. "We just prefer to complicate it because simplicity offers fewer hiding places." He gestured toward Laura. "She sees you clearly, Moses. Not just the doctor, but the man. That frightens you, doesn't it?"

Before Moses could respond, Laura stirred on her pallet, murmuring something indistinct in her sleep. Her brow furrowed, and she shifted restlessly. Without hesitation, Moses moved closer, taking her hand in his.

His thumb moved in small, soothing circles against the back of her hand. Laura's features relaxed, her breathing evening out once more as she settled deeper into sleep.

Moses continued to hold her hand a moment longer, then became aware of Pastor Lewis's thoughtful gaze and released it.

"You already know how to care for her," the pastor observed quietly.

Moses felt a peculiar constriction in his chest, as if something long frozen had begun to thaw, bringing both relief and pain with the process.

"I can't afford to care too deeply," he said, the words sounding hollow even to his own ears. "Not when—"

"When there are no guarantees?" Pastor Lewis finished for him. "Moses, there are never guarantees in this life. Every bond we form, every love we nurture, carries the risk of loss. But consider the alternative—a life without those connections. Is that truly safer, or merely emptier?"

Moses confronted truths he'd spent years evading. Laura had somehow slipped past his defenses, stirring feelings he'd convinced himself were long dead. The realization terrified him, yet beneath the fear lay a current of something else—something remarkably like hope.

The door opened quietly, drawing both men's attention. Clementine entered, carrying an armful of blankets and a small basket of herbs. Her shrewd eyes took in the scene before her. Moses's protective posture beside Laura, the pastor's gentle intensity, the unspoken words hanging in the air.

"Well," she said simply, setting down her burdens. "You two look worse than half the patients. Particularly you, Doctor."

Moses straightened, attempting to regain his professional composure. "I'm merely keeping watch."

"Hmm." Clementine gave him a look that suggested she wasn't fooled in the slightest. "Watch all you like, but you'll be no good to anyone if you collapse too. The same goes for you, Pastor."

She moved to Laura's side, placing a weathered hand on the sleeping woman's forehead. "No fever, breathing steady. The girl needs rest, not two worried men hovering over her."

"I'm not hovering," Moses protested, aware of how defensive he sounded.

"Of course not," Clementine agreed, with a hint of amusement. "You're merely sitting close enough to count her eyelashes."

Pastor Lewis coughed quietly in what might have been an attempt to disguise a chuckle.

Clementine turned her attention to the room at large, unfolding the blankets she'd brought and arranging them into pallets on the floor. "Most of the patients are improving," she announced. "The poison is leaving their bodies. Even the Abernathy children are breathing easier."

Relief coursed through Moses at this news. "And Mrs. Bellweather?"

"Still struggling, but holding her own," Clementine replied. "Her age makes recovery slower, but her spirit is strong."

She straightened, fixing both men with a stern gaze. "Now, both of you will rest. I've prepared pallets, and I'll hear no arguments."

Moses opened his mouth to protest, but Clementine held up a hand, silencing him.

"Bodies heal with rest and medicine," she said firmly, "but spirits heal through connection. All three are necessary, and all three are lacking if you drive yourselves to exhaustion."

"I should stay awake in case Laura needs me," Moses insisted.

Clementine's eyes softened slightly. "Your spirits recognized each other from the moment you met, though you both fought against it. Fighting only drains your strength, Doctor."

Moses felt heat rise to his face at her perceptive observation. "I don't know what you're talking about," he muttered.

"Don't you?" Clementine's expression suggested she knew better. "Sometimes the greatest healing comes from the most unexpected sources." She gestured toward Laura. "She came to heal bodies but has done much more than that, hasn't she?"

Moses didn't respond, uncomfortable with how easily Clementine had pierced through his carefully constructed facade.

"I will watch over all three of you," Clementine continued, her tone brooking no argument. "When you wake, there will be food—good, nourishing food to rebuild your strength. Until then, rest."

Pastor Lewis was the first to agree, recognizing the wisdom in Clementine's words. "Thank you, Clementine. Your assistance has been invaluable during this crisis."

He moved to one of the pallets, settling himself with the quiet dignity that was his hallmark. "Moses," he said gently, "even God rested on the seventh day. Surely, we mere mortals must do the same."

Caught between his concern for Laura and the undeniable logic of their arguments, Moses finally nodded reluctantly. "Wake me if there's any change in her condition. Or if any of the patients worsen."

"Of course," Clementine agreed, though something in her tone suggested she'd make that determination herself.

With a last glance at Laura's sleeping form, Moses moved to the remaining pallet, positioning it close enough to Laura's that he could reach her quickly if needed. He removed his boots, lying down atop the blankets rather than beneath them.

Clementine shook her head at his half-hearted concession to rest but said nothing, moving instead to settle herself in a chair.

From his pallet, Moses could see Laura's profile illuminated by the soft glow of the lamp. Even in sleep, there was a quiet strength in the curve of her jaw, the delicate arch of her eyebrow. She had arrived in Aspen Hollow like a breath of fresh air, unwelcome at first, then gradually, inexorably, becoming essential.

Pastor Lewis's soft, rhythmic breathing soon indicated he had fallen asleep. Clementine sat silently, her weathered hands steadily working herbs into a small poultice, her presence watchful but unobtrusive.

Moses lay awake, his mind turning over the conversations of the evening. He had spent years building walls around his heart, convincing himself that professional dedication was sufficient, that emotional connection was an unnecessary risk. Yet in the span of mere weeks,

Laura Smythe had somehow breached those defenses, awakening feelings he'd believed long buried.

What Pastor Lewis had said resonated uncomfortably: his fear of failing Laura was inextricably linked to his failure to save Rebecca. And perhaps, on a deeper level, to his estrangement from God. The parallel had never occurred to him before, but now it seemed obvious. He had withdrawn from both faith and emotional connection for the same reason—fear of vulnerability, and of powerlessness in the face of forces beyond his control.

But watching Laura tonight, witnessing her vulnerability and feeling the powerful instinct to protect her, had shifted something fundamental within him. Whatever happened, he realized, he could not return to the emotional isolation of before. She had irrevocably changed him, opening doors he had believed permanently closed.

His eyelids grew heavy as exhaustion finally overcame him. As consciousness began to slip away, a thought surfaced in the depths of his mind: Perhaps this is what faith feels like—trusting without certainty.

It was his last coherent thought before sleep claimed him.

Chapter 16

Moses awoke with a start, momentarily disoriented. Pale winter sunlight filtered through the small window of Pastor Lewis's study, suggesting it was well into morning. He sat up quickly, his gaze immediately seeking Laura's pallet.

It was empty.

Alarm shot through him as he scrambled to his feet. The room was otherwise empty as well—Pastor Lewis's pallet neatly folded, Clementine nowhere to be seen.

"Laura?" he called, moving toward the door.

It opened before he reached it, revealing Laura herself, a steaming cup in her hands. She looked markedly better than she had the night before. Her eyes were clearer, and her stance was steadier, though still with a hint of the pallor that had alarmed him.

"Oh!" she exclaimed, surprised to find him so close to the door. "I was just coming back to wake you up and bring you some coffee."

Relief washed over him, quickly followed by concern and a touch of frustration. "You shouldn't be up," he said, taking the cup from her hands and setting it aside. "You need to rest."

"I've rested plenty," Laura replied with a small smile. "I'm feeling much better, truly. Clementine said you fell asleep around two in the morning, and it's now past two in the afternoon, so I believe you have rested enough as well."

Moses ran a hand through his hair, shocked that he had slept so long. "The patients—"

"—are all doing well," Laura finished for him. "Several have shown significant improvement, including Millie and Felix. Even Mrs. Bellweather's fever has broken."

"And you?" Moses asked, studying her face intently. "How are you truly feeling?"

Laura's expression softened at his concern. "Much restored. My headache is completely gone. Clementine insisted I eat before doing anything else, and Mrs. Williams seconded the order so forcefully that I didn't dare disobey."

Moses felt his lips twitch into an almost-smile. "Wise of you. Mrs. Williams can be formidable when her maternal instincts are roused."

"So I discovered." Laura's eyes sparkled with humor. "She threatened to spoon-feed me if I didn't finish every bite of stew."

The lightness of the moment unwound something tight in Moses's chest. Laura was rested, the patients were improving, and for the first time in days, there was a sense that the crisis might be receding.

"You need to eat as well," Laura said, gesturing to the cup she'd brought. "I'll have Mrs. Williams bring you some stew."

"I can get it myself," Moses protested, but Laura shook her head.

"Indulge me, please. After you spent so much time watching over me, the least I can do is make sure you're properly fed."

There was something in her eyes, warmth and gratitude, that made it impossible for Moses to argue. He nodded his acquiescence.

"Thank you," he said simply.

Laura tilted her head slightly, a question in her gaze. "For the stew?"

"For taking care of yourself," Moses clarified. "For resting when you needed to."

A soft smile touched her lips. "Well, I didn't have much choice, did I?"

"You gave me cause for concern," Moses said, his voice growing serious.

Laura seemed to understand what he was struggling to express.

"I'm sorry I worried you," she said quietly. "It was foolish of me to ignore my limits, especially after lecturing you about the very same thing."

"Not foolish," Moses corrected. "Dedicated. Perhaps excessively so, but with the purest of motives."

Laura looked surprised at his words, an echo of what he'd told her the night before. "You said something similar when I began to realize how exhausted I had become. I wasn't sure if I'd dreamed it."

"You didn't," Moses confirmed, uncomfortably aware of how much he'd revealed. He reached for the coffee she'd brought, needing something to occupy his hands. "How are the water protocols progressing?"

Laura accepted the change of subject gracefully. "Very well. Deputy Diamond organized teams to collect water from the uncontaminated spring, and every household that can be reached has received word of the contaminated water. No new cases have been reported since yesterday."

Moses nodded, relief washing through him. "And Barnaby Flint?"

"His body has been prepared for burial," Laura said solemnly. "Pastor Lewis will conduct the service once the storm fully clears. He's been meeting with the mine foreman about implementing the drainage corrections Barnaby specified."

She hesitated, then added, "I hope you don't think me terribly naïve, but I've been praying for Mr. Flint's soul. Despite the harm he caused through negligence, I believe his final act, trying to reach town to warn everyone, showed genuine remorse."

Moses studied her face, marveling at her capacity for compassion, even toward someone whose actions had caused such suffering.

"Not naïve," he said finally. "Just... better than most of us."

Laura's cheeks colored slightly at the unexpected compliment. "Hardly that. I simply believe in grace, even... perhaps especially, for those who don't deserve it."

"Because none of us do?" Moses guessed, recalling their earlier conversations about faith.

"Precisely," Laura nodded, looking pleased that he understood. "That's the beauty of it. Grace isn't earned. It's given freely."

Moses considered this, sipping his coffee thoughtfully. There was a time when such talk would have irritated him, seeming like empty platitudes in the face of real suffering. Now, he considered her words with genuine interest rather than dismissing them outright.

"I should check on the patients," he said after a moment, setting down his cup.

"After you eat," Laura insisted, her tone leaving no room for argument.

Moses raised an eyebrow. "I see Mrs. Williams's influence has rubbed off on you."

Laura's laugh, bright and unexpected, warmed something in his chest. "Perhaps," she admitted. "Or perhaps I've simply learned from watching a certain physician's rather authoritative approach to patient care."

"I am not authoritarian," Moses protested mildly.

"No?" Laura's eyes danced with amusement. "'You will rest. You will eat. You will take your medicine.' Sound familiar?"

Moses opened his mouth to deny it, then closed it again, unable to counter her accurate impression of his doctoring style.

"I'm effective," he said instead.

"Indeed you are," Laura agreed, still smiling. "Now sit down and let me be equally effective."

With mock solemnity, Moses seated himself in the chair by the desk. "Yes, Nurse Smythe."

Laura turned toward the door, pausing with her hand on the handle. "Moses," she said, her voice growing serious, "thank you for taking care of me and watching over me."

There was a depth of feeling in those simple words that made him pause.

"I'm not accustomed to being cared for. Since losing my family, I've had to be quite self-sufficient. It was... comforting, knowing you were watching over me," she said.

Moses found himself momentarily speechless, moved by her vulnerability and honesty.

"You're welcome," he managed finally. "Though I hope you don't make a habit of requiring such care."

Laura's smile returned, softer now. "I'll do my best to avoid it." She tilted her head slightly. "Though I must admit, seeing the good doctor so concerned about a mere nurse was rather illuminating."

There was a hint of an invitation to acknowledge what had been growing between them in her words. Moses felt his heart rate quicken, uncertain how to respond. Part of him wanted to retreat into the safety of professional distance, while another part, increasingly insistent, urged him toward honesty.

Mrs. Williams's voice called from the hallway. "Laura? Is the doctor awake? I've brought his meal!"

The moment passed, the unspoken words remaining suspended between them. Laura gave Moses a small smile and opened the door, admitting Mrs. Williams with a steaming bowl of stew.

"Here you are, Doctor," Mrs. Williams announced, placing the bowl on the desk with a flourish. "Venison stew with root vegetables. You're to eat every bite, mind you. Can't have our healer falling ill."

"Yes, ma'am," Moses replied with unusual docility, earning a surprised look from Mrs. Williams and an amused one from Laura.

"I'll see to the patients while you eat," Laura said, turning to leave.

"Laura," Moses called, stopping her. She looked back, a question in her eyes. "Don't overdo it," he said. "If you feel tired—"

"I'll rest immediately," Laura promised. "Doctor's orders."

She slipped out with Mrs. Williams, leaving Moses alone with his thoughts and the fragrant stew. He ate mechanically at first, his mind still turning over their conversation, particularly Laura's admission about how it felt to be cared for.

He understood that feeling all too well. The unfamiliarity of allowing oneself to be vulnerable, to be tended to rather than being the one who tended others. Since Rebecca's death, and Jake's subsequent passing, he had maintained a careful distance from everyone, giving his medical expertise freely but guarding his heart jealously.

Laura had somehow breached those defenses effortlessly, not through any calculated effort, but simply by being herself, compassionate, determined, transparent in her faith and feelings. Her honesty had created a space where his own buried emotions could resurface, unwelcome at first, then increasingly undeniable.

By the time Moses finished his stew, he had reached a decision. The nature of his feelings for Laura could no longer be ignored or dismissed as mere professional regard. What he would do about those feelings remained uncertain, but acknowledging their existence was a necessary first step.

Bowl empty, Moses rose and straightened his rumpled clothing as best he could. He felt remarkably refreshed, given the circumstances, testament to the restorative power of deep sleep and good food. Stepping out into the sanctuary, the sounds of quiet activity indicated the ongoing care of patients.

The scene that greeted him was markedly different from when he'd last seen it. Windows had been opened slightly to admit fresh air, diluting the sickroom smell that had permeated the space. Several patients who had previously been confined to pallets now sat upright, accepting small portions of broth or tea. Volunteers moved efficiently between pallets, changing linens and administering medicines under Laura's calm direction.

Laura herself stooped beside Millie Abernathy's pallet, helping the young teacher sit up to drink some broth. The two women spoke quietly, their words inaudible from where Moses stood, but Millie's weak smile suggested improved spirits along with her physical condition.

Moses took a moment to observe Laura unnoticed. She moved with purpose and compassion, her gentle touch and encouraging words clearly bringing comfort to those in her care. There was nothing showy about her manner, just quiet competence and genuine concern.

Clementine approached him from the side, her silent movements surprising him slightly. "She is well. She rested sufficiently," the herbalist observed, following his gaze to Laura.

"Yes," Moses agreed. "Though she'll need to be careful not to push herself too quickly."

Clementine made a sound that might have been amusement. "Difficult advice to follow for someone who gives so freely of herself. Similar to another healer I know."

Moses glanced at her, recognizing the gentle rebuke. "Point taken."

"Is it?" Clementine's sharp eyes studied him intently. "You've both been called to heal, but in different ways. She heals through connection, you through competence. Both are necessary, but neither is complete without the other."

"You're very perceptive, Clementine."

"I observe," she said simply. "It's a gift my grandmother taught me. To see not just what is visible on the surface, but what flows beneath."

Moses thought of the contaminated water, the invisible poison flowing beneath a seemingly normal surface. "Like the creek," he murmured.

"Precisely." Clementine nodded approvingly. "The poison in the water is being addressed, but there are other, older poisons that still need healing."

Moses understood she wasn't speaking solely of the physical illness affecting Aspen Hollow, but of the barriers he had erected around his heart, the emotional toxins he had allowed to accumulate over years of isolation and doubt.

"Some poisons are more difficult to extract than others," he said quietly.

"True," Clementine agreed. "But the right medicine can work wonders, especially when administered by skilled hands." Her meaningful glance toward Laura left little doubt about what, or rather, who she considered the appropriate remedy for what ailed him.

Laura looked up and noticed him. Her face brightened visibly, sending an unexpected wave of warmth through his chest.

"Moses," she called, waving him over. "Come see how well Millie is doing."

He moved toward them, Clementine's words still resonating in his mind. As he reached Millie's pallet, the young schoolteacher looked up at him with gratitude in her eyes.

"Dr. Grant," she said, her voice weak but clear. "Thank you for taking care of me… for taking care of all of us."

Moses felt a flush creep up his neck, acutely aware of Laura's gaze on him. "It was my duty," he replied automatically.

"Well, I'm grateful to you, doctor."

"Millie's fever has broken completely," Laura reported. "And her lungs are clearing well. I believe she'll be able to return home within a day or two, provided she continues to rest."

"Excellent news," Moses said. He performed a brief examination, confirming Laura's assessment and noting the marked improvement in Millie's condition.

"What of the others?" he asked, turning to survey the room at large.

"Felix is much improved as well," Laura reported. "Mrs. Bellweather's fever broke early this morning. Tommy is already asking when he can return to school. Overall, sixteen patients show significant improvement, seven are stable, and only three remain in concerning condition."

The statistics were better than Moses had dared hope. "Remarkable progress," he murmured.

"Clementine and I both believe the worst has passed."

"We'll need to maintain vigilance for at least another week. Some might appear recovered, only to relapse if care isn't continued."

"Of course," Laura agreed readily. "I've prepared detailed care instructions for each patient, both for their time here and for when they return home."

Moses wasn't surprised by her thoroughness, but he was impressed nonetheless. "May I see them?"

Laura led him to a small table where she had meticulously documented each patient's condition, treatment, and progress. The level of detail and organization surpassed anything Moses had implemented in his years of practice.

"This is exceptional work, Laura," he said, genuine admiration in his voice.

Laura's smile widened, creating small dimples in her cheeks that Moses had never noticed before. The observation struck him as significant. He was noticing new things about her, beyond her professional competence or the challenge she presented to his established ways. He was seeing her as a woman, complex and fascinating beyond her role as a nurse.

The realization should have unsettled him, but instead, it felt like a door opening to a room long sealed shut, slightly alarming, but also fresh and full of possibility. The thought of returning to the clinic with Laura at his side, of continuing their partnership beyond this emergency, filled him with unexpected anticipation.

Pastor Lewis approached them, a smile warming his weary face. "It does my heart good to see both of you looking so much better," he said. "And to hear such positive reports about our patients."

"We're not out of danger yet," Moses cautioned, "but the tide does seem to be turning."

"Thanks be to God," Pastor Lewis said simply.

Moses nodded in agreement.

"The storm has finally broken as well," Pastor Lewis continued. "Deputy Diamond reports the roads should be passable in a few days if no more snow falls."

"That's excellent news," Laura said. "We can bring in additional supplies and perhaps arrange for the healthier patients to return to their homes where they can rest more comfortably and family can care for them."

Pastor Lewis smiled at her enthusiasm. "Already planning the next steps, Miss Smythe? You should be resting yourself."

"I've rested enough," Laura insisted.

"Have you?" he asked skeptically.

Laura shot him a look of mild exasperation. "I'm fine."

Pastor Lewis watched their exchange with barely disguised amusement. "I believe what Dr. Grant is trying to say, in his uniquely directive manner, is that your health matters to him, to all of us," he amended quickly.

Laura's expression softened. "I understand, and I appreciate the concern. I promise I won't overtax myself."

"I'll hold you to that. I should check on the patients," he said, needing to regain his emotional footing.

Laura nodded, seeming to understand his need for space. "Of course. I'll continue with the documentation while you do."

As Moses moved among the patients, his hands performing the familiar rituals of examination, his mind remained fixed on the woman across the room. He could hardly imagine the town, or his life, without her.

The realization both terrified and exhilarated him, like standing at the edge of a precipice, fearing the fall, yet sensing that something miraculous might occur if he found the courage to step forward.

Chapter 17

Laura tucked a stray bandage roll into the medical bag with practiced efficiency, her fingers moving swiftly across the organized compartments. Across the clinic, Moses sorted through patient notes, occasionally glancing up to watch her preparations.

"Carbolic solution?" he asked, without looking up from his papers.

"Packed. Along with Clementine's pine tincture, willow bark tea, and fresh bandages," Laura replied, fastening the clasp on the leather bag.

Moses nodded appreciatively. "The Abernathy's are first, then the Holcomb's if the path is clear enough to reach them."

"Deputy Diamond said the main roads have been cleared sufficiently for travel," Laura said, moving to stand beside him at the desk. She glanced down at his meticulous handwriting. "Though we should expect deep drifts on the path to the Holcomb homestead."

"We can reassess after visiting the Abernathy's. If it's too treacherous, we'll postpone until tomorrow."

The winter morning light filtered through the clinic windows, catching on the fresh pine branches Laura had arranged in a ceramic pitcher. The subtle fragrance permeated the room, dispelling the lingering medicinal smells.

"I see you've brought the forest indoors," Moses commented, nodding toward the greenery.

Laura smiled. "Pine helps freshen the air and has natural healing properties. Clementine taught me that pine needles can be—"

"—steeped for respiratory ailments," Moses finished with her, their words overlapping. A surprised smile passed between them. "She's a wise woman. As are you for recognizing it from the beginning."

Laura busied herself with adjusting her shawl, unexpectedly touched by his admission. "I've learned a great deal from her."

Moses rose from his desk, tucking the portfolio under his arm. His eyes lingered on Laura, noting how the winter light softened her features. "You've created a remarkably detailed care plan for each household," he said. "It must have taken hours."

"I couldn't sleep much last night," Laura admitted. "Everyone's improving, but I wanted to ensure they continue to heal properly after returning home."

Moses reached out and briefly covered her hand with his. "Thank you. You've saved me considerable work."

The touch lasted only seconds, but Laura felt warmth spread from that point of contact throughout her body. "You're welcome."

Moses withdrew his hand almost reluctantly, clearing his throat. "We should go. The Abernathy's will be expecting us."

As they gathered their things, Laura couldn't help reflecting on how naturally they now worked together. The initial friction between them had transformed into a seamless partnership that felt as comfortable as it was unexpected. Moses no longer questioned her methods or dismissed her suggestions. Instead, they had developed an unspoken rhythm, anticipating each other's needs and complementing each other's approaches.

Outside, the morning air bit with cold clarity, their breath forming small clouds with each exhalation. Moses helped Laura onto her horse, his hands steady at her waist as she settled into the saddle.

"The snow makes everything look so pristine," Laura observed as they rode toward the mercantile, the horses' hooves crunching through the packed snow of Main Street.

Moses looked around at the transformed landscape. Aspen Hollow appeared almost enchanted beneath its white blanket, smoke rising in straight columns from chimneys against the brilliant blue sky.

"It conceals as much as it reveals," he replied thoughtfully.

Laura glanced at him. "That's rather philosophical for so early in the morning, Doctor."

The corner of Moses's mouth lifted slightly. "Perhaps you're rubbing off on me."

"Heaven forbid," Laura responded with a smile.

They reached the Abernathy & Sons Mercantile within minutes. The store was open but quiet, with only Silas himself behind the counter. He brightened visibly upon seeing them.

"Dr. Grant, Miss Smythe! Welcome!" he called, coming around to greet them. "Your timing is perfect. Twila, just put coffee on."

"How are you feeling, Mr. Abernathy?" Laura asked, noting with satisfaction that his color had improved markedly since she'd last seen him.

"Much improved, thanks to your good care," he replied, leading them toward the staircase that led to the family's living quarters above. "The cough is nearly gone, and I've been able to mind the store since yesterday."

"Any lingering fatigue or weakness?" Moses inquired.

"Some tiredness by day's end, but nothing concerning," Silas assured him as they climbed the stairs.

Twila bustled forward to greet them as they entered the living quarters, her previously pallid complexion now healthy and pink.

"You're both a sight for sore eyes," she declared warmly. "Please, sit. The children will be so pleased to see you."

"How are they progressing?" Moses asked, setting his medical bag on a nearby table.

"Felix is up and about already, though still weak," Twila reported. "Millie improves daily, but tires easily. It will be a few more days before she attempts to open the school back up or return to the boarding-house. And Tommy is almost his usual self, though I'm keeping him inside for now."

As if summoned by his name, Tommy appeared in the doorway, his face lighting up when he spotted Laura. "Miss Smythe! You came to visit!"

Laura smiled warmly at the boy. "Indeed, I have. And I'm pleased to see you looking so well."

"I've been helping Ma with chores," Tommy announced proudly.

"A fine young man," Moses commented with unusual gentleness, surprising Laura. "Now, shall we check how your lungs are doing?"

While Moses examined Tommy in one corner, Laura went to see Millie, who was sitting up in bed with a book. Her face brightened when Laura entered.

"Laura! I'm so glad to see you," Millie exclaimed, setting aside her book. "Being confined to this bed is becoming terribly dull. I cannot wait to go back to my room at the boarding house. I miss my quiet time."

"Well, let's see if we might allow you some short walks soon," Laura suggested, sitting beside the bed. She took Millie's wrist, checking her pulse. "How's your breathing? Any tightness or pain?"

"Much better," Millie assured her. "Just some weakness and occasional coughing, but nothing like before."

Laura listened to Millie's lungs with a stethoscope. The improvement was significant; the congestion had largely cleared, though some residual inflammation remained.

"Your recovery is progressing beautifully," Laura confirmed, smiling. "I believe you can start taking short walks within the house, but don't overexert yourself. Your body still needs rest to fully heal."

Millie reached for Laura's hand, squeezing it gently. "Thank you for everything you did — for all of us. I don't think I properly expressed my gratitude during the worst of it."

"No thanks necessary," Laura assured her. "I'm just relieved to see you improving."

Millie glanced toward the doorway, where Moses could be heard speaking with Felix in the next room. Her voice lowered conspiratorially. "You've been good for him, you know. Dr. Grant. He's different when you're near."

Laura felt heat rise to her cheeks. "I'm not sure what you mean."

"Oh, I think you do," Millie replied with a knowing smile. "He's softer somehow. More present. Everyone's noticed."

Moses appeared in the doorway. "How is our patient?" he asked, his deep voice sending an unexpected flutter through Laura's chest.

"Improving steadily," Laura reported, quickly recovering her professional demeanor. "I've suggested short walks within the house, but continued rest otherwise."

Moses nodded, moving to Millie's bedside. He performed his own brief examination, nodding with satisfaction. "Miss Smythe's assessment is sound, as always. Your lungs are clearing well, though I'd like you to continue with the pine steam treatments for another three days."

"Yes, Doctor," Millie agreed, her eyes twinkling as they darted between Moses and Laura.

They completed their examinations of the entire family, with Laura providing detailed instructions to Twila about ongoing care. Moses observed her interaction with the family with quiet admiration. She spoke clearly but kindly, ensuring they understood each element of care without being condescending.

"Miss Smythe has prepared this for you," Moses said, handing Silas the written instructions Laura had meticulously crafted. "Everything you need to know about continued treatments and what to watch for is detailed here."

Silas accepted the papers with obvious appreciation. "This is mighty thoughtful. Thank you both for your care. The town owes you a debt we can't repay."

"We're simply doing our duty," Moses replied automatically.

"No," Twila interjected firmly. "What you did went far beyond duty, Doctor. You and Miss Smythe worked day and night to save this town. We won't forget that."

Moses appeared momentarily discomfited by the praise, and Laura stepped in smoothly. "We should continue on our rounds. The Holcombs are expecting us."

After warm farewells and promises to return in two days to check progress, Moses and Laura made their way back downstairs. The store had a few customers now, all of whom greeted them with newfound respect and gratitude.

Outside, Moses helped Laura mount her horse once more. "The Abernathy's are recovering well," he observed as they rode away from the mercantile.

"Yes, they're fortunate," Laura agreed.

They rode toward the edge of town, where the path to the outlying homesteads began. As they left the cleared streets behind, the snow deepened considerably; the horses struggling to maintain solid footing.

"The drifts are worse than I anticipated," Moses said with a frown, surveying the pristine expanse stretching before them. "We should proceed carefully."

They continued for another half mile, but the path grew increasingly treacherous. A particularly deep drift caused Laura's horse to stumble slightly, making her clutch the saddle horn to maintain her seat.

Moses reined in his mount. "This isn't safe," he decided. "We should dismount and lead the horses through this section."

Laura nodded in agreement, allowing Moses to help her down from the saddle. The snow reached nearly to her knees in places, making progress slow and difficult.

"Take my arm," Moses offered, extending his elbow to her. "The footing is uncertain."

Laura gratefully slipped her gloved hand into the crook of his arm, acutely aware of his solid presence beside her. They trudged forward, leading the horses through the deepest drifts, their breaths forming clouds that mingled in the cold air.

The wind picked up suddenly, sending a shower of snow from the pine boughs nearby. Laura shivered as some of it slipped beneath her collar.

"There's a stand of pines ahead that should offer some shelter," Moses said, nodding toward a dense thicket of evergreens. "We can wait there until this gust passes."

They guided the horses into the natural shelter of the pine grove, where the thick branches had prevented much of the snow from accumulating on the ground. The sudden stillness was almost palpable after the howling of the wind outside their sanctuary.

"This feels like a different world," Laura observed, looking up at the snow-laden branches that filtered the sunlight into dappled patterns around them. The pine needles released their fragrance with each gentle movement of the boughs.

Moses secured the horse's reins to a low branch and turned to face her. In the filtered light, his features appeared softer, the usual lines of concentration around his eyes less pronounced.

"Are you warm enough?" he asked, studying her with concern.

"Yes, thank you," Laura replied, though she wrapped her arms around herself involuntarily.

Moses frowned slightly. "You're cold. Here." He unwound his scarf and stepped closer, carefully arranging it around her neck. His fingers brushed against her skin momentarily, sending an entirely different kind of shiver through her.

"Thank you," she murmured, acutely aware of his proximity.

He remained close, his eyes meeting hers with an intensity that made her heart quicken. "Laura," he began, then paused, seeming to search for words.

"Yes?" she prompted gently.

"I've been... thinking about our conversation at the mining camp," he said finally. "About faith and... doubt."

Laura nodded encouragingly, recognizing the difficulty this topic presented for him. "I remember."

Moses glanced away, his gaze fixing on some distant point among the trees. "You asked if I'd given up on God entirely. I didn't give you a proper answer then."

"You don't owe me any explanations," Laura assured him.

"Perhaps not," he acknowledged, meeting her eyes again. "But I find I want to give you one, nonetheless." He drew a deep breath. "I've been trying to pray again. Not with much success, but... I'm trying."

The simple admission touched Laura deeply. She understood how much courage it must have taken for this proud, private man to share something so personal.

"Faith often returns in small steps, not great leaps."

Moses nodded slowly. "I'm not sure what I believe anymore," he admitted. "After Rebecca died and then Jake, I was so angry. It seemed easier to close that door entirely than to confront the questions her death raised."

"About God's goodness?" Laura asked gently.

"About everything," Moses replied. "I did everything right, Laura. Everything medical science knew to do. And she died anyway, in terrible pain. And then so did Jake. How could a loving God allow such suffering?"

"I don't have a perfect answer. I wish I did. But I believe God suffers with us in our pain, rather than causing it or watching indifferently."

"That's a comforting thought," Moses said, though uncertainty lingered in his voice.

"It's what helped me after my family died," Laura explained. "Knowing that God wasn't punishing me or them, but was present in my grief, somehow made it bearable."

"How did you maintain such certainty?"

"I didn't," Laura admitted with a small smile. "I had my own dark nights of doubt. But I found that even in questioning, I was still in a relationship with God. The conversation continued, even when it was difficult."

The wind picked up outside their shelter, but within the grove, they remained protected, standing close together in the quiet sanctuary of pines.

"I've been afraid," Moses said, so quietly Laura had to lean closer to hear him. "Afraid to trust again—in God, in medicine's limits, in... connections with others."

"Because caring means risking loss," Laura supplied, understanding illuminating her features.

Moses's eyes widened slightly. "Yes," he acknowledged. "Exactly that."

"Is that why you've kept me at arm's length, too?" Laura asked, her heart pounding at her boldness.

Moses looked startled by her directness, then a rueful smile touched his lips. "You see through me rather too clearly for comfort, Laura Smythe."

"Not always," she countered gently. "You remain quite mysterious in many ways, Dr. Grant."

His expression softened. "Moses," he corrected. "After all, we've been through together. I think you've earned the right to use my given name consistently."

"Moses," Laura repeated, enjoying the way it felt to say his name so intimately.

Without apparent thought, Moses reached for her hands, taking them in his larger ones. Even through their gloves, Laura felt the warmth of his touch.

"Are your hands are cold?" he asked, rubbing them gently between his own.

Laura couldn't look away from his face, from the unexpected tenderness in his expression. "The cold doesn't bother me much," she said.

"Nevertheless," Moses replied, continuing his gentle ministrations, "a nurse should take better care of herself."

"As should a doctor," Laura returned with a small smile.

The wind outside their sanctuary began to calm, the howling diminishing to a gentle whisper through the pine boughs. Neither of them moved to leave the shelter of the trees, suspended in a moment that seemed to exist outside of ordinary time.

"We should probably continue to the Holcomb's," Laura said finally, though with obvious reluctance.

Moses nodded, but made no immediate move to release her hands. "Yes," he agreed. "Though I find myself unexpectedly reluctant to rejoin the wider world."

The admission, simple but profound, sent warmth blooming through Laura's chest. "I know exactly what you mean."

Slowly, almost regretfully, Moses released her hands and turned to untie the horses.

They led the horses out of the grove and back onto the trail, which now seemed less formidable than before. The remaining journey to the Holcomb homestead passed quickly, with occasional comfortable conversation interspersed with periods of thoughtful silence.

The Holcomb family greeted them with enthusiasm, particularly young Jeb, whose critical condition had caused such concern during the height of the epidemic. His recovery, while still incomplete, was remarkable, given how close he had come to death.

"We've been following your instructions to the letter, Miss Smythe," Virgie Holcomb declared proudly as she ushered them inside. "The pine steam treatments twice daily and the tincture every four hours, just as you wrote down."

"And it shows," Laura replied warmly, observing the children's improved color. "Your diligence has made all the difference."

While Moses examined Jeb's lungs, Laura checked on Angela and Donnie, finding both well on the road to recovery.

"Your care saved our children," Willis Holcomb said solemnly as they prepared to depart. "We won't forget that."

"Miss Smythe deserves most of the credit," Moses replied, surprising Laura. "Her quick action and knowledge of proper treatments were invaluable."

Laura felt a flush of pleasure at his unexpected praise. "It was truly a partnership," she clarified. "Dr. Grant's experience and judgment were essential."

As they journeyed back toward town, the winter afternoon light began to soften, casting long blue shadows across the snow. Laura found herself sneaking glances at Moses's profile, struck by how much had changed between them in such a short time.

Moses glanced at her with an unreadable expression. "You've changed my practice, Laura. My approach to patients."

"Have I?" Laura asked, genuinely surprised.

"Indeed," Moses confirmed. "Mrs. Bellweather actually commented yesterday that I seemed 'less intimidating' than before. I'm not entirely sure if it was meant as a compliment," he added dryly.

Laura laughed, the sound bright in the winter air. "Mrs. Bellweather has a unique way of expressing herself."

They reached the edge of town just as dusk began to settle, the windows of buildings lighting one by one with the warm glow of lamps and fireplaces. The streets were mostly empty, with townspeople having retreated indoors as darkness fell.

At the clinic, Moses dismounted first, then moved to help Laura down. His hands encircled her waist as she slid from the saddle, her hands coming to rest on his shoulders for balance. The movement brought their faces unexpectedly close, close enough that Laura could feel the warmth of his breath against her cheek.

For a suspended moment, neither moved. Moses's gaze dropped briefly to her lips, then returned to her eyes, a question in their blue depths. Laura felt herself sway slightly toward him, drawn by an irresistible pull.

"Doctor! Miss Smythe!" Deputy Diamond's voice shattered the moment. They stepped apart quickly as the deputy approached through the gathering twilight. "Glad I caught you both. Mrs. Roman's baby is coming, and she's asked for me to fetch you both. Her sister's with her now, but they're mighty nervous with this being a first baby and all."

Chapter 18

Laura felt her cheeks flush. She stepped back, creating a deliberate space, her voice sounding a little too crisp, a little too formal as she answered.

"Of course, Deputy. We'll attend to Mrs. Roman immediately."

Moses, too, seemed to gather himself, his usual professional mask slipping back into place, though Laura noticed a faint pink tinge still high on his cheekbones. He nodded curtly.

"They're at their cabin just outside of town, Doc. Mr. Roman was in a proper state, pacing like a caged wolf when I left to fetch you," Deputy Diamond said.

"Do you have any sense of how far along her labor is?" Moses asked Deputy Diamond, his voice all business now.

"Her sister said the pains started strong a few hours back, getting closer now. Water broke just before she sent me."

"She's likely well into labor by now," Moses said, and turned his attention back to Laura. "Ride with me. There's no need for both horses."

Laura nodded in agreement. Moses assisted her onto his horse, and then smoothly mounted in front of her.

The ride to the Roman cabin was swift. The last vestiges of daylight faded, leaving a sky dusted with the first glittering stars of the night. The crunch of the horses' hooves in the snow, the rhythmic creak of saddle leather, the distant howl of a lonely coyote, the only sounds in the crisp, cold air.

Laura instinctively wrapped her arms around Moses's waist to steady herself as the horse picked up speed. The solidity of him, the warmth radiating through his coat despite the bitter cold, made her heartbeat quicken in a way that had nothing to do with their brisk pace.

"This will be your first birth in Aspen Hollow," Moses said over his shoulder.

"Yes, but I assisted with many deliveries during my training in Philadelphia. I'm confident."

Moses nodded. "Mrs. Roman is young, and this is her first. She'll need reassurance as much as medical attention."

They crested a small hill, and a cabin came into view, nestled against a stand of pines. Golden light spilled from its windows, casting warm rectangles onto the pristine snow. Smoke curled from the chimney into the star-strewn sky.

As they approached, the cabin door burst open. A man with a shock of red hair and a worried expression rushed toward them.

"Dr. Grant! Thank the Lord you've come," he called, his voice strained with anxiety. "Mary's hurting something fierce, and I don't know what to do."

Moses dismounted quickly, then reached up to help Laura down.

"Frank, this is Nurse Smythe. She'll be assisting me," Moses said, his tone calm and steady. "How frequently are your wife's pains coming?"

"Every few minutes," he replied, wringing his hands. "Mary's sister says that's good, but it doesn't sound good. Mary's crying out something awful."

"Regular pains are exactly what we want," Laura assured him with a gentle smile. "It means your baby is on its way, just as nature intended."

Frank nodded, not looking entirely convinced.

The cabin interior was small but welcoming, a single room with a curtained-off sleeping area at the back. A robust fire crackled in the stone hearth, casting dancing shadows across the rough-hewn walls.

From behind the curtain came a low moan that rose in intensity before falling away again.

A woman emerged. "Doctor, thank heaven," she said, relief evident in her voice. Her gaze shifted to Laura. "And you've brought a nurse?"

"Mrs. Tanner, this is Nurse Smythe," Moses introduced them. "She's highly skilled and will be assisting with the birth."

"Call me Laura, please," Laura said warmly, already removing her coat and rolling up her sleeves. "How is your sister doing?"

"Mary's strong, but frightened," Mrs. Tanner replied. "It's been about six hours since the pains started in earnest."

Another moan came from behind the curtain, longer and more intense than the last.

"I should examine her," Moses said. He glanced at Frank, who stood frozen near the door. "Perhaps you might wait outside for a bit."

"Outside?" Frank protested. "But it's freezing!"

"Then by the fire," Moses amended. "It's best for Mary's modesty and your peace of mind."

Laura was already moving toward the curtained area, her manner calm and purposeful. "Mrs. Tanner, would you heat some water, please? And do you have clean linens ready?"

"Yes, ma'am."

Laura slipped behind the curtain. Mary Roman lay on the bed, her face flushed and damp with perspiration, her rounded belly rising prominently beneath the bedcovers. Her eyes, wide with pain and fear, locked onto Laura's.

"Who are you?" she gasped, before another contraction seized her.

Laura moved swiftly to the bedside, taking Mary's hand. "I'm Laura Smythe, a nurse. I'm here to help you and Dr. Grant bring your baby into the world."

Mary clutched Laura's hand with surprising strength as the contraction peaked. Laura breathed steadily, encouraging Mary to follow her rhythm. "That's it," she murmured. "Deep breaths through the pain. You're doing wonderfully."

Moses entered as the contraction subsided. He set his medical bag on a small table and washed his hands in a basin that Mrs. Tanner had prepared.

"Mrs. Roman, I need to examine you to determine how far along you are," he explained, his voice gentle but direct. "Nurse Smythe will stay right beside you."

Laura positioned herself at Mary's shoulder, continuing to hold her hand. "I'll be right here," she assured her. "You can squeeze as hard as you need to."

As Moses conducted his examination, Laura kept her attention focused on Mary, speaking quietly about the baby, asking gentle questions about names they'd considered, creating a distraction from the discomfort.

"You're progressing well," Moses announced when he'd finished. "The baby is in a good position, and you're nearly ready to deliver."

Mary's eyes filled with tears of relief and apprehension. "Will it be much longer?" she asked, her voice quavering.

"Not long now," Laura assured her, smoothing back damp hair from Mary's forehead. "Your body knows exactly what to do."

Mrs. Tanner returned with steaming water and additional linens. "How is she?" she asked anxiously.

"Doing beautifully," Laura replied with a reassuring smile. She turned to Moses. "Dr. Grant, what preparations would you like me to make?"

Moses was already arranging his instruments on a clean cloth. "Ready the linens for the baby, and prepare a solution of carbolic acid for cleaning," he instructed, his voice low and steady. "Mrs. Tanner, we'll need more hot water, and perhaps some honey water for Mary when the time comes."

Laura worked efficiently, setting out the items they would need. She noticed how naturally she and Moses moved around each other in the small space, anticipating each other's needs without speaking. It was a dance they had perfected during the epidemic, this wordless coordination.

Laura returned to Mary's side as another contraction seized, more powerful than the last. She cried out, gripping Laura's hand and the bed frame.

"The pains are coming faster," Mrs. Tanner observed nervously.

"That's good," Moses assured her. "It means the baby is nearly here."

"You're doing so well, Mary. Each pain brings your baby closer to your arms," Laura said softly.

For the next hour, they worked together as Mary's labor intensified. Laura and Mrs. Tanner both remained a constant presence at her side, offering encouragement, wiping her brow, helping her change positions to ease the pain. Moses moved between careful observations of the progress and quiet consultations with Laura.

In a brief moment between contractions, Mary whispered, "I'm afraid."

Laura leaned close. "That's natural, Mary. But I promise you, you're not alone. Dr. Grant is one of the finest physicians I've ever worked with, and I'll be right here holding your hand the entire time."

"You won't leave?" Mary asked, her eyes wide.

"Not for a moment," Laura promised.

Moses, overhearing this exchange, glanced at Laura with an expression of quiet admiration. In the lamplight, her face was softened, her eyes reflecting both determination and tenderness. He was struck, not for the first time, by her natural grace under pressure.

Mary's labor entered its final, most intense phase. Moses positioned himself at the foot of the bed while Laura supported Mary's back, murmuring constant encouragement.

"I can see the baby's head," Moses announced, his voice steady with controlled excitement. "Mary, on the next pain, I need you to push as hard as you can."

Laura felt Mary tense with both fear and determination. "You can do this," she whispered. "God has designed your body perfectly for this moment."

The next contraction came with tremendous force. Mary bore down with a guttural cry, her face contorted with effort.

"Good, Mary! Again, just like that," Moses encouraged as the contraction subsided. "The baby's head is crowning."

"Your child is almost here," Laura said, supporting Mary as she gathered her strength for the next push. "Just a little more courage now."

Two more powerful contractions, two more heroic efforts from the exhausted mother, and suddenly the cabin filled with the indignant, miraculous cry of a newborn.

"A boy!" Moses announced, his voice thick with emotion. "A strong, healthy boy."

Mary collapsed against Laura, sobbing with relief and joy. "My baby... let me see him."

Moses worked quickly to clear the baby's airways and tack care of the umbilical cord. Laura prepared clean linens to receive the infant, her own eyes bright with tears at the beautiful culmination of their work.

Moses placed the squalling infant in Laura's waiting hands. She cleaned him gently, wrapping him securely in the soft fabric. The baby's cries softened as Laura swaddled him, his tiny face scrunching with the effort of his first moments in the world.

"Here he is, Mary," Laura said softly, placing the bundle in the new mother's trembling arms. "Your son."

Mary gazed down at the tiny face with an expression of wonder and love so profound it seemed to transform her. "Look at him," she whispered. "He's perfect."

Laura settled beside Mary on the bed, adjusting the pillows to support her as she held her child. "He is indeed," she agreed, gently touching the baby's downy head. "Ten fingers, ten toes, and a splendid pair of lungs."

Moses completed his care for Mary, ensuring everything was proceeding normally after the birth. He moved with quiet efficiency, but Laura noticed his gaze repeatedly drawn to the tableau of mother and child on the bed.

Once he was satisfied that Mary was stable and comfortable, Moses stepped back, watching as Laura helped position the baby for his first feeding. There was a tenderness in the way Laura guided Mary's movements, a gentle authority that came from knowledge but was softened by deep compassion.

"Should I get Frank now?" Mrs. Tanner asked, her own eyes damp with happy tears.

"Yes," Moses nodded. "He should meet his son."

As Mrs. Tanner slipped out to fetch the new father, Moses found himself unable to look away from Laura. In the soft glow of lamplight, with her chestnut hair escaping its pins and her face alight with joy for the new family, she was more than beautiful. She was radiant, with purpose and compassion.

Frank burst in moments later, his face a mixture of terror and anticipation. He stopped short at the sight of his wife and child, his expression shifting to one of pure awe.

"Mary..." he breathed, approaching the bed cautiously, as if afraid he might shatter the perfect moment.

"Your son," Mary said, her voice tired but filled with joy.

Frank moved to the bedside, sitting carefully on the edge. Laura stood and moved to stand beside Moses.

"He's so small," Frank marveled, gently touching his son's tiny hand. The baby's fingers reflexively curled around his father's much larger one, and Frank looked up, his eyes swimming. "Thank you," he said, looking from Moses to Laura and back again. "Both of you. I don't have words..."

"No thanks are necessary," Moses replied, his voice unusually gentle. "Bringing new life into the world is a privilege."

Laura felt a warmth spread through her chest at his words. This was a side of Moses she had never glimpsed, a man who found genuine wonder in the miracle of life.

They stayed a while longer, ensuring that both mother and baby were settled. Laura provided instructions to Mrs. Tanner about caring for Mary and the infant over the next few days, while Moses observed.

"I'll return tomorrow to check on them both," Moses promised as they prepared to leave. "Send for us immediately if there's any concern, no matter the hour."

Outside, the night had deepened. The sky was a vast expanse of black velvet strewn with stars, their light reflecting off the snow in glittering diamonds. Their breath formed clouds in the frigid air as Frank walked them to their horses.

"I don't know how to thank you enough," he said again, shaking Moses's hand vigorously. "God surely sent you both to us tonight."

"Your healthy son is thanks enough," Laura replied.

Frank nodded, his eyes still bright with unshed tears of joy. "I should get back to them. Good night, and God bless you both."

As Frank returned to the cabin, Moses turned to help Laura onto his horse. But instead of reaching for the reins or offering his cupped hands to boost her up, he stood motionless, his expression unreadable in the starlight.

"Moses?" Laura questioned.

He took a step toward her, then another, closing the distance between them. His eyes held an intensity she'd never seen before.

"Laura..." he began, his voice catching.

Without warning, he gathered her into his arms, holding her against his chest in an embrace so profound, so filled with unspoken emotion, that Laura felt her breath catch. His arms encircled her completely, one hand cradling the back of her head as if she were something infinitely precious.

Laura stood frozen in surprise for only a moment before her arms rose to encircle him, her hands resting against the solid planes of his back. She could feel the rapid beating of his heart through the layers of their clothing, matching the sudden acceleration of her own.

"I…" Moses attempted to speak, his voice rough with emotion. He pulled back just enough to look into her face, his features illuminated by starlight and the distant glow from the cabin windows. "What we just did in there—bringing that child into the world… I…"

Words seemed to fail him, his usual eloquence deserting him entirely. Instead, his gaze dropped to her lips, then rose again to meet her eyes. A question, and a revelation all at once.

Laura reached up, her gloved hand trembling slightly as she touched his cheek. "Moses," she whispered, her voice hardly more than a breath in the frigid air.

For a heartbeat, it seemed he might kiss her. The air between them crackled with possibility, with unspoken words and newfound vulnerability.

Then, as if suddenly remembering himself, Moses gently released her, though his hands lingered at her waist.

"We should return to town," he said, his voice still unsteady. "It's getting colder."

Laura nodded, unable to trust her voice. Moses helped her onto his horse, his hands careful and deliberate at her waist. When he mounted in front of her, she hesitated only a moment before wrapping her arms around him again, perhaps holding a little closer than was strictly necessary for balance.

They rode in silence through the star-spangled night, each lost in their thoughts. The steady rhythm of the horse's hooves in the snow, the occasional call of a night bird, and their mingled breaths were the only sounds accompanying them back toward Aspen Hollow.

Laura rested her cheek against Moses's back, grateful for the warmth and closeness in the bitter cold. The memory of his embrace burned bright in her mind—the fierce tenderness of it, the uncharacteristic openness in his eyes afterward. Something fundamental had shifted between them tonight, something neither of them had fully articulated, but both had felt with absolute clarity.

Moses rode steadily, his thoughts in turmoil. The sight of Laura helping to bring new life into the world, her gentle strength and boundless compassion, had broken through the last of his carefully constructed defenses. Holding her in his arms had felt like coming home to a place he hadn't known he was seeking. The realization terrified and exhilarated him in equal measure.

As they approached the outskirts of town, the familiar silhouettes of buildings appearing through the trees, Moses felt Laura's arms tighten slightly around his waist.

"Moses?" she said softly, her voice barely audible over the crunch of snow beneath the horse's hooves.

"Yes?" he replied, slowing their pace.

"Bringing that baby into the world, seeing his parents' joy—it's another reason why I became a nurse. To help create beautiful moments like that."

Moses was silent for a long moment, considering her words. When he finally spoke, his voice carried a depth of feeling that surprised them both.

"You didn't just help, Laura. You transformed the experience," he said. "Your presence, your compassion... you made a frightening ordeal into something beautiful for that family." He paused, then added more quietly, "And for me as well."

They reached the clinic soon after that. Moses helped Laura down from the horse, their eyes meeting briefly in the pale light spilling from the clinic windows.

"Good night, Moses," Laura said softly, her hand lingering on his arm.

"Good night, Laura," he replied, his voice gentle in a way she'd rarely heard before.

As she turned to walk toward the boardinghouse, Laura felt a curious mixture of emotion—uncertainty about what tomorrow might bring, but also a quiet, growing certainty about the man she was leaving behind. Something had awakened in Moses Grant tonight, something she had glimpsed in rare moments but had now seen in full glory—a capacity for tenderness and wonder that matched his skill and dedication.

From the clinic doorway, Moses watched Laura walk away, her slender figure gradually disappearing into the night. His arms still felt the phantom warmth of her embrace, his heart still thundered with emotions he had long believed himself incapable of feeling.

He had nearly kissed her beneath the stars, had wanted to with an intensity that shocked him. Yet something held him back, not the professional boundaries he had so carefully maintained, but a new and unfamiliar urge to do this properly, to honor the remarkable woman who had upended his world.

Chapter 19

Moses stood motionless on the boardwalk beside his clinic, his eyes fixed on the spot where Laura had disappeared into the darkness. The cold bit through his coat, yet he remained.

What had possessed him to embrace her like that? The question tumbled through his mind, though he knew the answer. It was everything. The miracle of birth they'd witnessed together, the way she'd guided Mary through her fear with such gentle strength, the look of pure joy on her face when she'd placed that newborn in his mother's arms. In that moment, his heart had simply crumbled.

Moses tilted his head back, gazing up at the vast canopy of stars scattered across the black velvet sky. The familiar constellations seemed to shimmer with new significance tonight, as if the heavens themselves were witnessing his transformation.

"I'm in love with her," he whispered to the night, the words forming a cloud in the frigid air.

The recognition of this truth wasn't a shock. Instead, it settled into his chest with the comfort of something that had been there all along, simply waiting to be acknowledged. From their first contentious meeting to tonight's shared wonder, Laura had been steadily dismantling his defenses, challenging his cynicism, and rekindling his faith through her unwavering example.

Moses began walking, not toward his quarters above the clinic as he should have at this late hour, but in the direction of the church. His strides were purposeful despite his mental turmoil, his boots crunching in the hardened snow. The town was silent around him, windows darkened, only the occasional lamplight suggesting life behind closed doors.

The church stood silhouetted against the starry sky, its simple steeple reaching upward. A soft light still glowed from the windows—not unusual, as Pastor Lewis often worked late, and two recovering patients remained there under volunteer care.

Moses hesitated at the steps, suddenly uncertain. It was late, well past a reasonable hour for a visit. Yet something drew him forward, a need for counsel that couldn't wait until morning. He climbed the wooden steps and knocked softly on the door.

Footsteps approached, and then Pastor Lewis appeared, surprise clear on his face.

"Moses? Is everything all right?" he asked, concern immediately replacing his surprise.

"Yes," Moses replied, then reconsidered. "Well, no. I'm not sure. May I come in?"

Pastor Lewis stepped back, opening the door wider. "Of course. Moses, you didn't need to knock."

The church was warm after the bitter cold outside. The main sanctuary, which had so recently served as an impromptu hospital, now held only two occupied pallets near the stove. Mrs. Monroe, one of the town's older widows, sat knitting beside them, keeping watch.

"Doctor Grant," she acknowledged with a nod. "Come to check on our patients?"

Moses moved toward the pallets, professional instinct temporarily overriding his personal turmoil. The two miners, both young men from the outlying camp, looked markedly improved from when he'd last seen them.

"How are they faring?" he asked, kneeling to check their pulse and breathing.

"Much better," Mrs. Monroe reported. "Both took broth for supper and have been sleeping peacefully. No more fever in either."

Moses nodded in satisfaction as he completed his brief examination. "They can likely return to their homes tomorrow. I'll make a proper examination in the morning."

"That's welcome news," Pastor Lewis said, standing nearby. "Mrs. Monroe has been a stalwart volunteer, but I know she'd appreciate returning to her home as well."

The older woman waved away the praise. "Happy to do my Christian duty, Pastor. These boys needed looking after."

Moses rose, his professional assessment complete. Now the real reason for his visit pressed forward again, creating a tightness in his chest.

Pastor Lewis seemed to sense his disquiet. "Would you care to join me in my study, Moses? I've got coffee still warm on the stove."

"Thank you," Moses managed.

Pastor Lewis gestured to one of the two chairs. "Sit, please. You look half-frozen."

Moses sank into the offered chair, removing his hat and placing it on his knee. He watched as the pastor poured two cups of steaming coffee, handing one to him before taking the second chair.

"You have the look of a man who's had an awakening of some kind," Pastor Lewis observed, blowing across the surface of his coffee. "Something significant enough to bring you to the church at this hour."

Moses stared into his cup, gathering his thoughts. "I delivered the Roman baby tonight. A healthy boy."

"That's wonderful news," Pastor Lewis smiled. "I know they've been praying for a safe delivery, especially after all the illness in town."

"Laura was with me," Moses continued, her name feeling different somehow as it passed his lips. "She was... remarkable. The way she attended to Mary and calmed her fears... guided her through the birth."

Pastor Lewis nodded encouragingly. "Miss Smythe has a natural gift for bringing comfort."

"It's more than that," Moses said, looking up to meet the pastor's eyes directly. "It's who she is—her faith, her compassion, her unwavering determination to help others regardless of the cost to herself." He set his coffee aside, untouched. "After the birth, when we were leaving, I... I embraced her."

If Pastor Lewis was surprised by this admission, he showed no sign of it. "I see," he said simply.

"It wasn't planned," Moses continued, feeling the need to explain something he barely understood himself. "It was as if something outside myself took control. All I knew was that I needed to hold her, to—" He broke off, searching for words.

"To connect," Pastor Lewis supplied gently. "To acknowledge what has been growing between you."

Moses nodded, grateful for the understanding. "Yes." He paused, the magnitude of what he was about to say weighing on him. "I love her, Pastor. I'm in love with Laura."

Pastor Lewis's face softened into a smile.

"And this troubles you?" he asked.

Moses ran a hand through his hair. "It...surprises me. I never expected to feel this way... about anyone. After Rebecca and Jake, after everything... I'd convinced myself that such feelings were behind me." He leaned forward in his chair. "How is it possible that in the span of a few weeks, she's changed everything?"

Pastor Lewis considered this. "Love often works that way, Moses. It arrives unannounced and transforms us before we've even recognized its presence." He took a sip of his coffee. "Though I must say, to those of us observing, your feelings for Miss Smythe have been evident for some time."

Moses looked up sharply. "They have?"

A chuckle escaped the pastor. "Indeed. The way you look at her when you think no one notices, how you've gradually accepted her methods and insights, your fierce concern when she was beyond exhaustion... these things speak volumes."

Moses felt heat rise to his face. Had he been so transparent?

"What do I do now?" he asked, the question emerging from the heart of his uncertainty.

"What do you wish to do?" Pastor Lewis countered gently.

Moses considered this, his thoughts coalescing into unexpected clarity. "I want to court her properly. She deserves nothing less than complete respect and honorable intentions."

The pastor's eyes crinkled with approval. "A commendable approach. Laura is indeed a woman worthy of the highest respect."

"But..." Moses hesitated, his practical nature asserting itself. "Is it too soon? We've known each other for such a short time. And what of our working relationship?"

"These are valid considerations," Pastor Lewis acknowledged. "Yet I'm reminded of something my father once told me. He said, 'Some-

times God's greatest gifts arrive in unexpected packages at unantici-
pated times.' Your feelings for Laura may have developed quickly, but
that doesn't make them any less genuine or significant."

Moses absorbed this, finding comfort in the pastor's words. "And
what of the practical concerns? Our work together?"

"I suspect your professional relationship would only be strength-
ened by an honest acknowledgment of your personal feelings," Pastor
Lewis replied. "Laura strikes me as a woman who values truth above
all else. She would rather know where she stands with you than be left
wondering."

Moses nodded slowly. The thought of speaking his feelings aloud to
Laura both terrified and exhilarated him. "I need to proceed carefully.
She deserves a proper courtship."

Pastor Lewis smiled, a hint of amusement in his eyes. "While I
certainly endorse honorable intentions, Moses, perhaps I might offer
one small piece of advice?"

"Of course."

"Life is short," the pastor said simply. "Particularly, here on the
frontier, where hardship and danger are constant companions. Sometimes in life, we need to trust our instincts and have faith that God has a
plan." He leaned forward, his expression earnest. "Don't let propriety
become a shield against vulnerability. If you love her, find the courage
to tell her so."

Moses felt the impact of these words deep in his chest. The pastor
was right. How many times in his medical practice had he seen life cut
tragically short?

"You're suggesting I shouldn't wait," Moses said.

"I'm suggesting that while a proper courtship is admirable, beginning with honesty about your feelings, might be the most respectful

approach of all." Pastor Lewis's eyes twinkled. "Besides, if I may be so bold, I believe Miss Smythe may share your sentiments."

Moses's heart quickened at this. "What makes you say that?"

"I observe my congregation closely, Moses. It's part of my calling. There's a particular light in her eyes when she speaks of you, a light I recognize well."

Hope bloomed in Moses's chest. "Even so, I want to do this properly. She deserves no less."

"Indeed, she does," Pastor Lewis agreed. "But remember, Moses, that propriety need not preclude passion or honesty. The greatest love stories in Scripture are tales of profound emotion expressed openly... consider the Song of Solomon. Love, real love, is both respectful and ardent. It honors the beloved while also expressing the depth of one's feelings."

Moses nodded, feeling a new resolve forming within him. "Thank you, Pastor. Your counsel is... illuminating."

"I'm glad to help," Pastor Lewis replied warmly. "Now, drink your coffee before it gets cold. Mrs. Monroe will think I'm a poor host if you leave it untouched."

Moses picked up his cup, taking an appreciative sip of the strong brew. They sat in silence for a few moments, the only sounds the occasional pop from the wood stove and the distant murmur of Mrs. Monroe speaking softly to the patients.

"There's one more thing," Moses said finally. "My faith... it's still a work in progress. Laura's belief is so central to who she is, so unwavering. Mine feels... unsteady in comparison."

Pastor Lewis considered this thoughtfully. "Faith isn't measured by its steadiness, Moses, but by its sincerity. Your journey back to belief may be incomplete, but it's genuine. I believe Laura sees that and values it."

"I hope so," Moses said.

"Besides," the pastor continued, "perhaps part of God's purpose in bringing Laura into your life is to help strengthen your faith. Just as your practical wisdom and experience complement her idealism."

The idea resonated with Moses, that they might each have something the other needed, that their differences might be complementary rather than divisive.

"When do you plan to speak with her?" Pastor Lewis asked.

Moses took another sip of coffee, considering. "Soon. After I've had time to... prepare myself properly."

Pastor Lewis smiled knowingly. "Don't overthink it, my friend. Sometimes the words that come from the heart at the moment are more meaningful than those carefully rehearsed."

"I will remember that," Moses replied, though the thought of speaking spontaneously about such profound feelings was daunting.

They finished their coffee, talking about the town's recovery from the epidemic and the plans for services on Sunday. When Moses finally rose to leave, he felt lighter somehow, as if articulating his feelings had relieved a burden he hadn't fully recognized.

At the door, Pastor Lewis placed a hand on his shoulder. "I'll be praying for you, Moses. For both of you."

"Thank you," Moses said sincerely. "For everything."

The night air felt less biting as Moses made his way back to the clinic, his mind whirling with possibilities and plans. How would he approach Laura? What words could possibly convey the transformation she had wrought in his heart?

He climbed the stairs to his quarters, shedding his coat and hat mechanically, while his thoughts remained fixed on Laura. The small rooms felt particularly empty tonight, the silence more pronounced than usual.

Moses moved to the window, gazing out at the town blanketed in moonlight and snow. In the distance, he could just make out the outline of Aspen Rest, where Laura would now be sleeping. The thought of her, perhaps dreaming beneath the same stars that witnessed his revelation, filled him with a tenderness that was almost painful in its intensity.

Without conscious decision, Moses kneeled beside his bed. The posture of prayer felt awkward at first, rusty from disuse, but as he closed his eyes, words began to form.

"Lord," he whispered into the quiet room, "I don't know if I have the right to ask for Your guidance when I've turned away for so long. But I need... I need Your wisdom now."

He paused, gathering his thoughts, emotions welling up unexpectedly.

"I love her," he continued simply. "I love her faith and her kindness, her stubborn determination and her gentle touch. I love how she sees the best in people, even in me, especially when I don't deserve it." His voice caught slightly. "If it's Your will, show me how to be worthy of her. Help me find the courage to tell her what's in my heart."

The prayer was awkward, halting, far from eloquent, yet it felt genuine. As Moses rose from his knees, a curious peace settled over him, not erasing his nervousness about the path ahead but tempering it with newfound resolve.

He prepared for bed methodically, but sleep was elusive. His mind kept returning to the moment outside the Roman cabin, when Laura had been in his arms and the world had seemed to hold its breath. He had nearly kissed her then, should have kissed her, perhaps, but something had held him back.

Fear, he realized now. Not fear of rejection, but fear of the irrevocable change such an action would bring. Once he crossed that threshold, there would be no returning to the safe, isolated existence he had maintained for so long.

Moses turned on his side, watching moonlight create patterns on the wall.

Chapter 20

The morning arrived with crisp clarity, the rising sun transforming the snow-covered mountains into a tapestry of gold and rose. Moses woke earlier than usual, his resolve from the night before still firm in the light of day. He dressed with particular care, choosing his newest shirt and taking extra time with his shaving.

As he studied his reflection in the small mirror, Moses hardly recognized himself. There was a light in his eyes that had been absent for so long, a vitality that spoke of renewed purpose.

The clinic wouldn't open for patients until nine, giving him time to visit the Roman family first. He prepared his medical bag automatically, his hands going through the familiar motions while his mind remained occupied with thoughts of Laura.

Would she be at breakfast? Should he seek her out at Aspen Rest? What would he say to her with others present? Perhaps it would be better to find a moment alone later in the day.

Stepping out into the crisp morning air, Moses breathed deeply. Aspen Hollow was already stirring to life. Smoke curled from chimneys, the scent of wood fire and breakfast mingling in the cold. A few townsfolk nodded respectfully as they passed.

"Morning, Doc," Deputy Diamond called from across the street. "Baby Roman doing well?"

"Just heading to check on them now," Moses replied.

"Please give the family my regards." The deputy touched his hat. "That little one's arrival is exactly what this town needed after all the hardship."

Moses nodded in agreement. New life after so much suffering did seem like a divine reassurance, a reminder that even in the darkest times, hope endured.

As he made his way towards the Roman cabin on horseback, Moses rehearsed what he might say to Laura when he saw her. Each potential greeting sounded more awkward than the last. How had he become so inept at expressing himself? He'd never struggled for words when delivering difficult diagnoses or explaining complex medical procedures.

But this was different. This wasn't medicine. This was his heart laid bare.

The Roman cabin came into view, smoke billowing cheerfully from the chimney. Before Moses could knock, the door swung open to reveal Frank Roman, his face bright with a joy that hadn't diminished overnight.

"Doctor Grant! Welcome, please come in."

"How are Mary and the baby?" Moses asked, stepping inside.

"Doing splendidly," Frank beamed. "Mary's tired but happy, and the little one has quite an appetite."

The cabin was warm and filled with the scent of fresh bread. Mary sat in a rocking chair near the fire, the swaddled infant cradled in her arms. She looked up as Moses entered, her face glowing with maternal pride despite her evident fatigue.

"Good morning, Dr. Grant," she said softly. "Would you like to meet Thomas Franklin Roman properly?"

"Thomas," Moses repeated, moving closer to examine the infant. "A fine name."

"After my father," Mary explained, carefully adjusting the blanket to reveal the baby's sleeping face. "And Franklin after his father, of course."

Moses performed his examination with practiced gentleness, finding mother and child in excellent health. The baby's color was perfect, his breathing regular, his tiny reflexes strong.

"He's thriving," Moses confirmed, straightening up. "You're doing everything right."

Mary's eyes searched his face. "We couldn't have done this without you and Miss Smythe. She was so... calming. I was terrified, but her voice, her presence... it made me believe I could do it."

"That's her gift," Moses said quietly. "Helping others find strength they didn't know they possessed."

"You care for her, don't you, Doc?" Mary asked directly.

Moses felt heat rise in his face. Was his transformation so obvious that even relative strangers could perceive it?

"I..." he began, uncertain how to respond.

"I'm sorry," Mary interjected quickly. "That's none of our business. It's just—the way you looked at her last night, while she was helping me. I've never seen you look that way at anyone."

Moses cleared his throat, oddly touched by their observation. "Miss Smythe is an exceptional nurse and a remarkable woman," he admitted. "And yes, I do... care for her. Very much."

Frank's face broke into a broad grin. "Well, I think that's just fine, Doc. Just fine indeed."

"Have you told her?" Mary asked gently.

Moses shook his head. "Not yet. But I intend to."

Mary smiled, a knowing look in her eyes. "Don't wait too long. Life is precious and all too brief." She gazed down at her newborn. "We should cherish love when we find it."

Her words, so similar to Pastor Lewis's counsel the night before, resonated deeply. Was the entire town conspiring to push him toward this leap of faith?

"I'll keep that in mind," Moses promised. He completed his examination, provided instructions for Mary's continued recovery, and prepared to leave.

At the door, Frank clasped his hand warmly. "Thank you again, Doc. For everything."

Moses nodded. "I'll return to check on you both in a few days. Send for me if you need anything sooner."

As he rode back toward town, Moses's steps felt lighter, his purpose clearer. The Roman family's simple joy, their unabashed delight in their new son, reminded him of what truly mattered in life—not professional accolades or stubborn independence, but love, connection, and shared purpose.

He headed, not toward the clinic, but toward Aspen Rest. The timing wasn't ideal; the boarding house would be bustling with breakfast activity. Yet suddenly, waiting another moment seemed impossible.

The boardinghouse was indeed lively when he arrived, the sounds of conversation and clinking dishes spilling out onto the porch. Moses hesitated at the door, straightening his coat and gathering his courage.

"Dr. Grant! Is everything all right?" Mrs. Williams asked as he entered.

"Yes, yes, everything's fine," he assured her quickly. "I was hoping to speak with Miss Smythe."

"Oh. I'm afraid Laura left early this morning. Said she wanted to check on the Holcomb children before the clinic opened. You might find her there."

Moses nodded, trying to hide his disappointment. "Thank you, Mrs. Williams. I'll try there."

"Dr. Grant?" Mrs. Williams called as he turned to leave. When he looked back, she was smiling warmly. "It's good to see you looking so... alive."

Moses managed a small smile in return. "Thank you."

He made his way toward the Holcomb homestead, rehearsing his words again. The crisp morning air filled his lungs, clearing his thoughts. Perhaps this moment of delay was providential—the Holcomb property lay beyond the bustle of town, offering a more private setting for the conversation he wished to have.

The journey passed quickly, his mind so occupied with thoughts of Laura that he hardly noticed the cold or the distance. As the Holcomb cabin came into view, Moses spotted a familiar figure emerging from the door. Laura stood on the porch, accepting a jar of what appeared to be preserved fruit from Mrs. Holcomb. Even from this distance, Moses could see the animation in her movements, the gentle way she leaned down to speak to young Donnie Holcomb, who had appeared at her mother's side.

Moses slowed his pace, suddenly aware of his pounding heart. Laura looked up, noticing his approach. Her expression shifted from surprise to a warm smile that seemed to brighten the entire snow-covered landscape.

She said something to Mrs. Holcomb, then descended the steps and mounted her horse. Moses paused on the snow-covered road, watching as she rode his way.

For a moment, neither spoke, simply regarding each other with a new awareness that seemed to charge the space between them.

"Moses," Laura said, her blue eyes searching his face. "I didn't expect to see you here. I thought you'd be at the clinic."

"I went to check on the Roman family first," he explained, drinking in the sight of her. She wore her hair slightly different today, with soft tendrils framing her face beneath her bonnet. The morning sun caught the chestnut highlights, making them glow like polished copper.

He dismounted his horse and took a step closer.

"How are they?" she asked, genuine concern in her voice, as she tilted her head.

"Thriving. They've named him Thomas Franklin."

Laura's face softened. "A good, strong name. And Mary? Is she recovering well?"

"Very well. She spoke highly of you—of your kindness during the birth."

A slight blush colored Laura's cheeks. "It was a privilege to be part of such a moment."

Moses nodded, understanding completely. An awkward silence fell between them, heavy with unspoken words.

"Laura, I—" Moses began.

"About last night—" Laura said simultaneously.

They both stopped, then smiled hesitantly.

"Please," Moses said as he placed his hands on her waist and helped her dismount.

Laura drew a deep breath, her eyes never leaving his. "About last night, when you... when we..." She faltered, then straightened her shoulders, resolve evident in her bearing. "I've been thinking about it all night. About what it might mean."

Moses's heart skipped. "So have I," he admitted.

"And?" Laura prompted softly, a vulnerability in her expression that made his chest ache.

At that moment, all of Moses's carefully rehearsed speeches vanished. What remained was the simple, unvarnished truth.

"I love you, Laura," he said, the words emerging with startling clarity. "I think perhaps I've been falling in love with you since you arrived in Aspen Hollow, though I was too stubborn to recognize it at first."

Laura's eyes widened, lips parting in surprise. Moses continued, the words flowing now that the first barrier had been broken.

"You've changed everything—how I practice medicine, how I see this town, how I understand faith and compassion. Last night, watching you as that beautiful child came into the world, I couldn't deny it any longer. I love your determination, your unwavering faith, your kindness, even your stubborn insistence on modern methods that once drove me to distraction."

A smile blossomed on Laura's face, radiant in the morning light.

"I know it hasn't been long," Moses continued, "and if you think this too sudden, too improper, I understand. But I couldn't keep it to myself another day."

"Moses Grant," Laura said, her voice trembling slightly. "Are you always this eloquent when you abandon your usual gruffness, or is this a special occasion?"

A startled laugh escaped him. "Apparently only when I'm terrified of rejection."

Laura's expression softened. "There's no rejection to fear." She reached for his hand, her gloved fingers twining with his. "I love you too, Moses."

Something tight in Moses's chest unfurled at her words. "You love me?" he repeated, hardly daring to believe.

"Yes," Laura affirmed, her gaze steady and clear. "With all my heart."

Moses lifted their joined hands, pressing her fingers to his lips in a gesture so tender it brought tears to Laura's eyes.

"I want to court you properly," he said. "To honor you as you deserve."

"I would like that very much."

The world around them seemed to fade, the snow, the mountains, and the distant sounds of the farm, leaving only this moment, this connection.

"May I kiss you, Laura?" Moses asked, his voice low.

"Please," she whispered.

He drew her gently closer, one hand coming up to cradle her cheek. With infinite tenderness, Moses lowered his lips to hers. The kiss was gentle at first, almost reverent, but deepened as Laura's arms encircled his neck, drawing him closer still.

When they parted, Moses rested his forehead against hers.

"I should have done that last night," he murmured.

Laura smiled. "Perhaps this was better. No shadowy confessions under the stars, but truth spoken in clear daylight."

Moses nodded, understanding her perfectly. In the honest light of morning, there was no room for doubt or misinterpretation. What they had acknowledged was real, substantial, and impossible to dismiss as a moment of heightened emotion.

"What happens now?" Laura asked, her hand still in his.

"Now," Moses replied, a smile tugging at his lips, "we open the clinic, see our patients, and somehow try to behave professionally despite my overwhelming desire to kiss you again."

Laura laughed, the sound clear and joyful in the crisp air. "That sounds challenging."

"Indeed," Moses agreed, his eyes crinkling. "And afterward, perhaps you'll allow me to take you to dinner? Perhaps the boarding house? Publicly, as a proper beginning to our courtship."

"I would be honored," Laura replied, her eyes shining. "Though I suspect Mrs. Williams won't be remotely surprised."

"I'm beginning to think no one in Aspen Hollow will be," Moses admitted ruefully.

"Moses?" Laura asked after a few minutes of contented silence.

"Yes?"

"Thank you for coming to find me today."

"I couldn't wait another moment."

Laura squeezed his hand. "Neither could I."

Epilogue

Moses stared at the tiny, squirming bundle in his arms, mesmerized by impossibly small fingers and toes, the wrinkled face still red from the effort of entering the world. With practiced hands that trembled only slightly, he wiped the newborn clean and wrapped him securely in the soft flannel blanket Laura had embroidered during long winter evenings by the fire.

"That's it, little one," he whispered, his voice rough with emotion. "Your mama wants to meet you properly."

The baby blinked, dark blue eyes briefly focusing on Moses's face before squeezing shut again as he let out a plaintive cry that seemed impossibly loud for such a tiny being. Moses lifted him carefully, cradling the small head in his palm as he turned toward the bed where Laura lay, exhausted but radiant.

A single tear slipped down Moses's cheek as he placed their son in Laura's waiting arms.

"Here he is," Moses said, his voice catching. "Our son."

Laura's face transformed with wonder as she gazed down at the infant. "Hello, my darling," she whispered, trailing a gentle finger along his cheek. "We've been waiting for you."

The baby quieted immediately at his mother's voice, turning his head instinctively toward her. Laura looked up at Moses, her eyes shining with tears and joy.

"He's perfect," she breathed.

Moses sat carefully on the edge of the bed, one arm around Laura's shoulders, the other hand gently touching his son's dark hair. "He is," he agreed, his throat tight with emotion. "Just like his mother."

Laura leaned against him, their heads bending together over their child, forming a tableau of family that Moses had once believed would never be his. For a moment, time seemed suspended, the outside world falling away as they existed in this perfect bubble of newfound parenthood.

"What a year it's been," Laura said softly, breaking the silence. "Sometimes I can hardly believe how much has changed."

Moses nodded, memories washing over him. Their wedding in the sunlit church just a month after that snowy morning declaration, the gradual expansion of their medical practice, the news of Laura's pregnancy that had filled him with equal parts terror and joy.

"The day you rode into Aspen Hollow, I had no idea my life was about to change forever," Moses admitted, pressing a kiss to her temple.

"You certainly didn't act like you were happy about it," Laura teased, her eyes crinkling with amusement despite her exhaustion.

Moses chuckled. "I was a fool."

"No," Laura disagreed, shifting the baby slightly in her arms. "You were hurt and wary. And look at you now, still a respected doctor, but a stronger man, and a now new father." Her voice softened. "And the most loving husband I could have imagined."

Moses felt emotion swell in his chest, almost too big to contain. He still marveled at times that this remarkable woman had chosen him, had seen past his gruff exterior to the man beneath. Their year of marriage had been one of ongoing discovery—of each other, of their shared purpose, and of a depth of love he'd never believed possible after his years of isolation.

A soft knock at the door interrupted his reflections. Clementine Hayes peered in, her sharp eyes taking in the scene with approval.

"The babe is strong," she announced, entering the room fully. "Born under a good moon."

Moses had long since ceased questioning Clementine's blending of medical observation and traditional beliefs. The herbalist had become not just a colleague but a true friend in the past year, her wisdom extending far beyond plant remedies to matters of life and connection.

"Strong like his mother," Moses agreed, his admiration evident. Laura had labored for nearly a day, her determination never faltering even when exhaustion had clearly taken its toll.

Clementine approached the bed, studying the infant with her penetrating gaze. "He has your eyes," she told Moses, "but his mother's spirit. I can see it already."

Laura smiled tiredly. "Is that a good combination?"

"The best," Clementine affirmed with a rare smile. "Strength and wisdom together." She placed a small cloth bundle on the bedside table. "Pine needle tea for your recovery, and angelica root to restore your strength. Steep it fresh morning and evening."

"Thank you, Clementine," Laura said warmly.

The herbalist nodded, her eyes lingering on the family for a moment longer. "I will tell the others that mother and child are well. They have been waiting anxiously."

"Others?" Laura asked, glancing at Moses.

He smiled sheepishly. "Word spread quickly when I sent for Clementine. Half the town has gathered downstairs and on the porch. Sera Williams is keeping them at bay, but they're eager for news."

"All of them care for you both," Clementine said simply. "That is the true medicine of Aspen Hollow, not the herbs or the doctor's tools, but the binding of hearts."

After Clementine departed, Moses adjusted the blankets around Laura and the baby. "You should rest," he urged gently.

"Soon," Laura promised, unable to take her eyes off their son. "I want to savor this moment a little longer." She looked up at Moses, her expression suddenly questioning. "We still haven't decided on his name."

They had discussed names throughout Laura's pregnancy, but had never quite settled on a final choice. Moses had been reluctant to name the child after any of his lost family members, not wanting to cast even a shadow of past grief onto this new life.

"What do you think?" he asked, studying the small face that somehow already seemed to contain features from both of them.

Laura hesitated, then said softly, "I was thinking of Samuel. It means 'heard by God.'"

"Samuel," Moses repeated, testing the name. It felt right somehow, solid and dignified yet warm. "Samuel Grant."

"Samuel Jacob Grant," Laura suggested tentatively, watching his reaction. "If that wouldn't be too painful for you."

Moses felt his breath catch. Jacob—his brother-in-law's name, the man who had followed Rebecca in death, leaving Moses with the double burden of grief and guilt that had hardened him for so long.

"You want to name him after Jake?" he asked, his voice barely audible.

Laura nodded, her eyes never leaving his face. "Jake was family to you, Moses. He was important. And from everything you've told me about him, he was kind and good-hearted. Those are qualities I'd wish for our son."

Moses swallowed hard, fighting back more tears. Over a year ago, he couldn't have imagined this moment, holding his own child, a living symbol of hope and renewal, named in part for the family he had lost. The gesture touched him deeply. Laura's understanding of how to honor the past without being bound by it.

"Samuel Jacob Grant," he agreed, his voice rough with emotion. "It's perfect."

Laura smiled, relieved. "I think so too."

Young Samuel, apparently satisfied with his newly bestowed name, blinked sleepily and turned his face toward Laura's warmth. Moses watched in wonder as his son's tiny features relaxed into sleep, overcome by a wave of protectiveness so fierce it took his breath away.

"I never knew I could love someone I just met so completely," he confessed, gently brushing a finger over the baby's dark hair.

"That's how it happens," Laura said softly. "In an instant, they claim your heart forever."

Moses leaned forward, pressing a tender kiss to Laura's lips. "Thank you," he whispered against her mouth.

"For what?" she asked, her eyes half-closed with exhaustion and contentment.

"For our son. For loving me. For everything."

Laura's smile was luminous despite her weariness. "I think I hear our visitors downstairs," she said, tilting her head toward the muffled sounds of activity below. "You should go tell them about Samuel. I know they're anxious for news."

Moses hesitated, reluctant to leave even for a moment.

"We'll be right here," Laura assured him, correctly reading his expression. "Samuel and I aren't going anywhere."

With a nod, Moses rose and made his way downstairs to the clinic's waiting area. In the year since their marriage, they had expanded the clinic considerably. What had once been Moses's sparse living quarters had been transformed into a welcoming home above the medical practice, with a nursery recently added in anticipation of the baby.

As he descended the stairs, Moses heard the murmur of voices—many more than he had expected. Opening the door to the waiting room, he stopped short in surprise. Every chair was filled with additional people standing along the walls. Faces turned toward him expectantly as conversations ceased.

Pastor Lewis stepped forward, his expression questioning. "Moses?"

Moses felt a smile spread across his face, broader than any he could remember. "Laura is well," he announced, his voice carrying clearly through the packed room. "And we have a son. Samuel Jacob Grant."

A chorus of congratulations erupted, accompanied by handshakes and back slaps from those nearest. Silas Abernathy pumped his hand vigorously, while Twila pressed a basket of food into his arms. Millie Abernathy, who had become one of Laura's closest friends, wiped tears from her eyes.

"A fine name for a fine boy, I'm sure," Pastor Lewis said warmly, clasping Moses's shoulder. "Congratulations, my friend."

"Thank you," Moses replied, still somewhat dazed by the outpouring of community support. "Laura's resting now, but she's doing well. The labor was long, but she was... remarkable."

"That doesn't surprise any of us," Deputy Diamond commented from near the door. "She has more strength in her little finger than most have in their whole body."

Murmurs of agreement spread through the room. Moses looked around at the gathered townspeople, suddenly struck by how much had changed in just over a year. When Laura had arrived in Aspen Hollow, he had been isolated, closed off from genuine connection with the community he served. Now, the clinic was filled with people who had become not just patients but friends.

"Doc, when can we see the little one?" Jasper McCoy called out from the back of the room.

"In a few days, perhaps," Moses replied. "Laura needs rest first."

"We've brought food," Mrs. Williams announced, gesturing to several covered dishes arranged on a side table. "Enough to last you a week, so you can focus on Laura and the baby."

Moses was momentarily overwhelmed by their thoughtfulness. "Thank you. All of you. Your kindness means more than I can say."

"You and Laura have been God's blessing to this town," Pastor Lewis said simply. "We're just returning the favor in our small way."

After accepting more congratulations and assurances, Moses watched as they left. Only Pastor Lewis remained, a wrapped package in his hands.

"I have something for you," he said, extending the parcel. "For the baby."

Moses unwrapped it carefully to reveal a beautifully bound Bible, its leather cover supple and rich.

"For Samuel," Pastor Lewis explained. "To grow into, with space in the front to record his family history."

Moses ran his fingers over the embossed cover, deeply touched. "Thank you, Pastor. We'll treasure it."

"I'm happy for you, Moses," the pastor said earnestly. "I remember our conversation that night after the Roman baby was born, when you first acknowledged your feelings for Laura. To see how God has worked in your life since then... it's been a privilege to witness."

Moses nodded, recalling that pivotal conversation. "I never imagined I could be this happy again," he admitted. "That night, I was terrified of what I was feeling, of opening myself to potential loss again. Now I can't imagine living any other way."

"Love is always worth the risk," Pastor Lewis said with a gentle smile. "I'll stop by again in a few days. Give Laura my love."

After the pastor's departure, Moses gathered the basket of food and the Bible and returned upstairs. He paused in the doorway of their bedroom, taking in the peaceful scene. Laura had fallen asleep, one protective arm still cradling Samuel against her side. The late afternoon sun slanted through the window, bathing them in warm light.

Moving quietly, Moses set down his burdens and approached the bed. With infinite care, he lifted Samuel from Laura's embrace, settling the sleeping infant against his chest. The tiny weight felt miraculous, a perfect trust that both humbled and exalted him.

"I've got you," he whispered, his lips brushing the downy head. "I've got you both."

Laura stirred slightly, her eyes fluttering open. "Moses?" she murmured sleepily.

"Right here," he assured her, settling carefully onto the bed beside her. "Everyone sends their love. And enough food to feed us for a month."

A tired smile curved Laura's lips.

"Pastor Lewis brought a Bible for Samuel," Moses told her, nodding toward the package on the dresser.

"We're well looked after," Laura observed, her hand coming to rest on Moses's arm where he cradled the baby.

"Yes," Moses agreed, marveling at how completely his life had transformed. From lonely isolation to this rich tapestry of family and community in just over a year.

"I was thinking," Laura said, her voice soft with approaching sleep, "about the clinic and our practice."

"What about it?" Moses asked, gently rocking Samuel when he stirred.

"When I'm recovered, I'd like to start something new. A weekly clinic specifically for women and children. Many of the women in town and from outlying homesteads are still uncomfortable discussing certain matters, especially with a male physician. And I've noticed the miners' wives rarely seek care until conditions are severe."

Even in her exhausted state, Laura's mind was working, seeking ways to better serve the community they both loved. Moses felt a surge of admiration for her unflagging dedication.

"I think that's an excellent idea," he said. "We could set aside a day each week."

Laura nodded, her eyes drifting closed again. "And perhaps Clementine could join us on those days. Many of the women trust her remedies implicitly."

"A true integration of traditional and modern medicine," Moses mused, recalling how far he had come from his initial skepticism of Clementine's methods. "We'll make it happen."

Laura's breathing deepened as she slipped back into sleep, her body demanding the rest it needed after the rigors of childbirth. Moses continued to hold Samuel, watching over them both, his heart so full it seemed scarcely containable within his chest.

He prayed silently, words forming without conscious thought: Thank you, Lord, for this gift I never thought to receive. For Laura's love, for our son, for this second chance at life and family.

The prayer was simple but heartfelt, a reflection of the faith that had been rekindled through Laura's unwavering example and his own gradual openness to grace. While Moses's relationship with God remained a work in progress, less certain perhaps than Laura's steadfast belief, it had deepened into something authentic and meaningful over the past year.

As dusk settled over Aspen Hollow, Moses remained in quiet vigil over his sleeping family, memorizing every detail of this perfect moment. The weight of his son in his arms, the gentle rise and fall of Laura's breathing, the peace that suffused their home. Outside, the first stars appeared in the darkening sky, bright pinpricks of light above the mountains that embraced their town.

Somewhere in the distance, a church bell rang, marking the hour. Moses thought of the community gathering below earlier in the day, the genuine joy they had expressed for his family's happiness. He thought of Pastor Lewis's steady guidance, of Clementine's wisdom, of the Abernathy's' friendship, of all the interconnected lives that now formed the rich fabric of his existence.

Most of all, he thought of Laura. Brave, determined Laura, who had arrived in Aspen Hollow with modern ideas and unwavering faith, challenging his every assumption and ultimately healing his wounded heart. Laura, who had seen beyond his defenses to the man he could become. Laura, who now slept peacefully beside him, having given him the miraculous gift of their son.

Samuel stirred in his arms, tiny hands flexing as he dreamed infant dreams. Moses bent to kiss his son's forehead, then carefully rose and placed him in the cradle beside the bed. For a moment, he stood watching the rise and fall of the baby's chest, marveling at how something so small could so completely transform his world.

Returning to bed, Moses slipped beneath the covers and drew Laura gently against him, careful not to wake her. She sighed in her sleep, instinctively turning toward his warmth.

"I love you," he whispered into her hair. "More than I ever thought possible."

Leave A Review

I f you enjoyed this book, please consider leaving an honest review on Amazon

Visit Our Website:

www.vivianbelle.com

Visit Our Amazon Author Page HERE

Find Us On Social Media:

Facebook

Facebook Author Page

Instagram